THE MERCENARY NEXT DOOR

Rogues and Rescuers Book Two

LUCY LEROUX

DISCLAIMER

This book is a work of fiction. All of the characters, names, and events portrayed in this novel are products of the author's imagination. Any resemblance to actual events or persons, living or dead, is entirely coincidental.

This eBook is licensed for your personal enjoyment only and may not be re-sold or given away to other people. If you would like to share this book with someone else, please send them to the author's website, where they can find out where to purchase a copy for themselves. Free content can be downloaded at the author's free reads page.

Thank you for respecting the author's work. Enjoy!

TITLES BY LUCY LEROUX

Knight Takes Queen
The Millionaire's Mechanic
Burned Deep - Coming Soon

Writing As L.B. Gilbert
The Elementals Saga
Discordia, A Free Elementals Story
Fire
Air
Water
Earth

A Shifter's Claim
Kin Selection
Eat You Up
Tooth and Nail
The When Witch and the Wolf - Coming Soon

Charmed Legacy Cursed Angel Watchtowers
Forsaken

CHAPTER ONE

Mason jerked, his eyes flying open as the brakes of the bus squealed. The lumbering vehicle came to a stop. He grabbed his pack and stood, exiting into the drizzling rain.

Rolling his shoulders, he drew the hood of his jacket up, trying not to be annoyed. *I just spent three weeks in a rainforest.* He should have been used to it. But rain in Los Angeles was a rarity. Finding it here had been a less-than-pleasant welcome home.

The city needs it. It always did. But that was cold comfort as a fat drop managed to work its way inside his collar, dripping down his neck and under his shirt.

Next time, I'll stash my car at the airport's long-term parking, he told himself, aware it was a lie. The bus stopped just a few blocks from his apartment. It seemed stupid to pay the parking fees when he could just ride home after an op.

You can afford it, a little voice told him. But the habits of a lifetime were hard to break. He was no longer a towheaded punk kid in the backwoods of Tennessee, scrabbling for every crumb. His missions paid well, and he saved every cent. For what... he didn't know, but it was secure in the bank until he figured out what to spend it on.

The few precious things he bought stayed under lock and key—

like his car. He didn't mean for it to happen, but Mason didn't question the instinct to hoard what he valued.

"What's the point of having a cherry sixty-nine Camaro if you never use it?" Ethan, one of his buddies, would ask.

"How do you think it stays cherry?" Mason would reply before changing the subject. A car like that was a magnet for thieves. It was safer in his gated slot in the basement when he was away.

The Camaro had been his first big purchase with his Auric Security paycheck. Most people who found out he worked in "security" assumed he was a bodyguard to the stars. He had the build and height for it. Plus, this was L.A., and he made those wraparound sunglasses look pretty damn good. Enough for people to come up to him and ask him what TV show he was shooting.

Shooting.

As if on cue, his mind flashed back to the jungle. The firefight outside that little village had been brutal. His other buddy, Ransom, had been shot, but Mason's elite Auric team didn't get paid the big bucks for nothing. They'd gotten their man out in one piece—mostly—and accomplished their mission, the extraction of a kidnapped oil executive and his wife. And Ransom hadn't been hit bad—just a flesh wound. He'd heal up in no time.

Mason had been telling himself that for a while, but his mind couldn't stop replaying the moment Ransom was shot. His friend was a bit of a hotdog. He'd been voted the squad's *most likely to get shot* three years running, but, this time around, Ransom had been tight, following orders flawlessly.

That was probably why it bugged Mason so much. They could train and run drills until their limbs gave out, but in their line of work, that meant jack. People could do everything right, yet still end up catching a bullet.

Ransom's injury had been a signal to the powers-that-be at Auric that Mason's team needed rest. They'd been on back-to-back missions for three months straight without a break. It was in the company's best interests to ensure their highest performing team didn't burn out.

The furlough had been unexpected, but he was going to make the most of it. A lot of his team lived locally, and tearing up L.A. with them was fun, but with this much time on his hands, he could finally see Ethan in Boston, maybe even visit a few of his cousins back home. One had a new baby. He should pay his respects to the new family member while he could.

His mind full of plans, Mason rounded the corner. His building rose on the far corner. It was one of those utilitarian seventies' monstrosities—completely hideous by today's standards, but it was secure and relatively inexpensive. He could have moved to a much nicer place long before now, but saving money was second nature.

Growing up dirt poor will do that to you. But he wasn't poor anymore. Quite the contrary. And though it was economical, his space had lots of light with a loft bedroom over an open living room and kitchen space. Mason had filled it with plants, his one indulgence. He paid Laila, his neighbor, to water them when he was away, probably too much, but it was worth it to be able to walk into a green living area.

His mailbox was empty, also courtesy of his neighbor. Laila may have been quiet and sometimes squeaked when she talked, but she was reliable.

He went up to his fourth-floor apartment via the stairs, bypassing the narrow two-person elevator in the lobby. Mason didn't have any friends in the building, but he liked it that way. Home was a sanctuary where if he didn't feel like talking to anyone, he didn't have to. Laila was the sole exception, but she was so shy and unobtrusive it hardly counted.

Mason had met the master's student a year ago, shortly after she moved into the building. The structure only had three units per floor —two double bedrooms, one of which was his. Then there was the tiny and lightless one-room studio crammed into the corner. That one was Laila's.

He scanned the door, checking for a light underneath, but the studio was dark. Most likely, she was at work or a night class.

She could be on a date. But that was less likely since Laila appeared too shy. He'd never seen her with anyone. Well, almost...

There had been one guy, a fellow student, who had helped her move in. He'd come back a day or two after, wasted. Mason had caught enough of his drunken ramble to understand the little shit believed moving a few boxes entitled him to some action. He'd banged on the door, getting belligerent when she wouldn't open it.

As a rule, Mason didn't get involved in other people's business. He hadn't even really known Laila at the time, but he'd quickly sized her up at their first meeting. The shy, almost skittish girl had been way out of her depth when it came to the drunk asshole trying to break down her door. So, Mason took care of the problem for her—his way. The punk wisely decided to stay away for the sake of his health.

The next morning, Laila had come over with a buttermilk pie to thank him. He'd tried to send her away without taking it, but that damn pie had weakened his defenses. He still had no idea how she'd guessed it had been his favorite dessert growing up.

He and Laila weren't exactly friends now, but when he went out of town, he let her water his plants, trusting her with a copy of his key. But he was careful to pay her. Mason didn't like owing anybody anything.

Not that Laila ever imposed on him. She was too shy for that. That, and she appreciated the cash. Laila was putting herself through school by working at a grocery store near the university she attended. She cooked for the bakery there.

Mason liked the mental image of that, more than he wanted to admit. It was too domestic for his taste, but made for a pretty picture, nonetheless.

Kind of like the rest of her. Not that he'd ever go there. Laila was off-limits. His life was too hard for someone that soft.

CHAPTER TWO

Laila ran to her door when she heard the distinctive heavy tread in the hall, somehow managing to bang her leg on the coffee table in the process.

Damn it, she thought as she limped to the keyhole, knee screaming. The door across the hall closed before she could figure out if it were Mason or their other neighbor.

Of course it wasn't him. She just imagined it had been because he'd been gone for weeks, and she was hungry for a glimpse of him. Six-foot-two, blond, with more muscles than she could count, Mason Lang was the most beautiful man she had ever seen.

Except beautiful was the wrong word for that kind of raw masculinity. Her neighbor looked as if he'd been hewn from granite by a master sculptor. A person could cut themselves on his cheekbones. The first time she'd seen him getting his mail, Laila went weak in the knees.

And to think I used to believe that was just an expression.

When she found out the man lived right across the hall, she had to have herself a lie down. Mason was way out of her league.

So what?

A little harmless fantasizing never hurt anyone. It wasn't as if she'd stripped naked and waited for Mason in his bed when he came home. She wasn't that pathetic...although some might disagree if they knew she baked for him, too, in addition to watering his plants. But that was no trouble. After cooking at Gardullo's bakery, whipping up a single batch of her special rocky road brownies or a lemon pound cake took no time at all. Besides, the extra treats were the least she could do considering how well Mason compensated her to look after his plants.

Twenty dollars a day was insane for fifteen minutes of work—although truth be told, some of his plants *were* fussy. The mosses and his dozen or so orchids were especially demanding. Too little or too much water, and they wilted or died outright.

Laila wasn't good with plants—cooking was her thing—but Mason had an incredibly detailed list of instructions she could follow, down to the number of sprays each orchid received. As long as she stuck to the list, the plants lived, even thrived. Whenever he was away for more than a few weeks, he rounded up whatever cash he owed her, telling her to put it to good use.

At first glance, Mason Lang didn't look like the type of man to grow flowers. At second glance, he didn't look like the kind, either, but his apartment was proof that appearances were deceiving. It was a miniature jungle, an oasis in the middle of their dry urban sprawl.

They never discussed his hobby, but she liked that. People would pass him on the street, they would see his perfect face and hard body, and they'd never know about his meticulously maintained garden. It was like a secret they shared.

And the man had several.

Laila didn't know what Mason did for a living. All she knew was that he would fly off at a moment's notice, and his trips could take anywhere from days to a few weeks. This last one had been the longest.

Laila often wondered where Mason went and what he did when he was there. But he never brought it up himself, and she was too tongue-tied around him to ask. Not that he ever engaged in prolonged conversation. She considered herself lucky to get a five-minute chat out of him at a time. But Mason's gruff manner didn't put her off. As far as she was concerned, it just added to his mystique. If they did have a real conversation that lasted more than a few minutes, it might shatter her illusions about him. Her crush would die a quick death once he proved he was just like everyone else.

Yeah, keep telling yourself that.

Feeling like a fool, Laila limped back to her couch where her dinner was getting cold. Stalking her hot neighbor was a giant waste of time. If he didn't like his plants so much, he'd probably never speak to her.

Turning on her TV for the company, she finished her meal...alone. Again.

❧

Mason cracked a lid, hyperaware he wasn't alone. He sat bolt upright in bed, surprised to find it was morning.

He hadn't meant to crash right after getting home. Mason had planned on ordering a pizza and watching some porn to round out the night, but the jet lag took him down before he could decide on toppings.

Now it was daylight, and someone was in his apartment. He listened carefully, pulling his hand away from the bedside table, where he kept his gun safe.

It's just Laila. He'd forgotten to text her to let her know he was back.

After rolling out of bed, he went to the stairs that led to the living room. He could hear her moving around, humming along to whatever music was pumping through her earbuds.

And there she was, appearing from behind his blood orange tree... wearing nothing but skin-tight yoga pants and the tiniest tank top he had ever seen.

His lips parted as she set down the sprayer he used on his orchids. He'd never seen Laila wearing so little. Mason typically saw her dressed for school, or on her way to work in the plain green polo and beige pants the store used as a uniform.

She'd always struck him as modest, or at least painfully shy—too shy ever to show any skin. And right now, she thought she was alone, which was why she was dancing around like no one was watching.

His lips lifted at the corners as she twirled unexpectedly, her creamy coffee curves highlighted by the bright sunlight streaming through the windows.

Laila reached out, touching one of the rounded oranges hanging from his tree. As she closed her eyes, her surprisingly lush lips parted as she bent and inhaled, drawing in the citrus scent.

Well, fuck. Mason could feel himself swelling as she patted and caressed the fruit. Then she moved on, picking up the watering can while humming a tune he didn't recognize. Pivoting on her heel, she turned to face the stairs, opening her eyes. Screaming, she dropped the watering can.

"Hey," Mason said, unable to stop his slow grin.

Laila pulled the earbuds from her ears with a quick jerk.

"Hi!" she said in a loud voice, her golden-brown eyes wide.

She quickly glanced down and then up, color staining her cheeks. Mason rubbed the back of his neck, belatedly realizing he was wearing nothing but a snug pair of boxer briefs that left little to the imagination.

For a moment, he contemplated going for a pair of pants, but, in the end, he shrugged and stood his ground. People wore less on the beach.

"I got back late last night. I meant to text you, but I forgot. Sorry about that."

Still blushing, Laila cleared her throat. She picked up the watering can, twisting and spilling water on the floor.

"Here." Mason went down the steps, going to the kitchen to fish a towel out of one of the cabinets. He handed her the towel. She took it without looking at him, and he realized how fucking rude he was being. The girl was ready to bolt out the door.

"I'll be right back," he said, hurrying upstairs for pants, kicking himself for embarrassing her. He also dug around his room for the cash he owed her, but he came up short.

Mason hurried back down, pulling a plain t-shirt on over his jeans. He thrust his hand out, offering her the cash just as she was about to bolt out the front door.

"I need to hit a cash machine later, but here's a down payment on what I owe you."

She turned around, peeking at him from under her lashes. "You don't need to rush. I can wait for it."

"It's not a problem. I'm going to be running errands all day, getting restocked." Turning, he caught sight of the fruit tree. "And by all means, take the oranges. They look ripe. I'm sure you'll make better use of them than I can."

He'd just eat them. But Laila could turn them into something mouthwatering.

She was about to refuse the offer, but he forestalled her argument by picking the oranges himself. He stacked them in her arms.

"You can return the key later," he told her.

"Sure thing," she said, struggling to hold onto the fruit. He opened the door for her, debating taking them back. But he didn't want to risk touching her bare arms. Something told him skin-to-skin contact would be a bad idea. Instead, he ushered her out and shut the door behind her.

❧

An orange rolled out of her arms and hit her foot. Accidentally kicking it further, she sighed, convinced Mason thought she was an idiot.

That's because you are one.

In her defense, nothing would have prepared her for the sight of the man in his underwear. Those abs alone were worth the price of admission. Who could blame her for gawking? Sure, there were plenty of attractive people in the world. Supposedly they were crawling all over Los Angeles. According to the gossip blogs, a rock couldn't be thrown without hitting a model or a starlet in this town, but Laila didn't travel in those circles. Despite living here for years, she'd never seen a celebrity, with the possible exception of Mark Ruffalo at an environmental rally. At least she thought it had been the actor, but she wasn't a hundred percent sure.

Nudging the fallen orange inside with her foot, she let herself into her cramped apartment. Her tiny studio was wedged into the corner of the building. It boasted a small, high window so that even on the brightest day, it was always dark. That was why she used a halogen lamp, even in the afternoon.

Gathering the fruit on the counter, she bent and took a deep sniff. Their fragrance had been teasing her for weeks, the scent more powerful than any fruit she bought in the store.

Laila had some time before her shift at the grocery store, enough to make something special with Mason's gift.

I can give it to him when I return his key. The key exchange was part of the routine...

Lips pursed, she wondered why that was the case. Mason was unfailingly polite, but the one time she'd suggested holding onto his spare key, so they wouldn't have to keep passing it back and forth, he'd shut her down, albeit it in the nicest way possible. But that was his right. It was his space, and he was protective of it.

Pulling out her industrial-sized bag of flour, she washed and cut the fruit, excited beyond reason to find they were blood oranges. Oh yes, she was going to make something special with these...

CHAPTER THREE

Mason had hit the gym, the bank, and the grocery store before the incipient jet lag hit him, forcing him to head back to his place. He fell asleep on his couch, basking in the warm sun and the familiar smells of his apartment.

Perhaps that was what woke him—a new aroma that made him ravenous. Then something brushed past him. He shot up, rolling and taking the intruder down with him.

Laila's muffled gasp was cut off as he ground her into the carpet in between his couch and coffee table.

"I'm sorry," she cried, throwing her hands up to ward off a blow.

"*Laila*," he hissed, blinking rapidly, realizing with a start that his arm was drawn back to strike.

Fuck. If he'd hit her, he would have smashed every delicate bone in her face.

Slowly, he put his arm down. "What are you doing here? How did you get inside?"

She gulped, her chest heaving underneath him. "I didn't think you were at home. When I knocked, you didn't answer, so I assumed you were still out running errands."

Lifting her arm, she pointed at his coffee table. "I was leaving your key and the cake I made with the oranges. I—I thought you weren't home," she repeated, stuttering slightly.

Adrenaline was still coursing through him, but he tried to get ahold of himself. "Did I hurt you?" he asked, studying her critically as if peering into her eyes would tell him if she had a head injury.

"N-No." Laila was still staring up at him. She cleared her throat. "I, uh, just had the wind knocked out of me."

He paused, gazing down at her. Her heart was thrumming like a hummingbird. He could feel it beating far too fast for his peace of mind.

He could also feel other things, like his own arousal, which was rapidly going from half-mast to rock hard.

Laila wasn't even trying to be provocative. She was wearing her grocery store uniform for fuck's sake. Compared to the yoga pants and tank top, it was shapeless and boxy, but that didn't seem to matter because now he could *feel* each one of her curves pressed against him.

To make matters worse, Laila smelled of sugar and vanilla. It made him want to open his mouth against that cinnamon skin to swallow her whole. Or at least lick her up and down.

Snapping out of it, he climbed off her, pulling her to her feet as he went. Once she was standing, he gave her another once over

"Are you sure you're not hurt?" He checked her back for bruises, then moved in front of her to flex her wrists.

"I'm sure," she said, looking up at him with huge honey-brown eyes. He'd never gotten this close, which was why he'd never noticed those little gold flecks in them before.

"Again, I'm so sorry. I would have never come inside if I thought you were home..." She ducked her head, stepping away.

It was only two feet, but Mason could feel her withdrawal like a punch to the gut. Her posture, the way she was physically drawing in on herself, told the story.

"You're afraid of me," he whispered. "Shit, I'm sorry. I didn't mean to scare you."

"I'm not scared," she assured him, her eyes skittering to his face and then away.

Wincing, he swore under his breath. "Fuck, again, I am so sorry. It's a hazard of the job. Some of the places I sleep in aren't always secure. When you brushed past me, I reacted."

She nodded a little too quickly. "As I said, I shouldn't have come in here without permission. I know better than to sneak up on a soldier." Her shoulders drew up, and she gave him a forced smile. "That is what you do, right?"

Well, he was wearing an old pair of fatigues. It was only natural she put two and two together.

"I *was* a soldier. Now I work for a private security firm. That's why I go overseas a lot. The missions I pull take me all over the world."

A small line formed between her brows. "Like a Blackwater-type job?"

He wanted to groan aloud. Of course she'd know that name. And it didn't bode well, given how the company was portrayed in the media.

"Auric isn't like the outfits you've heard about. The type of work I do involves protecting people. The last mission was a K & R."

"What is that?"

"Kidnap retrieval. My team went in to extract an oil exec and his wife from a hostage situation. We got them home to their three little girls."

"Oh." She blinked. "Wow."

Mason had never tried to justify what he did before, not to anyone. He wasn't ashamed of the work, but he knew how some people saw his kind. *Mercenary* was a dirty word in certain mouths. And this was Laila.

He hadn't realized until now that her opinion mattered to him so much. Enough for him to try to paint himself as a hero in her eyes— whatever he needed to undo the damage caused by throwing her to the ground like a maniac.

"That's amazing. Those people got to go home to their kids because of you," she added, giving herself a little shake. "But I, um, I should get going. My shift starts soon."

Nodding like a marionette, he let her go. But long after she was gone, he kept replaying the way she left, backing away as if afraid to take her eyes off him…because he was a threat.

CHAPTER FOUR

Laila looped her infinity scarf around her neck one more time, trying to draw it high enough to cover her ears. The nights were colder now than when it had been raining. But she had to be out here. It had been over a week since she last took a shift with the Night Witches, the group she helped found when she was an undergraduate at the school.

Named after a famous group of Soviet aviatrixes, their version had been created after she and Rosamie found one of their classmates passed out on the lawn halfway between the frats and their dormitory. Banding together with a few other girlfriends, they spread the word— anyone partying on campus could text them to get walked back to their dorm room at any time, no questions asked. The girls who volunteered worked in pairs, sometimes arranging to pick up a certain person in advance. They were a regular and unpopular sight on Greek Row, the street where the fraternities and sororities owned their houses.

Despite the fact she wasn't an undergrad anymore and lived off-campus, Laila still tried to volunteer at least once a month—twice if her schedule allowed.

It was just her luck she'd chosen what had to be the coldest night of the year. *If anyone had told me I'd be freezing in L.A., I would have laughed in their faces.*

Laila had grown up in Chicago. After eighteen years of chilly autumns and frigid winters, she initially laughed at what passed for fall and winter in California, but, five years later, it was as if her blood had thinned to the point where she was always cold.

"You're quiet tonight," Rosamie observed, walking beside her with her hands in the pockets of her faux-fur bomber jacket.

"Sorry," she apologized, aware she hadn't been very animated. Being out with Rosamie or their other friend Jasmine was one of the things that made the Night Witches enjoyable, even fun most of the time.

"I've had a lot on my mind."

"Is it your mom?" Rosamie asked, concern wrinkling her rounded features.

"No, although she's not great." Laila's stepmother was her only family. Joyce James suffered from a case of progressive dementia. She was currently in a home in the Chicago suburbs, close to the siblings who had never really accepted Laila as one of their own. "I spoke to her yesterday, and she was fine...at first. But she became confused and hung up on me after ten minutes."

That was how Laila judged her mother's state of mind—by how long Joyce stayed on the phone. Her dad's life insurance money ensured his second wife had the care she needed, which was a relief, even if it meant Laila had to pay her own way through school.

"Is that shorter than normal?"

A corner of Laila's mouth pulled down. There had been a time when she would have spent more than two hours on the phone with her stepmother. "A bit shorter, but only a few minutes."

The call before had lasted a quarter of an hour, but this kind of fluctuation had happened before. Laila knew better than to count the seconds. However, the overall downward trend was distressing.

But she can bounce back. It had happened before, and Laila lived in hope.

"Are you going to visit her this Christmas?" Rosamie asked.

Guilt weighing down her steps, Laila shook her head. "I can't afford the airfare if I'm going to pay for this year's classes." She was more than halfway through her associate degree, but she was struggling to make ends meet. The books she'd had to buy for this quarter had wiped out her reserves.

"That sucks. But you're always welcome at my place!" Rosamie was local. Laila had spent many a holiday with her big and boisterous Filipino family.

"I would love to go. If I don't have to work, of course." Since she couldn't afford to go home for the holidays, she was often scheduled to cover the holiday hours. But she appreciated the invitation, nonetheless.

"If it's not your mom, what's got you down?"

Laila stopped halfway down the path to Greek Row. "I, um, I had a run-in with my neighbor."

"What did that old fart say to you this time?"

"It wasn't Mr. Tran. I meant Mason."

Rosamie's eyes bugged out. "You mean Mr. Marvelous? He's back in town?"

Laila nodded. "I didn't even realize he was home. I was watering his plants, and he came out of his bedroom in his underwear."

Rosamie whistled. "Was it awesome?"

Laila tipped her head back to take in the night sky. She could compare Mason's beauty to the stars, but they couldn't see them. Too much light pollution.

"*Yes,*" she said, drawing out the word. "In the most literal sense of the word. He was magnificent..."

She trailed off, lost in the memory of all those glorious muscles.

"Did you stare at him too long, and it got weird?" Rosamie asked sympathetically. They'd been friends long enough to know that was a real possibility.

"No—I mean, yes. But also, no. He didn't seem embarrassed. It was later that I made a mess of things. I came back when I thought he was gone to return his key and to leave him a little something I made."

"*Again?*" Rosamie's nose wrinkled. She didn't approve of Laila's penchant to bake things for Mason. Her friend thought it was too desperate—because it was. *'The way to a man's heart isn't really through his stomach,'* she would say.

"I was making something for myself anyway," Laila lied. "But I shouldn't have let myself into his place with him back in town. He was there, but asleep. When I woke him, he—he sprang up and pinned me."

Rosamie stopped short in the middle of the walkway. "*What?*" she screeched.

The scarf was starting to feel too tight against her neck. Laila tugged, loosening it. "He moved *so* fast. It was crazy—one second I was on my feet trying to sneak out without waking him; then, the next, I was on the floor with him on top of me."

"I don't know whether to be pissed at him or jealous of you." Rosamie threw up her hand. "Both. I can be both. Did he hurt you?"

"No, I was just…shocked," Laila said, prevaricating.

She was a small woman, and the impact *had* stung. But the thick carpet had protected her head from the worst of it. True, her back was sore today. However, it was the memory of Mason's hard body over hers that she couldn't get out of her mind. She was going to remember how he'd felt—his hard length pressed against her for a *long* time.

"Anyway," she said after a moment, "he apologized, and I got out of there, but it was so embarrassing."

"*You* were embarrassed?" Rosamie smacked her lips. "What about him? Who does shit like that? Did he even apologize?"

"Repeatedly," Laila assured her. "He was worried he'd hurt me. As for why, he said the places he'd been sleeping in weren't always safe or secure. He is *not* a personal trainer or an actor like we thought—he's a soldier for hire. He'd just gotten back from rescuing this kidnapped couple. It sounded crazy dangerous."

Rosalie was incredulous. "*Really?* That guy? I could have sworn he was a secret porn star or something. It would explain why he was always taking off. I thought he was going off for marathon filming sessions. Instead, he's Clearchus of Sparta."

Laila frowned in confusion, and Rosamie shrugged. "Clearchus was a famous mercenary. I wrote a paper about him for my History of Ancient Greece class last year."

Laila rubbed her hair with her gloved hand. "As bad as Mason felt —and he obviously did—*I* was the one who felt like shit. I would have never gone in there if I thought he was home. Although, now I'm wondering if he has some kind of PTSD."

She would never have thought such a thing before. Mason always seemed so together. True, he didn't talk much, but he never appeared stressed or out of sorts.

But then again, how would she know? Laila was relegated to the periphery of his life. Despite her interest in him, she knew next to nothing about the man.

Rosamie wagged her finger in Laila's face.

"*Nu-no*," she said, over-enunciating. "Stop right there. Mason isn't some puppy that's been kicked. You can't take him in and make him all better. That's the kind of shit that almost got you kicked out of the dorm freshman year."

Laila winced. "I know Mason isn't some charity case. I'm not an idiot."

Rosamie nudged her with her hip. "I know you're not. And I don't want to kill your buzz—I really don't—but you've been lusting after this guy for ages, and he's never looked at you twice. Now you have your first real interaction, and he *tackles* you? *Run*. Run like he's the devil."

"C'mon, Mason isn't a bad guy," Laila protested. "He saves people."

"Or so he says." Rosamie scowled. "For all we know, he protects drug dealers and rich pedophiles. Mercenaries are just that—*merce-nary*. They do anything for money."

"I don't know. That doesn't read right to me. A man who cares for his plants so meticulously can't be all bad."

At least Laila hoped he wasn't.

"I didn't say he was, but now that you brought it up, how many people do you think he's killed?"

When Laila didn't answer, Rosamie sniffed. "Stick to college boys."

"In case you haven't noticed, there's not exactly a line of those beating down my door."

"That's because you never give them a chance. I don't know why not. You're *so* pretty." Rosamie waved at the distant row of Greek houses. "You could walk into any of those houses and have your pick of boys."

"*Ugh*," Laila said, bypassing the compliment. She knew she wasn't hideous, but she could only call herself passably cute if she put in the effort to do her face and hair. Most of the time, she was too tired. "Bad example."

As part of the Night Witches, the guys they regularly saw in the Greek houses were hostile and pretty gross. The smell of stale beer wafted from them in place of cologne. It made her stomach churn.

"You're right," Rosamie laughed. "But with a little effort, you could have anyone, not just the low-hanging fruit."

"I don't know why we're even talking about this," Laila said, resuming the walk to Greek Row. "My fantasies about Mason are just that. Not real. I know they're kind of sad—that much is true. But it's not like I have time to date anyone anyway. Between classes, getting enough hours at the store to cover rent and tuition, and the Witches, I have no time for a social life."

"Laila, I love you, but that song is getting *old*," Rosamie admonished, but she softened it with a smile. "At least get a fuck buddy. Any of the guys from the Pharmacology study group would do the job credibly."

The class was a killer, hands down the most intense requirement of her respiratory therapy degree.

Laila made a face. "I'm not sure I can handle a fuck buddy."

She didn't' come right out and say it, but Rosamie knew she wasn't experienced. Laila wasn't the type to go from zero to sixty without doing something stupid...like getting her heartbroken.

"You won't know until you try," her friend encouraged.

They stopped at the corner, and Laila grimaced at the row of houses. It was Friday night, so each one was lit and busy. Music blared as people milled in and out, going from house to house—a typical Friday night.

"Which one are we headed to first?"

Rosamie peeked at her phone at the text she'd received. "Alpha Omega."

Laila's groan was loud. "Those guys are the worst. I thought they were disbanded after what happened last month."

Alpha Omega, the wealthiest fraternity on campus, had come close to being shut down when an alleged case of hazing landed one of their pledges in the hospital with alcohol poisoning.

"Their alumni association paid through the nose to get them reinstated. Since the guy pulled through, the university was inclined to let them skate," Rosamie said with a sniff. "But things are supposed to be better now. They've just elected that new hotshot transfer student as president—the lieutenant governor's son. He's supposedly walking the walk, not just talking the talk. He even said the Night Witches were welcome anytime."

"Sure he did," Laila said skeptically.

"Only one way to know for sure." Shrugging, Rosamie twined an arm through hers. "Let's get this over with."

With a sigh, Laila trudged after her friend, wishing she had Mason's muscles between her and the drunken gauntlet of jerks who made up Alpha Omega.

CHAPTER FIVE

"You better not light that thing in here," Mason scolded, snatching the fat Cuban cigar out of Ransom's good hand.

His friend and coworker waved the other arm, sling and all. "What? You've got enough plants in here. They'll absorb the smoke. That's why you have so many freaking plants, right—because they clean the air? Or so you keep saying."

Mason grunted noncommittally. "Are you even allowed to drink or smoke? Aren't you still on antibiotics? What did Doc Valentine say?" he asked, naming the physician Auric Security kept on retainer stateside.

Ransom wrinkled his nose, picking up a beer. "He said to take my fucking pills, and I shouldn't scratch under the bandages," he replied, proceeding to do just that.

Mason didn't blame him. He'd been shot before, too, and he knew how itchy a healing bullet hole could get at this stage. Picking up his beer, he turned to the living room. The rest of his Auric team was milling about, setting up the poker table.

Ransom, Jace, Klein, Wes, Tyler, and Collins came over weekly whenever they were in town. But tonight promised to be more than their standard poker game—some of the guys had brought girls.

Wes and Tyler had already pushed the couch to the wall. Someone had dragged the folding chairs out of the closet, but Mason wondered why they bothered. One of the girls had taken a call, giving someone directions to his place aloud. Tyler had connected his phone to the Bluetooth speakers, and he was actively scanning dance music playlists.

Mason suppressed a scowl. "When you said you wanted to come over tonight, I thought we'd have a quiet night in. It's *Wednesday*," he stressed. "I have neighbors."

No sooner had he said the word than the image of Laila pinned underneath him flashed through his head. Her lips had been parted, and their unexpected lushness stayed front and center.

That had been a few days ago. Mason hadn't run into Laila since. He was concerned she was avoiding him.

"We'll keep it down." Ransom waved his concern aside, swigging his beer.

"Right." Grabbing one of the closed bottles of booze the guys had brought over, Mason headed to the door.

"Hey," Collins called. "Where are you going with my Jack Daniels?"

Ignoring him, Mason stepped outside, knocking on his other neighbor's—Old Man Tran—door. The bottle was accepted grudgingly, but Tran still threatened to call the cops if they got too loud.

"And tell your female friends to keep the screaming in the bedroom to a minimum. Don't forget I hear *everything*," Tran snapped before closing the door in Mason's face.

Behind him, Ransom laughed. "What was that about?"

"Our places share a bedroom wall."

Still laughing, Ransom rolled his eyes. "What a waste of whiskey." He turned to Laila's door. "And what are you going to give this one?"

An unwilling flush crawled up Mason's neck. "Never mind," he said, pointing to the door. "Go back inside. I'll be right there."

Mason lifted his hand to knock on the door, but he stopped when Ransom narrowed his eyes. "What?" Mason growled.

Leaning his good shoulder on the door with exaggerated casualness, Ransom smirked. "I'm curious about your mystery girl. This is the one you text whenever we're heading back, right?"

"Because she waters my plants," Mason said, lowering his voice. Though he'd never been inside, he knew Laila's apartment was small. If she were in there, there was no way she could miss hearing this conversation.

"Small little thing, dark hair and eyes." Ransom squinted as if he were scanning his memory. "Is she hot?"

"*Go-back-in-side*," Mason gritted from behind clenched teeth.

Ransom snorted. "No way. Don't think I haven't noticed how cagey you've been about her. It's like you don't want us to know she exists. I'm dying to see her up close."

"I never denied Laila exists," Mason said.

Ransom raised a brow. "So, you're not doing her?"

"*What?* No. And lower your fucking voice," Mason hissed, casting a nervous glance at the door.

"Well, then invite her over." Ransom shrugged. "The more, the merrier."

"Hell, no," Mason snapped.

"Why not?"

"*Because*," he said, imagining Laila mingling with his team. If Ransom didn't try to get in her pants, then Wes would be all over her. The only ones Mason could trust around her were Collins and Jace, but only because they were the ones who'd brought dates. Hell, maybe not even then.

None of the guys were married. Everyone but Klein played the field. Louis Klein had a boyfriend, Julio, and their relationship was the only steady one in the bunch.

Ignoring his friend, Mason pivoted to knock on Laila's door. He hoped she wasn't standing on the other side, listening to the entire mess.

What if she is... and she wants to come over?

Something in him balked at the idea. He didn't want Laila around his single friends.

"I guess she's not home," Ransom said after a minute or two passed.

Mason hid his relief. "Now stop stalling. I want to kick your ass at poker."

They returned to Mason's place to play a few hands. Mason lost the first two, but he won the pot on the third—mostly because the girl perched on Collins' lap distracted him during the game.

Shortly after the girl's friends arrived, they dropped the pretense of playing poker. Everyone started dancing instead. Choosing to drink instead of chatting with the two available girls, he backed off. He then behaved like a grumpy old man, making the occasional circuit around the living room to pick up dirty cups. He also turned down the volume on his speakers whenever anyone nudged it over the threshold he'd marked in red sharpie.

Tran was probably going to call the cops, but it was out of his hands now. Mason had done everything he could. Deciding the cat was out of the bag, he allowed himself to relax, the hum of conversation washing over him.

"What are you doing hiding in the kitchen?"

Mason glanced up to see Julio, Klein's boyfriend, holding a six-pack. Genuinely happy to see him, Mason pumped the other man's hand.

"I'm not hiding. Just kicking back," he said, taking the bottle Julio offered. It was from a local microbrew Mason sometimes visited.

"Thanks for this. I like this place. They have this killer Porter they only do at Christmas. Have you tried it?" Mason asked.

"No, but I'll make sure to check it out in December." Julio grinned, passing a hand over his blue scrubs.

"Did you come straight from the hospital?" Mason asked, pointing to the outfit.

"I did. I just got off a ten-hour shift, but I'm still wired. After Louis called, I decided to join in the fun. What happened to the poker game?" Smirking, he raised an eyebrow at the trio of couples grinding on the makeshift dance floor.

Mason shrugged before opening his beer. "You know how it is after a long op. They just want to blow off steam. I'm hoping they keep it down, though. The old man next door already threatened to call the cops."

Although Tran had a point about the noise being more disruptive if it came from Mason's bedroom, given their shared wall.

Guess it's a good thing I'm not getting any.

His thoughts immediately returned to Laila, and he winced. Covering, he took a sip, although this particular beer wasn't bitter enough to justify the grimace.

"Why don't you move?" Julio asked, leaning back against the kitchen counter. "Louis and I started looking at houses since he got back."

Mason drew his head back. "Really? A *house*?"

Julio nodded enthusiastically. "The last one we saw was nice. It's in a new development outside of Alhambra. It'll be a hell of a commute for me, but Louis and I want a yard, maybe a pool. You know what a fish he is. I'd rather just have a hot tub, so we're thinking of compromising and getting one of those spa-swim things, with a hot tub at one end and a motorized lap pool on the other. They're pricy, though, so it will have to wait for a year or two after we close escrow."

Escrow? Julio may as well have been speaking Greek. "Damn. I guess Klein's all grown up."

The nurse nearly snorted out his beer. Wiping his face, he laughed. "Not quite, but for this, he's motivated. We're tired of our neighbors, too."

"I didn't say that," Mason protested, thinking of Laila. "Not all my neighbors anyway. But buying a house is a big commitment. I'm not sure I'd be ready for that."

He had the cash thanks to his Auric paycheck, but the idea of shelling out such a large amount just to call a place his own didn't feel right. It was all so... permanent.

"Maybe you could rent one?" Julio suggested. "It's not like you need to be in town, right? Proximity to an airport is a bigger factor."

Mason thought about it before shaking his head. "I wouldn't want to give up the restaurants around here. I like being able to get Chinese food at two in the morning if the mood strikes."

Not that he did it all that often. But he enjoyed having the option.

Julio shrugged. "Suit yourself. But I'm telling you, I can't wait to have our own space with no landlord to answer to."

"That would be nice," Mason acknowledged, wondering when it had gotten so crowded.

His apartment was packed now. At least six other people had arrived when he wasn't paying attention, including Dusty, another Auric merc from a different team. Considering the square footage, it made for a tight squeeze.

"Where did Ransom go?" Mason asked, not seeing the big man.

"I don't know," Julio answered from around a mouthful of chips. "The bathroom?"

Mason waited to see if that was the case, but when the occupant came out, it was a girl he didn't recognize.

Suspicious now, he went out into the hall. A rush of heat swept over him as he caught his buddy leaning over Laila, clearly chatting her up.

Ransom's good arm was braced over Laila's head. Technically, she could still open the door, but to do so, she would have had to turn her back on the large stranger.

Laila wasn't wearing her grocery store uniform, but she held a brown paper bag with the store's logo printed on it.

"Hey, leave her alone," Mason said, grabbing Ransom's good arm. Roughly, Mason pulled his friend away from his tiny neighbor.

Ransom scowled as if to say, 'give me a little credit'. "I was just about to invite Laila over."

Laila swiveled her gaze between the two men. Her expression crestfallen, she smiled tightly. "I can't. I'm in the middle of midterms."

Mason wanted to swear. He didn't mind inconveniencing Old Man Tran, but Laila was another story. He was about to promise to keep it down when one of the girls who came with Collins exited his apartment, heading to the elevator with a wave of her unlit cigarette.

A burst of music and loud conversation followed her. Even after the door closed, they could still hear the bass.

Wincing, Mason turned back to Laila. "Let me get you a hotel room."

She pulled the grocery bag closer to her chest. "That's not necessary. I can put in some earplugs. I won't be sleeping much in any case. I have a lot of studying to do."

"And is that something you enjoy?" Ransom asked, nudging Mason in the back.

"Of course," Laila said, seemingly confused.

"Really?" Now Mason was surprised. He had done well enough in college, but the minute it was over, he'd been out of there like a shot. The idea of going back for an advanced degree, voluntarily entering a classroom or lecture hall, made him claustrophobic. But that didn't mean he and his friends were going to be the reason he messed that up for Laila.

"Go grab some clothes and your books, and I'll drive you to a hotel. Somewhere nice."

"But—"

"I insist," he interrupted. "You have to get a good grade, right?"

She hesitated.

"Please. Or else I'll feel terrible."

Laila looked as if she wanted to argue with him, but he just shook his head. When it came to stubbornness, he would always win.

"All right. I'll pack an overnight bag. It was nice to meet you," she said, flicking Ransom a shy glance from under her lashes before ducking inside.

Mason blinked. He had forgotten Ransom was there, which was why the other merc wore a smug, self-satisfied expression.

"What?" Mason grumbled when his friend kept quiet.

"You *do* like her."

Mason waved him back inside his apartment. "She's a nice kid who is paying her way through school. If Laila fails her tests, she can't afford to retake the classes."

"Uh-huh." Ransom's smirk only deepened.

Deciding to ignore him, Mason grabbed his car keys off the hook in the kitchen. But Ransom followed him.

"This explains so much. Like why you haven't been trying to hit that," he said, gesturing significantly to the crowd in the living room.

Mason glanced up. Angie, Dusty's sister, was here now, and she was on the dance floor. Her heavily kohled-eyes met his for a moment. Movements slowing, she started a rhythmic surge that high-lighted the exaggerated curve of her hips. Her red hair was perfectly styled, not a strand out of place.

"Angie?" he muttered in a low voice. "Why would I try to get with Angie?"

"You know she likes you."

Mason grunted noncommittally. She had flirted with him, but Angie used to '*like*' Collins. And before that, it was Ansel, the team leader of Dusty's Auric team. She was a merc groupie, who went from man to man in the organization—with her brother's blessing. Mason had always thought that was kind of gross, but if one of the guys said something to him, Dusty would shrug and say Angie was her own woman who could do what she wanted.

The latter, Mason could understand. He wasn't a hypocrite. Angie could run through all the Auric teams if that were what she wanted, but Mason had too much small-town Tennessee in him to approve of Dusty's laissez-faire attitude. Mason didn't have a sister, but he had female cousins he had been close to growing up, and he knew he wouldn't be that blasé.

Ransom was still talking. "So, if you don't come back, I can lock up."

"Lock up?" Mason echoed.

Ransom gestured around them. "Leave me your spare set."

The dots connected. "You don't need my keys. I'm coming right back."

"Sure, you are, buddy. Sure you are." With a flick of his fingers, Ransom dismissed him.

CHAPTER SIX

Laila tugged on Mason's sleeve. "This has to be some mistake," she said in a hushed tone.

It was instinct as if she were in a Cathedral instead of the lobby of a hotel. But this was like no hotel she'd ever been in.

The outside of the building was fairly nondescript. Mason had driven them in his red Corvette a mere ten minutes before stopping at a building with a sleek granite facade. At first, she'd thought they'd arrived at a bank, but Mason didn't exit to take out cash. Instead, he tossed his keys to a valet who had materialized out of thin air. Then he'd opened her door and ushered her inside.

Laila nearly tripped on the marble tile because she was too busy gawking to watch her step. The interior was the most opulent space she'd ever been in.

Her first impression was of sparkling golden-brown marble and elegant brass. A Chevron design in the art-deco style was embedded into each pillar at the edge of the wide lobby. Lush green plants dotted the room.

With subtle pressure on her lower back, Mason guided her to a wooden reception counter where a male employee in a navy suit waited.

"I never expected you to put me up in a place like this," she whispered as Mason handed his credit card to the man.

"That's why I'm enjoying this so much." Mason grinned, transforming his face from handsome to ungodly beautiful. It was like a blast of sunlight appearing from behind a dark cloud. The contrast to his typical stoic expression was like night and day. "And this place is close to campus. You can walk to your test tomorrow."

Lord have mercy. Laila gripped the polished counter, needing the support after being blindsided by his smile. She glanced at the man checking her in, but the hotel employee didn't react to the display of absolute masculine perfection.

"Where are we again?"

"The Caislean."

Laila had never heard of the hotel, but their locations were displayed on the wall behind the counter in raised brass lettering. Boston, Miami, Las Vegas, New York, Milan, Sydney... She stopped reading after Paris.

"It's too expensive," she protested. Laila had no idea what this place cost, but she could tell from the heavy stationery behind the desk and the shine of the counter that it was too much.

"Don't worry about it." Turning to the man, Mason leaned toward him. "She didn't get a chance to eat dinner. Will you please send something up? Whatever the chef's specialty is. Oh, and she's a baker, so please add something special for dessert."

"What are you doing?" Laila squeaked, grabbing his arm. "Dinner must be more than my entire paycheck."

Another quirk of his lip. "I said, don't worry about it."

"Would you prefer a king-sized bed for two or a double room?" the attendant asked with a polite smile.

"She only needs one bed. I won't be joining. I also have this," he said, handing over a second card.

The attendant's demeanor changed subtly. His expression had been welcoming and polite, but when he took the card, it became downright deferential. "Ah. Thank you, Mr. Lang. Why don't you give me a minute? Let me see if I can upgrade you to a suite."

He tapped on the keyboard, then looked up with a smile. "Good news. We've had a cancellation, so there is one available."

"Make sure to bill all expenses to that credit card," Mason added.

"Wait." Laila tugged him away from the desk. She held up the small paper bag she'd packed in a rush. "At least cancel dinner. I brought leftovers."

"Save them for later," he told her with a laugh. "When do your midterms end?"

"The day after tomorrow."

"Stay here until Friday then," he said. "When you're done with midterms, you can come back here to unwind a bit. Then text me. I'll pick you up."

Laila's eyes darted over the lobby. It was like being in her personal version of Aladdin's treasure cave. It was tempting, but she couldn't let him do this. "It's not too late to find another hotel. This place might cost your firstborn. And what was that card? Not the credit card. The other one."

Mason chuckled. She warmed, pleased she could make him laugh. He didn't do that a lot.

"The price won't be that bad, because that card was a special VIP identification."

Laila's drew her head back. "You stay here often enough to have a VIP card?"

"No. But my buddy knows the owners, and they hand out these member cards to their friends. You can put other people on them. The room isn't free, but it's heavily discounted and gives you access to many perks. I rarely get the chance to use it. Most of the places I work don't have fancy hotels—most don't have hotels period. You should make the most of it."

"Oh..." Laila didn't know what to say to that. "I guess I should then."

"Good."

Staring up into his perfect face, Laila racked her brain for something brilliant to say. But the man behind the desk signaled them before she could think of anything, indicating the room was ready.

Mason walked her to the elevators. "Do you have everything you need? You didn't forget any of your books, did you?" he asked, gesturing to her overnight bag.

"Books?" she echoed stupidly.

"To study for your midterms," he prompted.

"Oh." Blushing, she shook her head, lifting her bag. "I have them. Thank you."

Most of her midterm materials were on her computer in any case.

"Well, if you think of anything later, give me a call. I can run you back to your place to get it."

"That's kind of you. This entire thing is too generous," she said, gesturing to their surroundings.

He waved away her thanks. "Don't mention it. And sorry the party got in the way of your studies. It won't happen again."

"Well, you are setting a bad precedent," she joked weakly. "You can't rent me a luxury hotel suite every time you have a gathering."

"All the more reason to keep a lid on things in the future, but I don't mind treating you. You deserve to be pampered every once in a while."

His intense blue eyes bored into hers for a beat. The elevator doors opened, and he backed away. Feeling weak-kneed, she stepped inside the cabin.

Walking backward, he raised his hand. "Study hard," he called cheerfully.

Laila craned her neck to watch him leave.

"Oomph," she groaned as the elevator doors closed on her.

Flushing in chagrin, she pulled her head inside and pressed the button for her floor.

🐾

Laila was still flushed when she reached her floor, but the Caislean hotel suite did a lot to distract her from her embarrassment.

The door opened with a short hallway on the left, which dead-ended with a three-way mirror next to a built-in coat closet beside a sink with smaller mirrors fixed to the wall. Glancing into them confirmed they magnified her face. It was the ultimate set up to get ready for a night on the town, conveniently located next to the door and closet for last-minute touch-ups.

The rest of the suite was just as well designed. She flipped the light switch to the main room, charmed by the sight of a small sitting room with a comfy-looking couch and a loveseat with a sizable flat-screen facing them. Behind it, two steps separated a set of double doors. They stood open, revealing an impossibly wide bed covered by a sky-blue coverlet. It was angled so the occupants could watch the television while lying down.

Laila stroked the couch upholstery, marveling at its softness. In the bedroom, she found an ensuite bathroom. The toilet was in a separate room nearest the door. A walk-in shower stall stood on the other side of a huge oval tub.

Squealing, Laila climbed inside the tub fully clothed. Nestled in the far corner was an entire line of bath products stamped with the hotel's name and logo, including bath salts and a full-sized bottle of bubble bath.

In contrast, her apartment had a small shower stall right next to the toilet. It was all one room, tiled up to the door. A drain in the middle was supposed to make sure the room didn't flood, but she always had to place towels against the door just in case. Laila couldn't remember the last time she'd had access to a tub—probably since her stepmother had to sell their house.

Laila was about to fling off her clothes when a knock at the door announced the arrival of dinner.

"What is this?" she asked when the waitress delivering her tray whipped off the silver dish cover.

"Seared duck magret with polenta and fresh vegetables—today's house special as requested. We also have a slice of our signature pavlova cake. It's a personal favorite among the staff. I hope you enjoy it. Please call the concierge if there's anything you need."

The woman pointed out the hotel directory, encouraging Laila to look at the other amenities before leaving. Laila had her phone in her hand before the door closed behind her. Rosamie arrived less than twenty minutes later, just enough time for Laila to devour the main course and half the dessert.

Her friend zipped back and forth like a bumblebee on a sugar high, checking every nook and cranny of the suite down to the plush carpet fibers.

"Oh my God, this couch is amazing. I would give up my bed for this. I could live on this thing," she said, getting on her hands and knees to rub her cheek against the fabric. Using her feet, she pushed herself across the cushions, stroking them with her entire body.

"You better not be wearing foundation, Rosamie," Laila scolded, climbing on the couch next to her and handing her the cake plate. "Here, I saved you half."

Rosamie sat up in a hurry, checking each cushion to make sure it wasn't marked. "They're fine. I'm only wearing eyeliner, and it's the expensive smudge-proof kind." She got up on her knees, making a beeline for the plate. "Gimme!"

Handing over the plate, Laila giggled as Rosamie gobbled up the rest of the pavlova, moaning in ecstasy. "I'm only eating this because you can bake this with your eyes closed," she said between bites. "You can make this, right? I don't think I can go back to a world where I can't get this on the regular."

"I'm pretty sure I can make it." Laila laughed. "It's a basic meringue shell with whipped cream and fruit."

"Oh, sweetie," Rosamie said, her eyes rolling back into her head. "There is nothing basic about this. *This* is better than sex."

"I will have to take your word." Laila giggled. "Did you see the size of the tub?"

"Yes!" Rosamie bounced up and down on the plush cushion. "You'll be able to do laps in it."

"Almost," Laila agreed. "Hey, do you want to stay the night? It'll be like a luxury sleepover."

Rosamie groaned. "I would, but I promised my mom I'd help get my brothers to school in the morning. Mom has her annual check-up tomorrow—mammogram, pap smear—the whole nine yards. And

Dougie and Jerico never get up with their alarm. I'll have to drag them out of bed by their hair."

Laila shook her head. Rosamie's brothers were a handful, but she knew her friend loved them to bits despite the colorful epithets she used to describe them. "Well, then come back tomorrow night. There's a heated pool in the basement, and I know you love to swim."

Rosamie's jaw dropped. "Mr. Marvelous is paying for *two* nights?"

"Yes—until midterms are over. But he doesn't pay full price. He's got some sort of hookup that gets him a big discount."

The phone on the coffee table rang. She picked up the receiver, then had a short conversation with the concierge. "I'll let you know," she said, hanging up.

"Let me guess. There's a problem with Mr. Marvelous' credit card," Rosamie said with a wry twist of her lips.

"No." Laila wanted to laugh at her friend's pessimism. "They wanted me to know that Mr. Lang, Mason, has asked them to schedule a *massage* for me. I guess he's still worried about my back."

Rosamie swallowed the last bite of Pavlova before licking the spoon. "Well, that shows me what's what."

Confused, Laila frowned. "*What?*"

Her friend pointed the spoon at her. "Mr. Marvelous totally wants to fuck you."

Laila cringed. "He does *not.*"

Rosamie smirked. "Of course he does. A guy wouldn't go to all this trouble for a neighbor out of the goodness of his heart."

"He does have a good heart," Laila protested. "Not to mention that with me out of the way, he and his friends can be as loud as they want."

With as many women as they want... Laila pushed the image of the tall, attractive model-type woman airily waving her cigarette at Mason out of her head.

"That, and he must still feel bad about tackling me," she added with a shrug. Her happy buzz dampening, she rose to wash her hands in the bathroom. She came back, kicking off her shoes and taking a running leap onto the bed.

She hit with a soft crash, the mattress engulfing and supporting her at the same time. It was perfect. "Oh, yassss queen." She rolled over. "Get your bootie over here. You have to feel this."

Rosamie stood, copying her running leap to the bed. She landed with a crash that barely jostled the thick mattress.

"Holy crap! We have to steal it," Rosamie said, flopping next to her. "Seriously, do you think they would notice if we carried a humongous mattress out to my car just before check out?"

"I'm afraid they might, so we better make the most of it." Laila stretched out her arms and legs, pushing them up and down. "Look, I can make a mattress angel and not even come close to touching you."

Chuckling, Rosamie did the same, twisting and reaching out to brush Laila with her fingertips. "I have to stretch way over to reach your fingers. Is this a California king? Cause it seems bigger than that."

"I don't know, but it's the widest bed I've ever seen." Laila could roll over more than half-a-dozen times without falling off.

Rosamie sat up and grabbed a pillow, pointing it at the headboard, the couches, and a lamp in turn. "I love you, I love you, and I especially love you," she said.

"Don't forget about this," Laila said, getting up on her knees to touch the art-deco design on the wall above the headboard. The pattern was in shining tiles, similar in style to the one in the lobby but different in execution.

"The amenities folder over there says each room has a unique design. It gives this place that perfect personal touch."

"That is pretty cool." Rosamie wasn't even looking at the design. Her eyes were closed as she wiggled on the dense mattress. Eventually, she raised her phone to check the time. She groaned. "I better get going."

"But you'll come back tomorrow?" Laila asked hopefully.

"Try to stop me!" Rosamie laughed, heading for the door. Laila followed her, picking up the cake plate and setting it on the tray.

Her friend paused at the threshold. "Well, I'll come back *if* you're alone. However, if Mr. Marvelous decides to drop by to help you test out that mattress, be sure to let me know so I can make other plans."

The velveteen pillow Laila threw hit the closing door. Once Rosamie was gone, Laila hurried to make sure the pillow wasn't damaged. "There you go," she said, laying it gently on the couch as if it were a baby bird.

Spinning around, she twirled like a ballerina before hurrying to the bathroom, undressing as she went. Once there, she uncapped the bubble bath and took a deep sniff. Unused to the perfume, she couldn't identify the scent, but it was delicious. Impulsively, she grabbed the bath salts as well, determined to make the most of her time with the glorious tub.

When the bath was ready, she jumped inside, holding the iridescent bubbles in her palm before blowing them out of her hands with a giggle.

Then she lay back, trying not to fantasize about the man who'd gifted her this experience.

CHAPTER SEVEN

Gardullo's Gourmet Grocery, the specialty store where Laila worked, had a large lot relative to the size of the building. Mason locked his car and put his hands in the pockets of his bomber jacket, vacillating on whether to go inside.

You were just passing by and decided to get something for dinner. Laila might not even be working since it was close to closing time. Most of her shifts were earlier in the day so the goods she baked could be stocked fresh.

In all likelihood, she was on campus in class or at a lecture. He didn't know her schedule well enough to guess.

Mason was almost at the store's entrance when he stopped. He could still hear Ransom ribbing him about Laila.

His friend had made a lot of noise when Mason had come straight back to his apartment alone. Soon, his friends joined in, but he'd ignored them, kicking back with Louis and Julio in front of the flat screen and joking around about their house hunting or the types of patients Julio saw in the ER.

The party hadn't broken up until close to two, but another bottle had smoothed things over with Old Man Tran. His other neighbors didn't complain, although he was on the receiving end of a few glares in the laundry room.

As for Laila, Mason had fully intended to drive her home from the hotel after her exams, but she'd texted him early Friday to say she didn't need one. Then she'd slipped a sweet little thank-you note under his door this morning.

Chastising himself for his hesitation, Mason went inside, picking up a basket before wandering the aisles. He hadn't gotten a lot of sleep last night, wondering if she was okay, hoping her exams had gone well.

He was just going to check on her. It wasn't a big deal.

The grocery store was small compared to the major chains, but they made the most of the space. He started in the fruit, picking up rarities like dragon fruit and those little yellow mangos he had first seen in Mexico but had starting to pop up in local shops stateside a few years ago. The deli cases included meats and deliciously prepared meals. He selected a few before finally zeroing in on the bakery.

Gardullo's was one of those places that prided itself on its home-made fresh baked goods. To drive the point home, it put the whole operation on display. The industrial ovens were in another room, separated by an open arch. It was laid out so you could see the whole space, showcasing the labor of their bakers. A long counter bracketed the arch with a glass display case chock full of pastries, pies, and cakes.

Laila was bent over the counter. She was spreading what appeared to be honey over a tray of dough with a brush. A clear plastic container with ground pistachios rested on the counter next to her.

"Are you making baklava?"

Laila gasped, her head flying up. The brush flew out of her hand, hitting the container of pistachios with enough force to knock it over.

"Sorry." Mason winced. "I didn't mean to scare you."

Laughing, Laila scooped the pistachios into the container with one of her gloved hands. She dropped the brush into the sink before picking up a new one. "Unfortunately, I startle easily. My friend Rosamie loves running up behind me after class just to see me jump."

The flush on her cheeks sent a tingle down his spine. An image of her underneath him, lips parted, flashed through his head. But it wasn't a memory of when he tackled her in his living room. This time, she was in his bed.

He squeezed his eyes shut. *Stop that.*

"I was in the neighborhood, so I thought I would grab some grub," he said, holding up his basket by way of explanation. "How did your exams go?"

"Fine, I think," Laila said with a hapless shrug. "Well, at least I hope they did."

"I'm sure you did fine," he reassured her. "And you got back from the hotel okay?"

"Yes," she said brightly, but then blushed as if she knew she'd responded too eagerly and with a touch too much volume. "I hope you don't mind. That suite was too amazing not to share, so I asked Rosamie to stay with me after my exams. She drove me home the next day."

"Not at all," he said with a smile. "I remember the bathtubs were pretty nice."

"It was huge." Laila beamed, spreading her arms as wide as they could go. She wrinkled her nose. "But I'm surprised that's what stood out for you, considering the competition—that humongous bed."

His eyebrow rose.

"Not that I pictured you on the bed," she burst out suddenly. "Not like that. Just you know—tall and blond with skin."

"Skin?" he echoed, a trapped belly laugh making him shake.

She shook her head fiercely, tripping over her words. "No. I meant tall. Because long, err, body."

Her lashes fluttering wildly, she broke off, slapping a hand over her mouth.

Mason bit the inside of his cheek to keep from laughing aloud.

Holding up a finger, he cleared his throat, stalling until he could trust himself to speak.

"My feet do tend to hang over the edge of most beds, but I never had a problem at the Caislean, even in their standard rooms. But the tub stands out the most."

Laila struggled to compose herself. "Really?" she squeaked. She coughed twice, but then a corner of her mouth lifted. "You don't strike me as the bubble-bath type."

"Oh, you'd be surprised."

One of her fine eyebrows rose, and he shrugged. "The kind of work I do, it wears you down. I have to run through minefields, sometimes literally. I've been beaten to hell, shot, and stabbed. I also had this really bad splinter once." He widened his arms, imitating her earlier pose. "It was huge—the white whale of splinters."

He put his arms down when Laila giggled, her posture relaxed.

She reached into the case, grabbed something, and held it up. "Cookie?" she asked, pushing it toward him.

"Sure." He took it, intending on taking a single bite, but it was so good he couldn't stop himself from inhaling the rest. "Oh my God. That was so good. What flavor was that?"

"Salted caramel chocolate chunk," she said, clearly more comfortable talking about food. "Anyway, now that midterms are over, I've been picking up extra shifts. I'm not ducking you or anything."

"I know that," he said. "I got your note. No thanks were necessary, by the way. It was my fault you couldn't study at your place. I made the guys promise not to let things get that out of hand again, at least not during the week. But if you ever have an issue, let me know, and I can get you another room."

"That's above and beyond, you know," she said with a twist of her lips. "Especially since I'm guessing you didn't do the same for Mr. Tran."

"What do you mean? Old Man Tran was in the room next to you. Didn't you see him?"

She giggled. "No. I must have missed him."

Charmed, Mason leaned a little closer. When it came to Laila, he could afford to be generous. Tran would have to settle for cheap bottles of booze.

"Did you get the massage?" he asked, immediately regretting it. *Now I'm picturing her naked on a massage table.*

Laila opened her mouth to answer when a timer interrupted them. "Oh, just a sec."

She hustled to the ovens, opening a door and pulling out the rack. With quick, efficient movements, she grabbed handfuls of pastel-colored bits from a nearby tub, pressing them into the top of the pans. Then she pushed the tray back and closed the door, resetting the timer before returning to the counter.

"I'm interrupting your work. I should get going."

"Oh, don't worry about it. As long as we don't burn anything, the owners like it when people talk to us. I have a few retirees who love to watch me work. And I'm just prepping this for later," she added, waving at the baklava. "I'm going to freeze it and bake it tomorrow. My shift is over as soon as those brownies are done."

Mason perked up. "You're making brownies?" He loved Laila's rocky-road brownies.

"I am," she hedged. "But these may not be up your alley." The timer went off, and she held up a finger. "Let me show you."

Excusing herself, she went to the oven, returning with the tray. She held it up.

"Are those Lucky Charms marshmallows?"

"The commercial equivalent. You can buy these knockoffs in bulk. They are almost the same in terms of taste, but they don't have that pesky nutritious cereal getting in the way."

"I'm not sure the cereal part is all that nutritious," he said skeptically. "But you're right. I don't think I'd like those very much. I do, however, see a lot of other things I would like—including some old favorites."

He recognized her handiwork in the display case. There was the buttermilk pie—this time, adorned with powdered sugar in the shape of the store's logo. It sat next to a cake adorned with raspberries that were drizzled with white chocolate. A million things caught his eye, including the mini strawberry cheesecakes. And then there were the cookies. Were those her sugar pecan?

There were other fancier desserts as well, but Mason had made his choices.

When he asked Laila to pack them up for him, her eyes darted from side to side as if to check if they were being watched.

She stood on her tiptoes. "Are you sure you want to buy them? I could just whip up a few things at home for you. The markup here is a little high."

"I can afford it," he assured her. "Plus, you should be paid for your labor. Never sell yourself short."

"But the hotel room—"

"I owed you," he interrupted before blurting out, "Hey, if you're done, do you want a ride?"

Mason hadn't intended to ask, but if she were on her way home, it would be weird if he didn't offer.

"Sure. If you don't mind, that would be great. I'll just finish up here," she said, gesturing to the trays. "I might need ten minutes."

"Sounds good," he said, lifting the basket. "I'll just go pay for my stuff and wait by the car."

A few minutes later, Laila came outside, hurriedly tucking in her shirt and fussing with her hair. When she saw him, she stopped and smiled a touch nervously. He waved, stepping to the passenger side to open the door for her.

He'd done the same the night he drove her to the hotel, but this time she asked about it.

"Don't get me wrong—it's endearing but a little old fashioned," she observed. "I don't think I know of another person who does that."

Even her father had only done it for her stepmother when Janice was wearing heels and dressed for a night on the town.

Mason shrugged. "It's just the way I was brought up. In my part of Tennessee, men are brought up to be gentlemen, and a gentleman always opens a lady's door. At least that's what my aunt Martha taught me."

"You have an aunt named Martha?" Her lips quirked. "Her last name wouldn't happen to be Kent, would it?"

He held up a hand. "No Superman jokes. I get enough of that from my team."

She giggled. "Can you blame them?" Laila gestured at his muscled chest.

"Superman isn't blond."

"True," she said, subsiding. "Unless you're in disguise..."

The way she said it was so adorably cheeky he couldn't help but laugh.

They were only a few minutes away from their building when she cast a shy glance his way. "Do you, um, do you want to grab a bite to eat? I just got paid, and there's a new little ramen place my friend told me about that just opened a few blocks from us. My treat."

"Oh." He hesitated. "I was going to go for a run before opening up one of those," he said, pointing his thumb to the sack of groceries in his backseat.

"No problem," she said hurriedly, turning away. "I just feel like I still owe you after that hotel room."

"You don't," he assured her lightly, but his gut twisted. Laila had been gazing at him with such a warm and sweet expression, but she wouldn't even look at him now.

"I can get out here," she said as he pulled up in front of their building.

He glanced at the overcast sky. A few fat drops hit the windshield. "Why don't you let me pull into the garage? It's starting to rain."

"Don't worry, this is fine. I need to check my mailbox anyway," Laila replied, her head down as she unbuckled her seatbelt.

She was out the door before he could protest.

Mason watched her hurry inside, her shoulders hunched in over her chest as if to protect herself from a blow from above.

Every fiber of his being rebelled, the instinct to chase after her sudden and sharp.

"*Fuck.*" Mason banged his hand on the steering wheel. It smarted, but he couldn't help thinking it should have been his head. That needed a good whack.

It's too soon, a little voice in his head whispered. Ransom was hit on their last outing. It could have easily been him, and it could have been a kill shot. And Ransom had been following orders to a tee. Sometimes, people could do everything right and still catch a bullet.

How could Mason risk getting involved with someone like Laila with that hanging over his head?

But staying away was starting to become a real struggle. Especially when she had just put herself out there with that dinner invitation. Sure, they could pretend it had been a casual thing, a simple thank you on her part. But they would have been lying to themselves and each other.

Instinct told him that sweet invitation wouldn't come again. Laila was far too shy.

Swearing under his breath, Mason parked the car. By the time he got upstairs, Laila was already inside her place, the flickering light under the door telling him that she was moving around in her kitchen.

Mason stared at her door for a full minute, willing himself to knock. Instead, he pivoted and went into his place. He changed into his running gear, resolving that whatever else was true, he hadn't just lied to Laila about his plans.

CHAPTER EIGHT

Laila ran up the stairs, closing the door to her apartment as if she could shut out her embarrassment and leave it in the hallway along with the shreds of her dignity.

Everything is fine. Mason hadn't realized she was asking for a date. The Caislean Hotel was a highly rated luxury chain, or so she'd learned after her stay there. She would never have been able to afford a room on her own. It was only natural she would want to repay him in some fashion. Or at least that was what she kept telling herself. But her pulse insisted on racing, replaying the moment she'd made a fool of herself on a loop.

Groaning, she scrubbed her face with her hands. After a minute, she dragged herself into activity, forcing herself to put her things away before turning off her floor lamps.

Drops were pelting the small window above her bed with increasing force and frequency. Judging from the sound, the rain was turning into a deluge.

I guess Mason doesn't need an excuse to cancel that run. And it had to have been an excuse...

Laila groaned again, rubbing her fingers over her heart. *C'mon, this is ridiculous.* It wasn't aching. Not literally. This was a purely psycho-somatic response.

At least now she knew for sure. If Mason had been interested in her, he would have taken her up on her dinner offer. He hadn't—case closed.

Laila changed out of her damp uniform, pulling on a dry tank top and leggings. Planning to go to bed early, she didn't bother with a bra.

Heavy-hearted, she forced herself to fix some dinner, but a quick quesadilla was all she could manage. She'd just turned off the burner on her stove when there was a knock on the door. Mr. Tran was angling for leftovers from the bakery again, she'd bet.

Sighing, Laila picked up the bag holding a day-old cinnamon roll. She opened the door without looking through the peephole.

Mason stood on the other side. And he was wet, soaked to the skin with his blond hair plastered to his head.

Laila only had a few seconds to register his presence, and she spent most of it ogling his chest—every taut muscle visible through his now-transparent white t-shirt. He reached out, pulling her to him with enough force for her breasts to make an audible slap against his chest.

"D-did you lock yourself out?" she asked, stuttering slightly.

Mason shook his head firmly. Still holding her tight against his chest, he started walking them into her apartment. Then he kicked the door closed.

Startled and aroused, Laila stared up at him, her tongue glued to the roof of her mouth. She couldn't have uttered a word to save her life...but Mason wasn't holding her this close for the sake of conversation.

They stared at each for an endless minute. She counted a million heartbeats before his mouth came down on hers. The first touch was a feather-soft brush, a gentle swipe of his lower lip before pressing heavier and hotter.

Whimpering, Laila rubbed her chest against his. She didn't care that her thin top was being soaked through because the friction was the most pleasurable sensation she'd ever felt.

Then Mason's hands moved down her back, cupping her rear. He lifted her with sudden urgency, guiding her legs around his waist. Spinning her around, he pressed her against the door as his lips teased hers apart.

Half in denial that this was happening, Laila clutched Mason's shoulders, trying to catalog every sensation for posterity. But the minute his questing tongue slipped inside her mouth, her thoughts splintered. Mint and honey exploded across her senses. One taste, and she was lost.

Mason growled something against her mouth, but she couldn't make out the words. Not that she needed to hear to understand what he wanted. His grip on her thighs flexed, lifting her higher until she rubbed against his hard length. Her leggings were no protection since his heat bled through the thin material. She shuddered, her core spasming involuntarily.

Heartbeat thrumming in time with her quickened breaths, Laila clenched her inner thighs, climbing Mason like a tree.

His breath grew ragged in response. Shifting to support her weight with one arm, he used his free hand to pull the straps of her tank top, tugging them down until they hit her elbows.

Cool air hit her exposed breasts, making her gasp. Nipples hardening, she tried to tug the top the rest of the way down, but Mason stopped her. His right hand caught the cloth against at her lower back. Wrapping the material around his fist, he used it to restrain her arms at her sides.

The feeling of being bound and helpless in Mason's arms damn near made her pass out.

"*Please,*" she rasped. Laila didn't care that she was begging. She needed his touch.

His eyes met hers, and she almost swallowed her tongue. Mason's blue eyes were so light and intense they gleamed almost silver in the low light. Laila wasn't very experienced, but she recognized the hunger in them.

Then his gaze dipped down, feasting on her bare skin. Mason dragged her tighter against his body, raising her breasts to the level of his mouth. His lips closed over her nipple, his tongue rasping over the tight bud before he drew on it hard, suckling before biting down.

The nip was gentle, but it was enough to send a bolt of electricity down her body. Crying out, she threw her head back, accidentally whacking it against the hard wood.

Mason made a low, commiserating sound in the base of his throat, the noise suspiciously close to a purr. He cupped the back of her head, and the world spun as he carried her deeper into the room.

Her apartment was a cramped one-room studio. It didn't leave him much room to maneuver. When Mason bumped the lightweight paper screen that separated her bed from the rest of the room, the rickety assemblage fell over with a loud whack.

Mason didn't react at all. His single-minded focus was on making her pant and moan. His mouth moved from one breast to another, licking, sucking, teeth grazing one nipple before shifting to the other.

Her eyes opened when her back hit the mattress. Mason towered over her, his gaze hot enough to blister. With quick work, he tugged her leggings and panties down, then tossed them away while she lay completely bared to him with only her tank top wrapped around her waist.

Too awed to speak, Laila watched as Mason stripped his shirt off. Dark sweatpants swiftly followed it. Unable to stop herself, she sat up, her hand reaching out to stroke the glorious work of art that was his muscled chest. His eyes closed as her hands roamed, but when she strayed too low, he caught her wrist. Pushing her back on the bed, he came down on top of her, naked skin pressing against naked skin. But that wasn't enough for him. Mason pulled away long enough to tug the tank top down, working it over her body until it slipped over her feet, nudging it off the bed with his foot. His boxer briefs followed suit.

Heated steel pressed against her thigh as he settled between her legs.

Laila pressed hot kisses to every part of Mason that she could reach until he took her mouth again. His tongue stroked hers aggressively while his hands roamed all over her body. His touch left a hot tingling trail on the surface of her skin.

Mason pressed his face into her neck, inhaling deeply. "You smell so good. Like vanilla and sugar." His tongue licked up and down, sending her temperature skyrocketing. "Tastes like sugar, too."

His voice didn't sound normal. It had picked up this panty-melting drawl that was all the more disarming because she'd never heard it before. She doubted many people had. *This is his Tennessee coming out.*

Laila squirmed, arching up in a silent plea for more contact. When Mason broke the kiss, she protested. He turned aside, reaching for something. When she heard the crinkle of plastic tearing, she glanced down to see him rolling a condom over the head of his cock.

Oh my God, this is happening. This is really happening.

"Laila?" Mason's beautiful face hovered over hers. "Are you checking out on me?"

"No!" She reached up, grabbing the nape of his neck and pulling him down. "*Never.*"

Laila put everything into that kiss—the first time she'd ever seen him outside their building while he'd been stretching for a run like a sun-kissed Greek god, all those times she intentionally brushed his fingers with hers when he handed over his keys...and every time she touched herself while thinking about him, alone in this very bed.

The kiss was all the answer he needed. His body moved over hers, breaking over her like a wave. His pecs started low, brushing her stomach and gliding up until they abraded the sensitive tips of her breasts.

"Holy God," she said, a squeak escaping. Mason's sudden grin was deliciously naughty. Bending his head, he bit her lower lip, sucking it into his mouth as he settled between her legs, his thighs flexing to push them open wider.

Then she felt his long, thick length, the tip of his cock running back and forth over her slick folds.

Wet and aching, Laila hissed as her channel pulsed and clenched down on nothing. Understanding her need, Mason shushed her, soothing her with a hot, open-mouthed kiss. But his hands weren't so gentle. He took both her wrists in one of his, pinning them over her head.

"I'm going to take you now," he whispered in her ear. Laila gulped, nodding in wordless agreement when he paused, hovering.

Mason muttered something that sounded like *'Thank Christ'* before flexing his hips, driving his cock past the threshold of her aching sheath. But it wasn't an easy breaching. Her core wasn't precisely untried. A slim vibrator was lying in a shoebox under the bed, but her little toy was just that—a toy. At least it was when compared to the thick reality pulsing against her skin. So, despite her almost-desperate welcome, her body resisted him.

Laila could feel Mason hesitate. Determined not to let him stop, she wrapped her legs around him, pulling him close. A whimper escaped as the broad head of his cock pushed past the tight entrance of her channel.

Mason sucked in a breath, freezing with predatory stillness. Laila's heart nosedived in her chest. For a split second, she worried he was going to withdraw, leaving her alone and cold.

Apparently, though, she misread his intentions. Whatever internal battle Mason's brain waged, he'd already lost. "Sugar, look at my cock. Watch me take you."

Whimpering at that testosterone-filled order, Laila glanced down, her eyes fixed on his shaft, which was slowly disappearing into virgin territory. "Oh God, please, *please*," she cried out incoherently as his hips pressed flush against her.

"I'm going to give you what you want, sugar. Never doubt that," he said roughly.

Crying out in relief, she clutched at him as he began to thrust, sinking deeper and deeper. Whatever pain she felt began to fade with each slippery glide.

Mason was too tall to kiss her lips in this position, but that didn't stop her from kissing him. Laila opened her mouth against his chest, grazing his collarbone with her teeth.

Even though Laila still hurt, her hunger was stronger than the pain. She had been in love with this man for the better part of a year.

If she could have, she would have taken a bite of him, consumed him whole.

Her small show of aggression seemed to inflame Mason. He picked up the pace, pumping faster. His rhythm wasn't easy or gentle, but she didn't care. Laila had waited too long for this. She was too hungry. Acting on instinct, she tightened her inner walls experimentally, squeezing hardest when he was deepest. Mason swore, his head thrown back.

"Be careful what you wish for, baby," he warned with a hiss, his eyes molten silver. Hitching her legs tighter around him, Mason started to thrust, one hand holding her wrists pinned to the bed.

Frantic now, Laila threw her hips at him, meeting him thrust for thrust. Bliss fizzed in her veins as she rocked with him, greedily absorbing every surge and stroke until she, too, was moaning, pulsing and fluttering all around him.

He let go of her wrists, maneuvering her knees a little higher.

"Are you close?" he breathed in her ear. "Or do you need me to fuck you harder?"

Laila cried out as Mason ground against her, pelvis stroking her clit in time with his thrusts. Blindly bucking against him, she gasped as the knot of pleasure in her core began to tighten like a spring winding tight.

"That's it," Mason breathed, his hips driving into her relentlessly. "That pink pretty pussy needs it deep. It needs my thick cock to fuck it hard, doesn't it?"

"Yes, *yes*," she pleaded, her nails digging into his back.

The tight coursing pleasure splintered, breaking her open as she screamed out Mason's name.

It was nothing like the brief climaxes she'd experienced on her own. This was nothing less than rapture, a paroxysm of pleasure. And it went on and on because Mason kept pushing, grinding and stroking with his hands and cock until she collapsed underneath him in a sweaty, boneless mess.

But Mason hadn't come yet.

Laila hadn't known if she would be aware of the moment Mason orgasmed. Rosamie had frequently complained about her ex's stealth climaxes. Most of the porn videos she'd watched on lonely solo nights also seemed to corroborate the fact men didn't do big finishes. But there was no doubt with Mason. He didn't come—he *exploded.*

Swearing a blue streak, Mason buried his hands in her hair as his thick shaft jerked and pulsed inside her, setting her throbbing again. His arms and chest went rigid before he buried himself to the hilt once, twice, and three times before he let gasped out, '*Fuck,*' and collapsed on top of her.

Still trembling, Laila wrapped her arms around Mason's chest, her legs jerkily rubbing over his muscled calves and thighs.

Belatedly, she realized he was talking to her.

"Hmm?" she asked drowsily.

Mason rolled over, taking her with him. She ended up plastered across his chest and arm. "I asked if you were okay, sugar?"

His usually mild accent was thicker than molasses.

Loving the Southern drawl more than words could say, she moved her head to kiss whatever she could reach without having to move her useless limbs—in this case, his shoulder. His cock was soft and sated now, but still substantial enough to fill her. It moved deeper inside her, a teasing echo of the night's activities.

"I'm good," she murmured. But all too soon, her neurons began to fire again. "I should get off you. I must be heavy."

"You're about as heavy as a feather, sugar. Stay just a minute longer," he drawled, pressing a hand right above her ass.

It felt as if he'd reached into her chest and squeezed her heart. Glowing, she rested her cheek on his chest, drifting off with a smile.

CHAPTER NINE

Laila had positioned her bed where the early morning light would hit her face. She was a heavy sleeper, and she worked long hours, both in the store and at her classes. Burning the candle at both ends, she always needed a little help getting up, and the sun was the one thing that never failed to rouse her.

Mason, however, didn't even stir when the rays hit his face. But Laila didn't mind. It gave her a perfect chance to study him in repose.

His face was lit up, the fine down next to his ear sparkling like pure gold. It almost hurt to look at him. He was too beautiful to be real—like an archangel, complete with scars earned in battle.

There was a long gash down his side, a scar she hadn't noticed the first time she saw him shirtless. Below that, there was a round puckered mark on his abdomen. It was bigger than a cigarette burn would have been, although it could have been from a cigar. But she didn't think that was likely, given his occupation. Laila suspected it was a healed gunshot wound.

There were other marks scattered over his body, including an inch-long burn scar below his wrist. Sympathy welled up in her, but she resisted the impulse to reach out and stroke the marks with her finger.

Despite the events of the previous night, Laila had a hard time believing Masson was lying there next to her—well, crammed-in. Her full-sized mattress had always been more than enough for her short ass, but Mason hadn't been kidding about being too tall for most beds.

His head wasn't hanging over the end because he was lying at an angle, his knees bent with his feet pressed against the wall.

Damn, even his toes are perfect. As was the rest of him.

Mason was gloriously naked—although her sheets hid the best parts. He couldn't have displayed that gorgeous body more effectively if she'd posed him herself.

And she couldn't have asked for a more sensual, special night for her first time.

Laila was a practical modern woman. She hadn't been waiting for true love, and she also didn't ascribe to archaic gender norms. Virginity wasn't a true medical condition, or so she'd learned in her women's studies class. Given her determined efforts at self-pleasure—her vibrator was top of the line—she wasn't even sure she'd met the technical definition of a virgin before last night. Her stepmother would have said she wasn't one. That last would have been pronounced with a scowl, but Laila tried not to think about that part.

Regardless, these details hadn't mattered before. She'd simply been too shy around men to act on her desires. Also, after seeing how they behaved on Fraternity Row, she was cautious around the boys on campus. She'd seen first-hand how a perfectly behaved study partner could turn into a raging ass with a little alcohol in him.

However, last night had been a revelation. Her first sexual encounter had been quickly followed by her second, when she'd drifted awake to sparks of pleasure to find Mason stroking her ass, dipping his fingers between her legs to brush over the lips of her sex and clit.

She didn't know if Mason had realized the true extent of her inexperience, but she suspected he'd been aware on some level. He'd been too attentive after the first round, asking if she was too sore for more. Laila had wanted him too much to care, so she'd told a little white lie.

But when Mason took her again, he'd been gentle, his touch tender but sure. The heat had built languorously, sweet but not overwhelming—up until he brought her to another screaming orgasm.

Laila was a novice, but her heart told her that they had shared something more special than sex. It had felt like lovemaking.

Now what do I do? She was naked, lying in bed with the man of her dreams. Nothing in her short life had prepared her for this experience.

What were people supposed to do the morning after?

Breakfast. I should make him breakfast. But Laila couldn't bring herself to move just yet. She was afraid of breaking the spell. Then Mason sighed and turned around, flipping over on his stomach. His arm moved up, putting his watch closer to his face.

Laila held her breath, waiting for him to open his eyes and say something. But he didn't do that. His arms and leg, which had been relaxed in sleep against her, turned to corded steel. His entire body stiffened, transmitting his uneasiness as he realized where he was.

Stung, Laila pulled in her limbs. Heart sinking, she tried to decide whether to bolt out of bed or pretend to be asleep.

Just face the consequences like a big girl. This didn't need to be a painful ordeal. She would just wait for Mason to turn around and make some excuse to leave.

But he stayed put, his head turned away while his body screamed with unspoken tension. When he didn't shift, she began to edge away, preparing to run to the bathroom to hide until he left.

Mason's arm shot out, grabbing her by the wrist. His silver-blue eyes ensnared her, stopping her more effectively than his restraining hand. "Do you have to go to work?"

His voice was rough with sleep, but the expression in his eyes was clear, calm. Then his gaze moved down, skimming over her naked body.

"N-no," she whispered.

"*Good.*"

Shifting his hold, Mason stroked down, his large hands wrapping around her hips. A squeak escaped as she slid toward him. When he had her where he wanted her, Mason pushed her knees up, wrapping his arms around them to pin her to the bed.

Then he dived in.

Laila gasped as his lips settled between her thighs. His mouth closed over her clit like it was candy. Grazing the nub of flesh with his teeth, he licked and probed with his tongue, alternately laving and sucking as his fingers clenched into the flesh of her hips.

Stunned, Laila writhed, moaning and gasping from the sensual onslaught. Could pleasure make people blind...because she was pretty damn close to it.

Laila had always thought descriptions of sex in print were over-wrought. She should have known better after last night. Her body was engulfed with a pure squirmy sensation.

Waves of pleasure coursed through her, too intense and powerful for her to stay still. Her instinct was to get away, but Mason wouldn't let her. He had her exactly where he wanted her—exposed and at his mercy.

"*Holy shit*," she cried, bucking when his teeth closed over her clit. Mason chuckled, the sound buzzing her sensitive flesh with a deep vibration.

"I can't stand it," she confessed in a ragged gasp, whipping her head from side to side. "It's too much. I can't—"

Mason lifted his head. "Shh..." He soothed her with a hand, stroking lightly over her stomach, hips, and ass before he returned to his feast, fucking her in earnest with his tongue.

Laila's hips rose and fell in time with the rhythm he set. Lost in the pulsing pleasure, she made sounds she never had before. Broken gasps and low moans filled the room. But her noises seemed to please Mason.

"Louder," he urged after a particularly vocal whimper. Redoubling his efforts, he moved his fingers to her clit, stroking in circles as his tongue penetrated her, working in and out.

Twisting and convulsing, Laila hurtled off the edge with a keening cry. Mason continued to stroke and lick her through the bone-rattling pulses, stopping only when she collapsed on the mattress, too weak to do anything but lie there and try to catch her breath.

Her lids flew open when Mason kissed her stomach. Their eyes met over the naked expanse of her chest. She felt more than saw the smile he pressed against her midriff. He worked his way up her body, lips lingering on her breasts. But what set her off again was his shaft, hard and hot against the sensitive skin of her inner thigh...

Laila tried to work a hand between them to guide him inside her when the phone rang. The ringtone sounded distinctive, classical, and ominous.

"Fuck." Mason jerked into a sitting position. "I'm sorry," he apologized as he leaned over to reach for his pants. "Sorry, this is work."

Hitting redial, he climbed off the bed.

"Lang here," he said into the receiver, not bothering to grab his pants or shirt.

Mason Lang is in my apartment, buck naked. Laila pinched herself, but the unlikely apparition stayed right where it was.

And he's not even a little bit shy, is he? Well, why would he be? The man was a golden god. Modesty was for lesser beings.

A little wrinkle appeared between Mason's brows.

"Oh, really?" He glanced at his watch again. "I guess. Yeah, sure. I can be there in thirty minutes."

Hanging up, he turned back to her, his mouth tight. "I have to go."

Laila pulled the sheet up, covering her breasts, although she wasn't sure why. He'd already seen, stroked, and licked every inch of her. "Do you have to leave town?" she asked tentatively.

"I'm not sure. They didn't say so, and they would have, I think. I'm being called into headquarters."

She blinked, concerned because he was. "Is that not normal?"

"No," he said, the furrow deepening. "We usually get a message to gear up and head for the airport, or we meet at our training facility first for a run-down if the powers that be think one is necessary. We don't get called into the downtown office very often. That's for schmoozing the clients."

He broke off, staring at her. Laila bit her lip, willing for him to say something...*anything.*

"I guess I should go find out what they want."

"Uh, yeah," she said awkwardly. "I hope everything is okay."

"I'm sure it's nothing. If I were getting fired, I would have some clue. My team lead, Dominic, isn't the kind to mince words if you're fucking up on his watch."

Laila nodded her head like a stupid bobblehead doll. "That's comforting."

Mason picked up his pants, getting dressed in a blink. He grabbed his keys.

"Do you want something for the road?" she asked, her head spinning at how fast he could pull on his clothes. Was it a job hazard?

Mason jerked. "What?" A slow grin spread across his face.

Blushing, Laila realized how those words must have sounded. She jerked her thumb at the kitchen counter. "I brought some day-old muffins and a cinnamon roll from work. They're in that bag."

Laughing, Mason nodded. "I am starving," he said, reaching in and taking out the banana nut muffin. "I, uh, I guess we'll talk later."

Laila nodded again, still hiding under the sheet. She waited until the door closed behind him before throwing herself face-down on the bed.

"Oh my God." Burying her face in the pillow, she let out a short, muffled scream.

"Laila?"

Whipping around, she saw Mason at the threshold. He'd come back. *Shit.*

"Are you okay?"

"Yes," she squeaked, mortified.

"Good, good."

"Did you forget something?" she asked.

"Yeah." Crossing the room, he strode up to her, gathering her in his arms. He pressed her close, kissing her within an inch of her life.

"Damn," she gasped, collapsing on the mattress when he let go. Every part of her tingled.

"We *will* talk later, okay?"

"Okay," she agreed, dazed.

CHAPTER TEN

Mason stepped into the elevator before pressing the button for the twentieth floor. Auric headquarters was at the top of an L.A. Highrise. The sleek offices were where the company founders—Ian Quinn and Elias Gardner—met with private companies and government contractors.

The two men were cousins. Gardner came from a much wealthier background than Quinn, but that didn't matter to them. They had been tight since childhood. After doing stints in different branches of the military—Quinn had been a ranger, Gardner a Navy Seal—the ambitious duo joined forces. They founded Auric while still in their twenties, recruiting their closest friends as team leaders.

The interior of the office was designed to impress. Minimalist without being bare, the rooms were professionally staged to convey affluence and stability—the way a bank tried to make its customers believe it had been there for decades, if not longer.

Aside from their work for Uncle Sam, most of Auric's clients were big companies—including one or two multinationals. Some were in the oil business, but not always. The world grew more interconnected by the day. The need to secure people and places would only increase.

Though the Auric offices weren't as flashy as the Caislean, Mason always felt a little out of place whenever he came here. Employees at his level didn't see the main hub too often, usually only when they signed their contracts or updated their wills...which may have explained his mild disquiet.

Every member of Auric was required to have a last will and testament, updated every year. Mason recognized the wisdom of the policy, but it still made him uneasy. Despite regularly facing his mortality on the job, it was never as real to him as when he saw it in black and white while revising his will with the company lawyer—his annual trip to purgatory.

Other than the dreaded paperwork, the bulk of Auric's business was conducted at their training facility near Glendale. Only the team heads came to the offices regularly—not that Quinn and Gardner discouraged visits. But they weren't necessary. Both men still trained with their employees, making themselves accessible should someone want to have a quiet word. When Mason first started at Auric, they used to go on missions, but the business was growing fast, so they did so less and less. The last time Quinn had coordinated an op was over a year ago.

Nevertheless, the cousins' past military experience was one reason Mason had decided to sign up with Auric. It was important to him that the founders weren't fat cats or straight-up pencil pushers. Quinn and Gardner knew what it meant to serve. He trusted them. And before today, he thought that went both ways. Now he wasn't so sure.

Mason didn't know why he was being called in, but he must have done something wrong and not realized it.

It was the only thing that could have distracted him from thoughts of Laila at that moment.

He stopped short of the entrance to Auric offices, images of her slim naked form wrapped around him, flooding through his brain.

Fuck. Stop that. Right now, Mason had to deal with the fact he might be getting fired for some godforsaken reason.

Grunting, he passed a hand through his hair before straightening his posture and opening the glass door the led to the reception era.

Whatever was going on, he could count on Quinn and Gardner to be straight with him.

"Hello, Mr. Lang," Laurie, the receptionist, greeted him. In her early twenties, Laurie was the object of much speculation among the men. A few had asked her out, though without success.

Her bright smile could have been in a toothpaste ad. "They're expecting you," she said with a graceful gesture of her hand.

He inclined his head, intent on going in and getting it over with, but Laurie hopped to her feet behind the desk. "Can I get you something before you go in? Coffee? A bottle of water?"

"No, thank you, ma'am," he said, stiff-necked. The touch of Tennessee in his drawl was proof of his anxiety.

"Be sure to let me know if you change your mind," Laurie said cheerfully before she sat, returning to her work.

A hand clapped him on the shoulder. "Hey, man. Thanks for coming in so fast." Dominic Santos, his team leader, drew him away down the hall. Once they were away from the reception desk, he smirked, nudging him. "You know Laurie never offers to get *me* anything. Nor does she offer refreshments to any of the team heads—I know because I asked. She only fetches for Quinn and Gardner, the clients, and, apparently, you."

Mason ignored the bit about the receptionist. It wasn't hard given the sight that greeted him on the other side of the glass conference room doors.

"Now I know I'm in trouble," he said, looking askance at the group around the oval table. Ian Quinn and Elias Gardner sat with two other men in suits so sharp they could probably draw blood.

"What makes you say that?" his team leader asked.

"Why else would you be here?"

Dom was a solid guy, a former ranger like him, but he was also a family man with a young kid at home, so he didn't socialize much with Mason or the rest of the team. But Mason could still read him. And, right now, Dom was amused.

"Relax. It's nothing like that."

Scowling, Mason wanted to ask him what it was like then, but

Dom forestalled him. "Let's just get in there," he said, pointing to the door with his thumb. "It'll all be clear soon enough."

Wiping his expression clean, Mason followed him inside. The newcomers turned to him. They appeared to be the same age as Quinn and Gardner. They were also fairly fit, but that was where the similarities ended. These were gym bodies wrapped in ten-thousand-dollar suits. Mason was generally good about spotting fellow former soldiers. And these men didn't have the bearing that marked past military experience.

"Hey, Mason, come on in." Quinn waved him over. "This is Rainer Torsten," he said, pointing to the man with red hair. "And this is his associate, Garret Chapman."

Chapman, a dark-haired man just under six feet, put his hand out to shake. Torsten followed suit.

Mason greeted them with a murmur, but he refrained from launching into the dozens of questions he had. It must be a new op, something sensitive enough to require a face-to-face interaction.

Everyone took a seat around the polished oak table. After making a few bland inquiries about Torsten and Chapman's flight here, Quinn turned to him. "I'm sure you're wondering why we called you in here."

Mason nodded, his eyes darting to study the other men before returning to Quinn.

Ian leaned forward. "Though we're a relatively new company, our reputation has grown at a steady rate. The business has been solid, and we've landed several big contracts. However, we're getting to the point where we have had to start turning down jobs. The demand is that high."

Mason nodded. Dom had told him as much, but Mason hadn't considered what that meant beyond having basic job security.

"So, there's a deal on the table," Quinn confided.

Mason leaned back. Dom was right—this wasn't about a screw-up. But he still didn't know what he was doing here.

"We have three teams running now," Quinn continued. "But we could be fielding twice as many. Doubling our current operations has been our long-term goal, as is opening an East Coast office, but those things are a few years out—at least three, perhaps four. Or they were until Torsten and Chapman approached us about investing, allowing us to expand our operation. With their help, we can do it in two."

He gestured to the men. "I've known Garret for years. We were a year apart at university. He and Rainer have partnered on deals before. They've been looking to invest in a company like ours for a while, and while we have been hesitant to take outside funding, they are a known quantity."

"Is that right?" Mason asked, his tone conversational. He was fairly certain his expression was as bland as the day was long, but Quinn and Gardner quickly addressed the first question that jumped to mind.

"Neither wants to get involved with daily operations, just a solid company to invest in. They would be *silent minority* partners," Quinn stressed.

"The other guys will be happy to hear that," Mason said with brutal honesty. "No offense meant, but a lot of us signed on to Auric because we knew our bosses were former military themselves. They understand our mindset, and neither is cavalier with our lives."

Garrett Chapman leaned forward in his chair. "Naturally, we're not interested in messing with perfection. Auric is doing very well without us. We just want to help it grow. But we do have some ulterior motives for investing in a security company specifically," he said, giving the redheaded man a significant nod.

"Um…" Caught off guard, Torsten hesitated, but Quinn gave him an encouraging nod.

Torsten's fair complexion reddened to the point where the bridge of his cheekbones almost matched his hair. His mouth closed. He reached for the bottle of water in front of him, taking his sweet time to take a drink. "Well, this is a little embarrassing, but I had an incident last year."

"A security breach?" Mason prompted, a tiny bit surprised to find himself sympathetic for a millionaire.

"In a sense," Torsten acknowledged. He smiled sheepishly. "I, um, I met a woman."

"*Ah,*" Mason said aloud, leaning back in his chair.

The man cleared his throat. "I was introduced to her by one of my museum contacts—I have an extensive antiquities collection."

Torsten's mouth quirked, and he shrugged. "Eileen was charming, and she had great credentials in the art world. And, well, she was stunning. I wanted to spend time with her...alone. She returned my interest, but she balked at having an audience. So, I dismissed my security personnel for the night."

"Hmm." Mason didn't need the man to draw him a picture. "Were you injured?"

"No. Just drugged. She wasn't looking to violate my person—her interest lay elsewhere."

Torsten had a distant light in his eye like he was riffling through his memories, examining each one in turn and setting it aside.

It must have weighed on him something fierce. Torsten would have been helpless. He could have been killed, particularly since he'd gotten up close and personal with his assailant and could easily identify her. He was lucky she let him live.

Yeah, something like that would have been hard to shake off.

"I've explained to my insistent friend here that the woman didn't steal anything of value," Torsten said, indicating Chapman. "All she did was copy some information about one of my art purchases. Considering the lengths she went to get it, the details were pretty innocuous. I still have no idea why she wanted the data."

"Are you concerned this Eileen will come back?"

"No. I'm sure she won't," Torsten said, sounding certain.

Mason raised a brow in question. "Then, are you worried about the integrity of your current security? Do you want us to vet your people?" Auric sometimes did that, although team leaders typically handled the assessments.

"Not exactly," Chapman answered. "We want you to train *us.*"

Mason drew his head back. He raised an eyebrow at Quinn and Gardner, who nodded.

"We may not want to be involved in the day to day," Chapman said.

"But we do like to dive into companies to learn what makes them tick. It makes for more informed collaborations."

That didn't sound particularly hands-off to Mason, but Torsten's story explained why they would want to 'dive in'. Mason just hoped their involvement would end there. Auric wasn't a boot camp for bored billionaires.

"So, you want me to take some time to run them through our training routines?" he asked politely, addressing his team lead and the big bosses.

"Actually, we want you to train them alongside your *new* team," Quinn corrected.

Mason sat up straighter. "Excuse me?"

"That's the real reason we brought you in today. We want to start recruiting a fourth team now, and we'd like you to take the lead—on a trial basis, of course."

Gardner tapped his fingers on the table to get Mason's attention. "We are evaluating a few candidates for team leads, but that's for teams five and six. If we're serious about expanding, we need to hit the ground running. It makes sense to promote from within. And given your performance, it would be stupid not to make you an offer."

"That's great," Mason said. "At least, I think it's great."

"You've been with us a long time," Gardner continued. "The men respect you. When Dom had to delegate the lead to someone else, you've stepped up with excellent results. If you'd stayed with the Rangers, you would have been promoted a long time ago."

Mason blinked. He hadn't thought about it that way, but then the military wasn't something he'd signed up for because he was looking for a career. It had merely been a placeholder. *Kind of like Auric.* Or at least that was what he'd been telling himself up until now.

Gardner nodded to the two investors, drawing his attention back to the present. "Garrett and Rainer will only be with you through the first phase of training, where you run through candidates and put them through their paces. We wouldn't finalize the new team until after. I don't have to tell you how important it is for the group to gel.

We wouldn't want the presence of these two to interrupt the new group's dynamics."

No, Mason didn't need that spelled out for him. Even more so than the army, Auric teams were well-oiled machines. Each one was a cohesive unit. They got that way through training, a polite phrase for the endless and grueling drills, courses, and exercises each team went through until they operated seamlessly.

Mason took a deep breath. Part of him was still reeling. *Me a team leader?*

"So, a crash course in hand-to-hand and marksmanship is all you're looking for?" Mason asked Torsten with a raised brow. "It won't change what happened to you," he added a bit more gently.

"I know that," Rainer Torsten said with a self-deprecating little shrug. There was an air to him—chagrin mingled with frustration.

He doubts his judgment. Mason could relate.

"Garrett thinks it's high time I learned how to shoot and fight hand-to-hand," Torsten said. "And I guess it wouldn't hurt to learn how to handle myself a bit better, get some real offensive and defensive techniques down. When you have as much money as I do, it's hard to find someone willing to hit you."

Mason laughed despite himself. If he walloped the man during their sparring, he'd sure as hell be worried about it afterward.

But he couldn't help the cheeky grin. "Be careful what you wish for."

CHAPTER ELEVEN

Mason trudged up the steps of his apartment, bypassing the elevator out of habit. How was it that paperwork was more draining than running ten miles?

He hadn't been prepared for the reams of documents the Auric lawyers had laid in front of him. Leveling up at work meant a fucking metric ton of new contracts. And the promotion and its concomitant pay bump were still over a month away.

Fuck. He still couldn't believe he was going to head a team. More to the point, did he even want to?

Something I should have asked myself before I signed the contracts...

It wasn't that he couldn't lead. That was something that came naturally. But he'd never actively sought out the role, not in the army and not at Auric. He'd taken an honorable discharge from the Army over re-enlisting when he'd been tapped for a promotion.

Here at Auric, he'd done his job, and he'd done it well. But that wasn't enough now. Taking this promotion meant fully committing. Mason couldn't treat this job as a paycheck anymore, not if he were fielding his own team. The men and women under him deserved more than that.

Mason had signed the papers, but he still had an out. There was a six-month trial period, longer if his new team didn't pull a mission at that time. If Mason didn't meet expectations, he would be demoted. Unless he resigned, of course, but Quinn and Gardner didn't foresee that as a possibility.

Maybe it wasn't one. Not at the pay raise he was about to receive.

Feeling better, Mason hit his floor with a spring in his step. That money was *real* cash. Instead of bankrolling his next venture, he could retire a millionaire in five years. Maybe less if he earned a few bonuses.

Wait until I tell Laila.

Mason stopped short behind the door leading to his floor.

Fuck. He was deeper than he thought if he planned on confiding in her before his actual friends.

What Mason needed to do was call Ethan to hash over this promotion with him. His oldest friend could turn over a problem and examine it from every perspective. It was what made the man a hell of an FBI agent. As for Laila, it wouldn't hurt to tell her about the promotion. Mason wanted to gauge her reaction. A lot was riding on it...

But his plans to discuss things with Laila were put on hold. When he reached their floor, his apartment door stood open.

Bracing himself, he paused at the threshold, suppressing a groan as he glanced in.

"Congratulations!" Ransom yelled, waving a bottle of beer. His other teammates were behind him, cheering and yelling random shit.

Mason snorted. "I see Dom called."

"Hell yeah he did." Ransom pounded Mason on the back with his good hand. Wes tossed him a beer from the kitchen. Across the way, Collins lit a stogie.

"Oh, come on. Didn't we just talk about this?" Mason laughed. His teammates jeered in response.

"What?" Ransom asked with a shit-eating grin. "You can't possibly give us hell for wanting to celebrate the fuck out of this news. Plus, it's Friday. Your neighbors can't give us shit for making a little noise."

"The hell they can't, but you're right. We gotta commemorate this night." He'd been to hell and back with these guys. Mason was one of them. His promotion was as much their victory as it was his. "But we're not doing it here. Get your shit. We're going out to a real bar."

That announcement was met with enthusiasm. Mason hustled his team out the door and to the stairs, peeking over his shoulder at Laila's door. Was she home, maybe watching him through the peephole?

"Aren't you going to invite your girl?" Ransom teased after the rest of the guys had marched down the stairs.

Mason considered it for half a second, but then he shook his head. What he needed to say—and do—to Laila required absolute privacy. But what he said was, "And subject her to you lot? No. I'll catch up with her later."

Ransom smirked. "I knew it," he crowed. "I knew there was something up with you two!"

"Yeah, yeah," Mason said, pushing his smug friend to the stairs. "You're a deductive genius—a regular Veronica Mars."

"Ouch, at least let me be Hercule Poirot." Ransom winced.

"Keep dragging your feet, and I'm demoting you to Nancy Drew," Mason said, giving Ransom another hard nudge. "C'mon. Let's get our drink on. I'm buying the first round."

Those were the magic words. Ransom relented, letting himself get herded out of the building.

*

Mason woke up with cotton mouth and a headache, but the pain was receding as his dick was enveloped by warm heat and pressure.

Laila. He'd fantasized exactly this plenty of times without admitting he was thinking about her. But this daydream was the most vivid yet.

Hands moved over him, pumping his cock once or twice before her lips closed over him again, taking him deeper. Mason pushed his head back against the pillow, determined to enjoy the sensation, but the more it went on, the less enthused he became. It felt a little too real. That and his fantasy girl was using a bit too much teeth.

Shit. This wasn't Laila. It was also not a dream.

Mason's eyes flew open. He sat up, pushing at the woman in his bed at the same time. The wet pressure retreated, and a hazy red blob pulled away.

"What the fuck?" he exploded, blinking to clear his vision. The blurry fire-haired woman coalesced into a recognizable face.

"Angie? What the fuck are you doing here?"

Angie's head drew back, and her lips pursed. "Good morning to you, too."

Mason's jaw clenched. "I repeat… what the fuck are you doing in my room? In my *bed?"*

Angie's perfectly painted red lips puckered. He was relieved to see that, unlike him, she was dressed. *Thank heaven for small miracles.*

His uninvited guest raised an eyebrow. "Don't you remember last night? You bought me quite a few drinks."

"Yeah, I remember." Mason scoffed. "I had three beers, so there's no way I'd forget I didn't invite you in here. Also, I bought *everyone* a few drinks."

He gestured to the living room beyond his closed bedroom door. "Some of the guys came here to crash because they were too drunk to go home. You were not among them."

Angie sat up, pressing her arms together in front of her. The gesture plumped up her cleavage. "I came back to congratulate you on your promotion. What's the big deal?"

Mason's face contorted. "The deal is I went to bed alone. I expected to wake up that way."

Angie huffed, brushing her hair back behind her ear. "Well, this is a first. I usually get a much warmer reception."

"I'm sure you do," he said, reaching over to grab the pair of pants he'd tossed on the floor before crashing. He shoved his junk back into his boxer briefs and stood, keeping one eye on Angie as he yanked his jeans on. "But you won't find it here. Sorry."

Face tight, Angie turned away. "I got it," she snapped, getting up to snatch her purse from the floor.

Mason's stomach churned. From what he'd heard, Angie's claws could draw blood, but there was no hiding the hurt that flashed across her expression. He had just insulted her pretty badly.

"Look, it's nothing personal," he said, picking up his shirt. Sniffing it, he made a face and tossed it in the hamper. "But I'm not free to carry on with someone else like this. I'm taken."

The words just came out. He didn't even have to think about them.

Angie shot him a glare. "You don't have to make shit up to spare my feelings. I'm a big girl."

Mason suppressed a wince. How was it that he was the one feeling like the asshole? "No, really. It's new. Just starting up, but also a long time in coming."

Mason knew that now. In the back of his mind, he had been silently struggling against the idea. But he wanted Laila, and now that they'd been together, he was done fighting it.

"Whatever," Angie mumbled with a scowl, throwing his bedroom door open.

Mason followed her. If Dusty, Angie's brother, had crashed last night like he'd been planning, there might be trouble. The man claimed he didn't care what his sister did, but Mason preferred to test that theory now rather than find out later, like when his team depended on Dusty's for support ass-deep in the desert.

However, when he got downstairs, it was empty. Those guys who'd stayed last night had either changed their minds or cleared out earlier. He hoped it was the former. If Angie's humiliation was private, then there was a chance this might blow over.

Please let this go away. He didn't need this kind of shit in his life.

The door closed on Angie's back, and Mason sighed with relief. He started going around the living room, picking up stray beer bottles and Solo cups when someone started banging on the door.

Wincing, Mason stalked to the door and threw it open. "What?"

"I need my fucking keys, don't I?" Angie snapped. "I must have dropped them in your bedroom."

She pushed past him. Mason scrubbed his face roughly, wishing her a million miles away.

He put his hands down, his stomach sinking when he saw movement out of the corner of his eye.

Laila stood by the elevator, holding a paper bag of groceries to her chest. She blinked at him, turned her head, and shook it as if nodding to herself. Suddenly, Mason was very aware he was shirtless, his fly still partially unzipped.

Fuck. Laila didn't say anything. She just hunched her shoulders down before hurrying to her door.

Angie brushed past him, shifting to face him briefly. "Thanks for nothing," she snapped in a low voice.

Wild-eyed, he tried to sidestep around her. *"Laila."*

But it was too late. Her door clicked shut. The unmistakable sound of the deadbolt sliding home like the fucking nail on the coffin.

Making a disgusted noise, Angie pivoted on her heel and stalked off.

Ignoring her, Mason knocked on the door. "Laila, open up. It's not what you think. Please, let me explain."

But it was no use. He kept knocking, calling to her, but she didn't answer. And there was no way she could avoid hearing him. Her place was too small.

"Laila, *please.*"

Silence.

"Shit," he swore under his breath.

I can't even take the door off its hinges. They were on the inside. He also couldn't scale the fire escape because Laila didn't have one. Short of breaking down her door, there was nothing he could do.

The mission-alert ringtone on his phone sounded. *"Fuck!* Not now," he grumbled, turning the alert off.

But that did no good since it just repeated in a loop, worse than the world's most annoying morning alarm. With one last regretful glance at Laila's closed door, he stepped into his apartment to call Dominic.

"Are we really getting called up?" Mason asked.

"Yeah, sorry if I caught you hungover, but we have a situation in Columbia—one of our regular contractors needs extraction ASAP," Dom said, sounding a bit surprised to hear from him. "I would have preferred to give you a day to sleep off the celebrating, but when the shit hits the fan, we gotta move and do it fast. The good news is you'll have time to sober up on the way."

Mason's hand tightened reflexively into a fist. "I have a problem. How much time do we have before wheels up?"

"An hour."

Mason gritted his teeth. With traffic, that was barely enough time to grab his gear and get out to the airport.

He was quiet so long that Dominic got suspicious. "Are you thinking of sitting this one out?" his team leader asked, a slight hint of warning in his tone.

Technically, it was an option. Missing an op wasn't ideal, but contractually Auric gave them a couple of hall passes, allowing them to miss up to two missions a year. No one ever used them unless they were down with the flu, or there was a death in the family.

"How bad would that look?"

Mason could almost hear Dom shrugging across the line. "Unless you're dying, don't do it," his boss advised.

Mason swore under his breath. He hadn't even gotten used to the idea of the promotion, but jeopardizing it less than twenty-four hours later seemed like a stupid idea.

"I'll grab my gear and head out now," he said.

"Good man," Dominic said, clearly relieved. Noises resumed in the background, signaling the team leader had already moved on and was continuing to prep for their mission.

Mason murmured a distracted goodbye before clicking off. "*Fuck, fuck, fuck,*" he chanted.

Grinding his teeth, he grabbed a sheet of paper off his desk. He scribbled a note to Laila, explaining what had happened in the plainest terms possible.

He paused, vacillating between adding something else. In the end, he just wrote down his cell number, even though she had it already.

I'm going to call you, he added in a postscript. *Please pick up.*

Grabbing his go bag, Mason locked up his apartment.

Shit, the plants.

He groaned aloud. Would she even bother watering them after this? He wouldn't be surprised if Laila poured boiling hot water on his orchids, but what else could he do?

"Laila," he tried one more time, knocking plaintively. Closing his eyes, he rested his forehead against the wood, willing it to open.

But it didn't. He slipped his spare key underneath the gap at the bottom, pushing his note in behind it.

§

Vung Tran shuffled down the hall, shaking his head when he saw the crumpled piece of paper his neighbor had just dropped on the floor. It didn't matter how many bottles of alcohol that young man brought over, it still didn't give him a license to litter.

Stooping with a grunt, he picked up the trash. It was almost wedged under the door, but he yanked, and the bulk of it came out. Cursing the young, he added the fragment to the garbage bag he was carrying to the dumpster and headed down the stairs.

CHAPTER TWELVE

Laila was trying to juggle the heavy grocery bag while checking her texts at the same time. The phone slipped out of her hand, clattering down the concrete stairs and hitting the wall with a cringe-worthy smack.

She put the bag down, then hurried to retrieve it.

"Oh, no," she moaned. The screen was shattered, the display dark. A tentative attempt to restart it failed.

First, she had missed her bus and had to take the thirty-eight line that left her four blocks farther from home, and now this. The universe was trying to burst her bubble.

Well, it was going to have to try harder. She had been floating on cloud nine the entire day, reliving every detail of the night she had spent with Mason. In her mind, she'd savored the feel of his skin, the way his mouth tasted, the grip of his strong hands on her waist and thighs. All her daydreaming came with a price—she'd burned an entire tray of brownies and been reprimanded by the store manager. But even that had failed to deflate her.

And then she opened the door to her hallway, and her entire world came crashing down.

Mason had stood at the threshold of his apartment, shirtless and hair mussed, talking to a tall redheaded woman.

Laila heard the woman say, "I must have dropped them in your bedroom." That was all she caught before the ringing in her ears overwhelmed her. She had just stood there like an idiot.

The redhead pushed past him. Mason glanced up, noticing Laila's frozen form. His expression changed, the flash of guilt unmistakable.

Laila felt her heart break, busting wide open in her chest. It felt remarkably like a punch to the gut.

Wilting, she had felt herself shrinking as she turned away, not wanting to glance in Mason's direction. She couldn't handle seeing him kiss the woman goodbye.

Her blood roared in her ears as she made a break for her door. She closed it just as he started calling her name.

Dropping the grocery bag on the floor, Laila slid down the length of the door until she crumpled on the floor, tears streaming down her cheeks.

Her head pounded, and she had trouble catching her breath. Laila pressed her hands to her face, trying to hold in the sobs that wanted to rip out of her chest.

Belatedly, she registered Mason knocking and calling out to her, but the sound was weirdly distant and tinny as if she were underwater.

That would explain the lack of oxygen. Laila couldn't breathe. And she definitely couldn't deal with *him* right now.

Mason could never see her like this. If she opened the door, there was no way she could hide her devastation. It would take months, maybe years, before she could look him in the eye and not want to burst into tears.

Laila was wrecked, all the hopes and dreams of the past year floating down like ashes. *Stupid. So stupid.* How could she have believed that night meant anything to him?

Holding her breath, she reached up behind her, flipping the button to lock the door. She had already slid the deadbolt, but that didn't seem like enough.

Get away from the door.

Crawling on all fours, she made it to the couch, knocking her grocery bag over next to the door.

Ignoring the scattered produce, jars, and cans, Laila decided the couch wasn't far enough. She staggered to the bed before remembering *he* had been there. His smell was still on the sheets.

There was no way she could lie there until she washed the bedding, or, better yet, burned it.

Laila turned to the couch, collapsing across it. She tugged one of the threadbare throw pillows over her head for good measure.

Not that it mattered. Sometime in the last few minutes, Mason had stopped knocking. The only sound was her too-loud heartbeat.

Calm. You have to calm down.

Some undefined amount of time later, Laila finally summoned the energy to get off the couch. Night had fallen outside her tiny window. The studio was dark. Red-eyed and puffy-faced, she flicked on the secondhand desk lamp on her side table before taking stock of the scattered groceries by the door.

Laila picked up a can of diced tomatoes, finding Mason's spare key underneath it.

Oh. He was gone. And she had to water his plants… Laila closed her eyes, taking a deep, shuddering breath.

At least now she knew what he was knocking about—not an apology or an explanation for the redhead. That was obviously too much to ask for. She was a one-night stand, who, unfortunately for them both, lived next door. Other women didn't have to be explained to one-night stands.

There was a piece of paper on the floor next to where the key had been. She picked it up, heart pounding.

For a split second, she thought it might be from Mason because it didn't match any of the labels from her shopping. But the scrap of paper was blank. Shaking her head for getting herself all worked up for nothing, Laila tossed it in the garbage.

CHAPTER THIRTEEN

Two weeks later

"Get up, Lazy Jones," Rosamie said in her bright, overly cheerful voice, bouncing up and down on the mattress right next to her head.

"Remind me why I let you come over today?" Laila muttered, half her mouth flattened against the pillow.

"Because you promised you were going to come out with me," Rosamie said, continuing to bounce.

Laila shot her friend a bleary-eyed scowl. "You said you were bringing a bottle of wine over. I thought that meant we were staying in."

"I did bring a bottle." Rosamie grinned. "But it's tequila, and it's strictly for our prep round."

"Prep round?"

"That's right. You and I are going to forget about all douchebags—starting now. First, we're going to that bar down the block, then we're taking the bus to Club Casim to get our groove on."

Groaning, Laila dragged the pillow over her head, but Rosamie pulled it off. "You have got to stop moping over the mercenary."

"I'm not moping," Laila lied. This desolation was several degrees removed from such a commonplace term.

Laila felt...hollow. But she didn't blame Mason. No, the fault was hers.

Laila had set herself up for this pain, mooning over a man who was totally out of her league. *She* had been the one to extend that dinner invitation, and when he'd come to her later, she hadn't said no. Mason would have stopped if she had told him to leave.

And Mason hadn't made her any promises of fidelity. Well—there hadn't been time for conversation. Everything had happened so fast. Too fast.

How would you have known he would jump into bed with someone else the very next day? Unless it had been intentional...Perhaps Mason had sought out another woman to show her their night wasn't special.

Mason had responded to her unspoken invitation without thinking about the complications. He must have realized sleeping with his mousy neighbor, a woman who had clearly been pining for him since they met, was a huge mistake. So, he wanted to make sure she didn't read more into their sexual encounter—cue the redhead.

He could have just said as much. In fact, hadn't he told her they needed to talk? And despite that parting—and very misleading—kiss, he must have decided it was easier to *show* her how little their night had meant to him.

Still, parading another woman in front of her had been unnecessary. All right, maybe she did blame him for that—a lot. But it wasn't a problem. She could take the hint. Or, in this case, the hammer to the head.

Blinking back tears, Laila tuned back in to find Rosamie riffling through her closet.

"Trust me on this," her friend said, taking out a little black dress and discarding it with pursed lips. "Hooking up with another man—any man—is the answer. You know what they say. The best way to get over someone is to get under someone else...or on top. Or in front while on your hands and knees. Or—"

Limbs too heavy for anything more athletic than shuffling to the fridge, Laila forced herself to sit up. She held up her hand. "I get the picture. But I'm not sure I'm up for a club."

"Please," Rosamie pouted. "I have big news, and I want to celebrate."

Laila forced a smile. It felt like a grimace, but she needed to try for her friend's sake. "What's your news?"

Rosamie drew out a deep yellow sundress from the closet—one fit for high summer. "Put this on, and I'll tell you."

Laila made a face. "It's not warm enough for that dress. The black one is better for this weather."

"You'll get plenty hot after we dance until we drop. And forget all those drab dark colors. This color makes your skin pop. Add a little lipstick and eyeliner, and no man will be able to resist you."

Laila snorted at the absurdity. Rosamie sat next to her, then threw an arm around her shoulders. "Okay, I'm going to tell you the news so you can appreciate it—I heard from the housing office. I got a room in Wardley!"

"*What?*" There wasn't a lot of graduate housing available at their school. Wardley was the sole dormitory reserved for their use, which was why it was notoriously difficult to get into. But if a student did get in, it was worth it. The university subsidized the housing, so the room was around a quarter of the amount to rent the average L.A. apartment. That and it was close to campus, just a block over. And it was two blocks from Gardullo's Grocery.

Most of the rooms in Wardley were earmarked for students that came from abroad. Only a few were available to California residents. Students had to win a lottery to get a room. Unfortunately, the odds of winning the real lottery were slightly better.

Laila hadn't realized Rosamie had even bothered to put her name down—the competition was that intense. Also, her friend saved money by living at home.

"How did that happen?" It was mid-quarter.

Her friend beamed. "Well, it seems a certain dynamic duo got caught sleeping with their advisor and had to leave the Biochem program after an attempt to bribe *her* with the pictures they secretly took." Rosamie waved her hands about. "It was a whole thing."

Wow. Laila had been in her own world, so she hadn't heard. She listened open-mouthed as Rosamie detailed the scandal. When she was done, Laila gave herself a little shake. "And is your mother okay with you moving out?"

Rosamie laughed. "She knows she can't stop me. Nor does she blame me, not with the way the twins have been acting lately. We're slowly being suffocated by testosterone, zit cream, and teen angst. I think she secretly wishes she could move out with me. But she can't because *you* are."

Laila started to get dizzy. "Huh?"

Rosamie bounced on the bed again. "I put your name down in the lottery along with mine. We got a double!"

"Oh my God." Laila felt staggered. "But what about my apartment?"

Rosamie shrugged. "I know you have a few more months on the lease, but the dorm is way cheaper. In the end, you'll save money by letting it lapse. You might even get someone to take over the lease. This area is always in demand." Rosamie's expression sobered. "You know it's for the best. There's no way you're going to get over the scum-bucket formerly known as Mr. Marvelous if you are still living here."

"I would," Laila said. But it felt weak, even to her ears.

"Can I ask you something?" Rosamie pressed her lips together before clicking her tongue. "Are you still watering his plants?"

Wincing, Laila didn't answer.

Rosamie pointed at the door. "It just goes to show you how unbe-lievably dense some men are. Mr. Marvelous must think he's God's gift to women. I can't believe he still trusted you with the key after the shit he pulled. We should go over there and cut out the crotch in whatever pants he left behind."

An unwilling laugh escaped Laila. Rosamie patted her leg. "We can move into Wardley as early as next week. You never have to see Mason again."

Laila took a deep breath. How could one phrase fill her with relief, yet hurt like hell at the same time?

"I'll have to find someone else in the building to water his plants," she said eventually.

Mr. Tran wasn't reliable, but there was a nice-enough retired lady on the floor below them. Mrs. Turnbull would do it, especially once she learned how much Mason compensated for the simple task. Plus, Mrs. Turnbull's son was a cop. She wouldn't rob Mason. Mr. Tran, on the other hand, would drink everything in the liquor cabinet if she chose him.

There are always empty boxes by the recycling bin. Very few of her neighbors broke down their delivery boxes. Most of what she owned could fit in her extra-large suitcase and a few of those cartons—half a dozen at most.

Laila shook out her hair. "We can go to the club, but I'm not hooking up with anyone. I'm going to need to be up early tomorrow to start packing."

"That's the spirit!" Rosamie beamed. "Now, go jump in the shower because your hair is a greasy mess."

Forcing herself up, Laila paused to salute before crossing the room, stripping her clothes off as she went.

CHAPTER FOURTEEN

Mason's thick blond lashes screened him from the worst of the burn, but the overhead fluorescents still managed to scour the inside of his brain.

He licked his dry lips. "Where am I?" His voice came out as one long, dry wheeze.

"It's about fucking time you woke up."

"What?" Mason's lids scraped his eyeballs like sandpaper.

Ransom sat in a chair next to him. Mason laid in a hospital bed, the nondescript utilitarian decor and furniture giving little clue as to his actual location.

He tried to sit up, but he couldn't. His head hurt like hell, and his body wouldn't respond. He started to panic when he registered that his entire chest was wrapped in a cast that stretched down his arm to his wrist. "What the hell happened?"

Ransom leaned in, concern in his eyes. "You don't remember going all Captain America and saving everyone's butt?"

Gingerly, Mason shook his head. "It's a blur."

The mission had been a shitshow from the start. Auric's oil company client had severely underplayed their situation. The local state of affairs in Columbia had blown sky-high. Used to small-scale flare-ups, the client had downplayed their problems. When Mason's team hit the ground, they realized they needed backup, but there hadn't been time to wait. Four of the client's people had been taken hostage, with a dozen more under threat.

His team had managed to extract the latter with relatively little trouble, but the hostage situation had taken a bad turn before their support team could arrive.

"Last I remember, we were brainstorming ways to get those executives out."

"*Your* plan worked," Ransom said pointedly, giving credit where credit was due. However, the words did jog something in Mason's memory. Hopefully, after his head stopped aching, he would remember what it was.

"We took a few knocks and a hostage was shot, but it was just a flesh wound," Ransom continued. "But getting them out of the country was a hot mess. Insurgents attacked your position. There were no good egress routes. You and Dom split the civilians between you two. His half went first, and he managed to get out with the help of some locals. We paid a king's ransom for their vehicles, but you had to hole up and wait for them to double back."

Ransom sat deeper in the chair. A swizzle stick appeared in his hands from God-knows-where. He used it to dig under the seam of his cast, scratching some otherwise unreachable itch.

"I'm not sure what happened after that. Your position was compromised somehow. The teammates who stayed behind with you —Wes and Klein—said you had to move out fast. You sent them ahead with the fittest and fastest hostages while you took the rear, defending the stragglers. There was an IED explosion. Somehow, you got your little ducklings to cover."

Ransom threw his free hand up, pointing at Mason with the swizzle stick. "Man, I think you pulled a car out of your ass or something. The vehicle got blown over. It caught you in a glancing blow— pinned part of you against the wall. Your ribs are broken. One punctured your lung, and your arm is broken to boot. You also took a good knock to the head. Dom had a hell of a time getting you evaced in one piece."

Grinning, Ransom pointed to Mason's cast. "At least now you can't give me shit for this. Yours is bigger than mine—the only time you're going to be able to say that."

An unwilling laugh shook Mason's body. It hurt like hell. Ransom chuckled, too, but then his face sobered. "Buddy, you're looking at months of recovery and PT."

"Fuck," Mason swore. He swiveled his head gingerly. There was a window, but it faced a brick wall, giving no clue to its location. "And where is this?"

"Mexico City," Ransom supplied. "Quinn knew a guy who knew a good doctor. I flew in when you got here, about two weeks ago."

"Two *weeks?*" *Holy shit.* Mason's head spun, doing the math. He'd been on the ground over a week with Dom and the rest of the guys. "I lost a lot of fucking time."

"You weren't in a coma. You kept coming in and out. But you couldn't hold any conversations for a while. You'd drop off in the middle, then couldn't remember them afterward. But I think this one is going to take."

"Hell, I hope so." Mason's stomach soured. "When can we fly back to the States?"

"Not sure, but it may be a while."

Mason shook his head. It still hurt. "I gotta get back to L.A. Where is my phone?"

"It's here." Ransom fished it out of his pocket. "But no worries. I've been keeping the home office updated."

"That's not who I'm worried about," Mason said, pressing the power button on his phone. It stayed dark. The battery was dead. "Have you got the charger on you?"

Ransom sucked in a breath. "No. You didn't have it on you. It must be with your gear."

"Can you find me another one?"

"Yeah," Ransom agreed, but he didn't seem happy about it. "But I don't think it's going to do any good."

"What?" Mason wrinkled his nose, still mashing the buttons on his phone as if that would magically get it to restart. "Why?"

"You've been asking for Laila."

Mason blinked. "I have?"

Ransom's face twisted. "Yeah. You keep calling out for her in your sleep."

"Oh."

Uncomfortably, his friend shifted in his seat. "It was enough that I tried to call her with your phone before it ran out of juice. She didn't answer or respond to any texts. I couldn't find her on social media because you don't have her last name down in your contacts—and I scoured pics of every Layla living in L.A. on Facebook. Nada." He swiped at his nose with his cast. "I even had one of the guys swing by her place a few days ago. He knocked for a while, but she wasn't home."

Mason tried to shrug. It hurt too much to finish the gesture. "She works a lot."

Ransom grunted. "Look, I don't mean to get in your business, but this girl is no good."

The IED hadn't killed Mason, but the irony might. "Laila is the definition of good."

Ransom scoffed. "If she can't be bothered to answer the phone while you're in the goddamn hospital, then she isn't worth shit."

God, Mason didn't want to talk about this. But he couldn't let Ransom think the worst of Laila. "She must have blocked my number. And she probably did it before we went wheels-up to Columbia."

Confusion creased his friend's face. "Why's that?"

Mason sighed. "Things went tits up before I left."

"That was fast." Ransom raised his brows. "You don't usually make 'em run screaming until a few months in. Didn't you just start things with Laila?"

"One night," Mason muttered, sounding like an emo fuckboy. "All I got was one damn night."

The memory of waking up next to Laila was vivid and a little fucked up. How could he have freaked like that? The night before had been mind-blowingly intense, but he'd known then and there his life would never be the same. And then one stupid mistake—one *he* hadn't even made—and it had all got blown to smithereens.

Mason studied the view out of the window. "Did you ever save someone for later?" he asked in a low voice.

"What do you mean?" Ransom looked like he was trying to compute complex calculus in his head. But he was a neck-or-nothing type. Mason doubted Ransom ever thought about holding anything back in any aspect of his life.

God, this sucked. Mason's chest ached, and not because of his ribs. *Great. I am an emo fuckboy.*

"I mean…did you ever avoid spending time with someone, not because you didn't like them but because you liked them too much? Well, that's what I did with Laila. I tried not to think about her. And I was damn good at not thinking about her, but she was always there in the back of my mind."

Mason wished his arms were free because he wanted to strangle himself. "I knew if I let my guard down, that she'd be it for me. The whole nine yards—marriage, house, kids—and I wasn't fucking ready for it."

He was kicking himself for it now. All the time he'd wasted…

"I kept telling myself *later*. Laila was for later—once I was done with this job and cashed out. Then I'd ask her out properly. It was a mistake. She was there the whole time…waiting."

Seemingly at a loss for words, Ransom just stared at him.

"Am I making any sense, or is my brain so scrambled this is coming out as gibberish?"

"Nah, I get it." Ransom raised his cast, his face screwing up. "You had a someday girl, but you fucked it up before it ever got going. I'm still waiting for that story, cause that's the part I can't figure out."

"Well, I had help with that last bit." Mason reluctantly told Ransom about Angie, downplaying what had happened in his bedroom.

Nevertheless, Ransom filled in some of the dots. His friend's eyes nearly bugged out of his head. "Man, I didn't hear jack shit about that.

When I left your place that morning, she wasn't there. Wes was still crashed out on the floor, though. Maybe he let her in."

"Or he forgot to lock the fucking door, and she let herself in." Mason sighed. "Doesn't matter. Because Laila saw her, and it didn't look good. Like *really* bad. I don't blame her for not picking up when my number flashed across her screen."

"I guess that makes sense," Ransom grunted. "I know I only talked to her once, but she seemed...delicate. Real shy. A girl like Angie would roll over Laila like a steamroller."

Yes, Laila was shy and sweet...fragile. He didn't need to ask if she would be crushed, seeing him with someone else. He'd seen her reaction, the way she'd shut down. The pain he'd caused had been all over her stricken face.

"I need to get home," he repeated.

Mason was in the worst shape of his life—literally broken into pieces. But all he could think about was getting back to Laila and fixing what had gone wrong between them.

Ransom winced. "I hate to be the one to break it to you, but that's not going to happen anytime soon. The docs are being cagey, but I think they're worried about you re-puncturing your lung or some shit like that. They have a billion and one tests planned."

Mason groaned loud enough for a concerned nurse to poke her head in the door. After she took his vitals, Ransom swung back to Mason's least favorite topic. "How mad are you at Angie?"

"I don't know. It depends on the time of day," he confessed, but Mason wasn't a complete asshole. He knew nine out of ten guys would have welcomed that kind of wake-up call, but he wasn't one— even if there hadn't been another girl in the equation.

And it hadn't been just any girl. It had been Laila. Just thinking about her made Mason ache. It hurt worse than the broken ribs.

Mason dragged himself back to the present. "Do me a favor. Don't tell Dusty or anyone else about what happened. If Wes managed to keep his mouth shut, let's not spread shit around."

Ransom shrugged. "Sure, no skin off my back. I'm just surprised it happened at all. Angie doesn't seem like the type to go in for the kill unless she's sure of her reception. I also can't believe you're not more pissed at her. If a woman blew up my happily-ever-after, I'd be getting ready to read her the riot act the minute I got back."

Mason tried to shrug, but he soon regretted it. The cast kept him immobile so he didn't hurt himself, but the lack of response from his muscles and bones, something he'd always taken for granted, was profoundly disturbing.

Mason's mastery of his body was absolute. Even when he'd gotten sick with the flu or something bad enough to knock him off his feet, he'd never been down long enough to feel weak or incapacitated. All he'd ever felt was a brief frustration, along with a certain restlessness to get back up and be active again.

"I'm not going to do anything to Angie," he said, trying to sound as if he didn't deeply resent her. "She took a shot when she shouldn't have. I'm sure all of us have made the same mistake."

It was more generous than she deserved, but just talking about her pissed Mason off.

Ransom shrugged, then leaned back in the chair. "For what it's worth, I think you're smart to avoid that whole hot mess."

"I wouldn't call Angie a hot mess," Mason said, uncomfortable about defending the woman responsible for wrecking his love life.

"Not Angie—the situation," Ransom rolled his eyes. "I just mean that Dusty isn't as calm about Angie's activities as he pretends to be. Personally, I think those two should just bone and get it over with."

Mason's face curdled, feeling as if he'd smelled rotten milk. "With each other? Did the blow to the head make it okay for brothers and sisters to...er...you know."

"Nah, man." Ransom chuckled. "Their parents married each other in their teens. I think Dusty had graduated from high school already. They're not related by blood," he said.

Surprised, Mason only stared.

"Anyway," Ransom continued after a long pause. "I'm gonna stick around for a while, at least until the end of the week."

Mason groaned again, this time with his good hand theatrically pressed to his chest.

His friend fished a paper out of his pocket, a receipt of some kind. He balled it up, then threw it at Mason's face.

"I was going to offer to check in on your girl when I head back to the States, but now I'm tempted to let you sweat that one out until you get home."

Mason knew when he was beaten. "I take it back," he said quickly.

"Yeah, I thought you would." Ransom smirked, but he sobered fast. "Although, I don't know how much good it will do. Honestly, it kind of sounds like something you have to fix yourself."

"Just find me a charger for my phone, so I can explain where I am," Mason said. "Laila will take my calls if she knows why I can't be there in person."

At least, he prayed she would.

CHAPTER FIFTEEN

Laila pulled the tray of lemon bars from the oven, sniffing them deeply. It was a simple recipe compared to some, but, in her opinion, few people did it well. She had spent weeks tweaking hers, experimenting with different varieties of lemons while adjusting the amount of butter until the shortbread crust was a perfect shade of gold.

She even made the powdered sugar, crushing the bright sanding sugar to get various colors. After getting the consistency she wanted, she would sprinkle it over the lemon bars through stencils to make designs related to the season.

At the moment, she was making turkey and cornucopia shapes. Her boss had tried to steamroll her to move straight to reindeer and Santa hats, but Laila steadfastly refused to start on Christmas themes before Thanksgiving had passed. The autumn leaf garland decorating the front of her display case was her silent way of telling him to stuff his jingle bells where the sun didn't shine.

"I will hold the line at Thanksgiving," she told herself, sticking her index finger into the handle of her empty sugar shifter. She twirled it around like a gunfighter before setting it down and picking up a paintbrush. Bending, she swept some excess sugar off a slightly misshapen bird. "Your sacrifice will not have been in vain," she assured the twisted turkey.

"Well, now I don't think I can eat them, knowing they're your friends."

Laila's head snapped up to meet the twinkling blue eyes of a brown-haired man around her age. Dressed in an expensive polo and tailored khakis, he grinned, flashing bright white teeth.

He had Greek-Row elite douchebag written all over him.

"Then again, they look so good I may have to buy them. And whatever those are, too," he said, waving at the neat row of cylinders in the front of the display case.

"Those are *canelés*, a pastry from the Bordeaux region of France," she said, slipping into her professional mask. "A very good choice."

The guy's lips stretched. "Then I would like one, please."

Laila didn't respond to his megawatt smile. She wrapped the *canelé* in wax paper before handing it to him.

His fingers brushed hers as he took the pastry from her hand. Instead of fishing out his wallet, he raised the pastry to his mouth, then bit through the dark brown and golden crust.

"Oh my God, this is amazing," he said, gazing down at it as if it were a revelation.

Thank you," Laila said, warming incrementally at his praise. Getting the caramelized crust crispy without drying out the tender and soft center had been tricky. She was rather proud of how they'd turned out.

"What's in these?"

"Booze," she answered.

He laughed. "I don't taste it, and I consider myself an expert."

I bet you are, she thought a touch snidely. From the popped collar of his shirt to his hundred-dollar loafers, this guy oozed privilege from every pore.

"I use cognac, although rum is standard. But it's cooked off, so it's quite harmless."

Her customer leaned against the counter. "Got anything stronger?"

"That would be aisle six, the liquor section," she said, starting to pack away a batch of edible glitter she'd made for tomorrow's petit fours.

"Not even a tiny *baba au rum?*" he asked, naming a liquor-soaked cake, also from France.

Laila stepped back in surprise. "We couldn't sell those without carding customers."

"Well, honestly, they're not that great," the man said magnanimously. "I had a few in France on a family trip when I was fourteen. I made a point to eat them for dessert every night—because of the rum. I thought I was so cool and grown-up. But they weren't a fraction as good as these," he said, gesturing to the *canelé*. "I'm going to have to have at least a dozen more."

"Sure thing." Laila pulled out a box, then began packing it with the pastries. She was hyperaware that the customer watched her every move, his eyes running up and down her figure.

Her job's dress code dictated she wear the store's branded shirt with dark pants, but since she worked for the bakery at the front of the store, her manager had encouraged her to wear skirts when he hired her. She'd ignored the suggestion for years, but after moving in with Rosalie on campus, she'd taken to dressing a touch more femininely.

Since it was cold, she was wearing tights with her short skirt, which she paired with vintage Doc Marten boots. The last wasn't girly, but they didn't hurt her feet after hours behind the counter.

"You don't remember me, do you?"

Laila's brow creased as she snuck a peek at the man from under her lashes.

He held out his hand, but when she merely handed him the box and moved to the register, he stepped back and bowed. "Joseph Dubey, at your service."

"Have we met?" she asked, ringing him up.

"No, but not for lack of trying on my part. You never stay long at our parties. Not that I blame you—it would kind of defeat the purpose of the Night Witches."

"Oh, you're *that* Joseph Dubey." Joseph, or Joe, as his brothers called him, was the new president of the Alpha Omega fraternity. He was the rich-as-sin, politically connected son of some political bigwig. No doubt he would follow in his father's footsteps.

I'm probably looking at a future congressman. It did not make her see him any more favorably.

Several of the Night Witches had reported that, under Joseph's leadership, the atmosphere of Alpha and Omega had changed. The brothers now rolled out the red carpet for them—literally the first time. It was a stunt that had gotten them written up in the school paper. Laila had been suspicious of the new fraternity president ever since.

"I've seen you at Club Casim, too," Joseph said. "You wouldn't dance with me."

"Oh," Laila said. "Sorry. I don't remember that."

Joseph's laugh was easy, a small bonus in his favor. "That's all right. I was in good company. You shot down every guy who asked you to dance—I saw you do it. You preferred to dance on stage with your friend."

Heat filled her cheeks. "Yeah, well, I just go for fun. I'm not looking to meet anyone."

Or get groped.

The charming megawatt grin dimmed theatrically. "That's too bad because I'd love to take you to dinner sometime."

Laila cocked her head as she checked his expression. He appeared completely serious.

"I know an excellent French restaurant downtown," he continued. "Or any other country if you'd rather branch out. There's a great little Italian place not far from it that does authentic Venetian tapas."

"Venice has tapas?" That was news.

Joseph's eyes flared. "They do! I know people only think of Spain when they hear tapas but Italy, Venice in particular, has its own tradition."

"I didn't know that," Laila said, feeling strangely removed.

The entire conversation had taken a surreal tinge. Against her better judgment, Joseph, the big man on campus, was succeeding in intriguing her. If someone had asked her the day before—even the hour before—she would have said it wasn't possible.

It also wasn't possible that a guy like Joseph would want someone like her. Yes, she could look cute if she put the effort in, but she wasn't exotic or busty like the girls who frequented the Alpha Omega parties.

Don't get carried away. He's talking about food. Food was a hook for everyone.

"Thank you, but no. I meant it. I'm not interested in meeting anyone."

Joseph seemed unfazed. "Are you seeing someone?"

Mason's face flashed through her head. "*No.*"

Joseph leaned in. "Bad break-up?"

"Also no." There would have to have been a real relationship first.

But the words vibrated, too loaded with emotion. Even a superficial frat boy could pick up on it.

Joseph tsked in commiseration. "So, it's complicated. Been there." He sighed, glancing at the massive watch on his wrist. "I have to get back to the house, but at least I'm not leaving empty-handed."

He lifted the box, then made a show of smelling them. "I may not be leaving with your phone number, but at least I have these." He paused to wink at her. "I'm not leaving with your phone number, am I?"

"Again, no," she said, but she couldn't help but laugh this time. He was a practiced flirt.

Joseph began to walk backward toward the door. "Not today, maybe, but I'll be back. Now that I know this place exists and has goodies like this, I won't be able to stay away." He threw another toothpaste commercial-worthy grin at her. "Of course, I'll have to jog here or else there's no shot of me getting a date with you, not unless you're willing to roll me around."

He backed out the doors, ducking out of view. Laila was shaking her head in amused disbelief when he poked his head back in. "But I will be back," he called before waving and disappearing.

CHAPTER SIXTEEN

Four months later

"I can't believe you're thinking of saying no!" Rosamie said, holding up a mustard-yellow dress under her chin. She turned Laila to face the mirror nailed to their dorm room wall.

"Why are you always trying to get me into a shade of yellow?" Laila made a beeline for the black cocktail dress.

"Because you're an autumn with gold undertones. Yellow should be your signature color. And stop trying to change the subject," Rosamie chided.

"She's right," Jasmine, their other friend, said from the bed in between checking Rosamie's many different eye-shadow palettes for coordinating shades. "Your super-hot, super-rich boyfriend just asked you to move in with him. Yet, for some reason, you're hesitating."

"Do you want me to move out that badly?" Laila pretended to pout.

"Of course not." Rosamie leaned back, critically examining the dress draped across her front. "But we're talking about Joseph Dubey here. The only acceptable excuse for not moving in with him is temporary insanity. That or you just discovered he's an ax murderer."

"Neither is the case," Laila replied. "Unless you mean he is insane—because I have doubts about him being in his right mind. We haven't been together long enough for him to ask me to move in."

Just thinking about her life lately made her head spin. Laila barely recognized it. It was as if the last few months had happened to someone else.

Joseph Dubey had come back to the store as promised—or rather threatened—a few days after their first meeting. He became a regular, stopping in three or four times a week.

Every time he came in, Joseph did his determined best to get her to go out with him. But given what had just happened with Mason, she was suspicious of his regard.

Then Laila's cell phone contract expired. She'd never been able to get the phone to turn back on after she dropped it in the stairwell. But given the constraints on her budget, she hadn't been able to afford to replace it out of pocket. Instead, she'd used her computer to message her friends, going so far as to take it with her to work to stay in touch. She called her mother's care home from the breakroom phone at Gardullo's.

The minute her old contract was up, she had gone to the mall to sign up for a new one. After shopping around for the best plan, she decided to switch to a different carrier, one that offered a better smartphone for free with a new contract. She had planned to keep her old phone number, but she could not transfer it to the new carrier because they didn't have an interconnection agreement with the previous one.

The assistant at the shop had generously let her put her old sim card in a compatible phone to check if there had been any calls or texts that she'd missed while her phone had been inactive.

Laila had held her breath while she scanned the logs...but there had been nothing. Just a few messages from the phone company itself, reminders to pay her bill, and a few special offers, but that was it.

Nothing from Mason.

A little secret piece of her had died at that moment. Whatever stubborn ember of hope still glowed in her heart had been smothered.

She'd thrown the broken phone and obsolete sim card in the trash on the way out. Then she took the bus back to her dorm, heading straight to bed despite the fact it was only mid-afternoon.

She woke before dawn the next day, resolving never to think about Mason Lang ever again. The next time Joseph had come to the store and asked her out, she'd said yes.

It had started as an act of defiance, a little screw-you to the memory of Mason's smile. But Joseph had proven to be a surprise. To begin with, he was far more mature than she'd initially given him credit for. It may have helped he was a few years older than his frat brothers, thanks to multiple years off traveling abroad.

Joseph wined and dined her, courting her in an almost old-world fashion. He brought her flowers and took her to nice restaurants, trying to spend time with her despite her busy schedule and his status as a big man on campus.

And Laila had let him do all that, at first because she was angry and then because she was numb. But, eventually, she began to feel better. And then Joseph's attention started to be fun. The new man in her life was charming, the son of a good family, who realistically entertained political aspirations. He lived hard and played harder, but seemed to keep his head about him at all times.

Joseph had surprised her when he first told her about his off-campus apartment. Then he'd downright stunned her when he'd asked her to move into it with him.

"How is it that Joseph has a place off-campus?" Rosamie asked, jarring her back into the present. "Aren't all frat brothers supposed to live at their frat house?"

"When there is room, but even Alpha Omega has an overflow code."

Frats were little fiefdoms unto themselves, with their own rules of governance. While some didn't allow their members to live outside of their home, some required it because they didn't have enough space. Alpha Omega was one of the fraternities that let some of its most senior members live off-campus to make room for the newer recruits.

Laila didn't think that rule applied to the president of the fraternity. Indeed, it didn't. Joseph had a room at Alpha Omega, which he jokingly referred to as the presidential suite. But he still wanted his own space, and despite the fact real estate was at a premium in L.A., he could afford to pay for the privilege of privacy—or, rather, his parents did.

Joseph visited Alpha Omega every weekday between classes, but he only slept there on Friday and Saturday nights. The rest of the time, he stayed at his high-rise penthouse apartment, a gorgeous place he wanted to share with her.

Laila was tempted to say yes for the bathrooms alone. *And who could blame me? There are three!*

Rosamie threw her arms around Laila. "You know I don't want you to move out, right?" she said, kissing her on the cheek. "It's that I don't want you to miss your chance. Joseph is who you should be setting your cap on."

Laila smiled. She could always tell when Rosamie had been reading historical romances before bed.

Jasmine hesitated. "Or could you be reluctant for some other reason? You aren't still pining for the mercenary from next door, are you?"

"Of course not." Neither of her friends mentioned Mason by name anymore. "I've taken your persistent and strongly worded advice—I moved on. That's not the reason I haven't told Joseph yes. I just believe this step is too big for such a new relationship."

"But he's not even there half the time," Rosamie said, almost bouncing with her trademark enthusiasm. "It would be like time-sharing a glorious apartment or having a part-time gigolo—one that only comes by Sunday through Thursday."

Laughing, Laila shook her head. "I'm going to tell you the same thing I told him—I promise to think about it."

"Fine, fine." Jasmine sniffed. "I suppose that's all we can ask."

Laila raised a brow. "*We?*"

"Jas, Joseph, and I just want the best for you," Rosamie said with a grin. "I think he's good for you, and you're good for him—especially given his desire to follow in his father's footsteps. Dating you is a good move for him politically. Marrying you would be even better."

Laila scowled. "How do you figure that?"

She didn't come from money or had no connections a future politician could exploit.

"You're smart, photogenic, and most importantly—brown. Unless he plans to leave California, most of his constituents will be the same."

"How…romantic," Laila deadpanned.

Rosamie shrugged. "Among the upper-class, marriage is still a business. But nowadays, we can be both romantic *and* practical."

"Okay, now I know you have been reading too many Regency romances," Laila said flatly. Screwing her face up, she pointed at another dress laid out on the bed, this one a simple A-line silhouette in a burnt-orange color. "How about that one?"

Grinning, Rosamie snatched it up and tossed it over to her before running to their shared bathroom. "So glad you asked about it. I have the perfect earrings to go with it."

Jasmine held up a makeup case. "And I have the perfect eyeshadow color to match."

"I can't wear makeup to work," Laila protested. The heat from the ovens made it run into her eyes, and Joseph was picking her up directly after her shift.

Rosamie came back, then handed her the earrings.

"Let me see the eye shadow," she told Jasmine. Jas opened the case, displaying a colorful palette.

Rosamie whistled. "Those are perfect. Good choice."

"Again, I can't wear makeup near the ovens unless I want to go blind," Laila reminded them.

"Don't put it on until you are ready to leave," Rosamie said, handing her the case. "Trust me—it will make this dress."

"If you insist," Laila conceded, throwing the palette into her bag.

Rosamie smirked. "I always do."

CHAPTER SEVENTEEN

Laila didn't answer her door. Mason knocked for a solid five minutes before he gave up, vowing to try again once he'd settled in. It was midmorning on a Saturday. She would be at work, serving the wealthy patrons of Gardullo's their weekend indulgences.

Frustrated to be so close to his goal, yet still so far, he set down his bag, struggling to insert his key in the lock with his left hand. His right arm rested in a sling against his chest, still useless for the time being.

The arm *should* have been fine by now. However, a few weeks into his recovery, X-rays had shown the break wasn't healing right. They'd had to re-break his bones to reset them properly. Thankfully, they'd given him ample drugs at the time, so it hadn't been unbearable. But it had extended his stay in Mexico.

The full chest and arm cast had come off a few weeks ago. Now, a smaller plaster cast kept his arm immobile. Mason was dying to get the damn thing off, but he was following the doctor's orders to the letter. He didn't want to risk his future mobility by being impatient.

When he finally opened his door, he sucked in a breath of pained surprise. His plants were dead. Almost all were shriveled and wilted.

Fuck. Scrubbing his face with his good hand, he reminded himself he'd been half-expecting this. Ransom hadn't been able to get ahold of his neighbor the entire time Mason had been laid up. His friend had even stopped by the building personally, but Laila hadn't been home either time.

Mason hadn't thought to send his key along with Ransom, so he hadn't been forewarned about the state of his apartment. Tossing his bag on the couch, he spun around in a slow circle, taking stock.

He really couldn't blame Laila for not watering the plants. Given the way she steadfastly refused all his calls and texts over the last few months, it was obvious that she wanted nothing to do with him. It still hurt, though.

After taking a moment to regroup, Mason ordered take-out before fishing a few garbage bags of out his supply closet. He started to throw away the dead plants, salvaging the few that might be revived.

That was a little weird, he thought, stacking the now-empty pots. All the plants were in bad shape, but it almost appeared as if some had been watered a bit more recently than he'd supposed. If Laila hadn't set foot in here since he left, then all the greenery would be dead. Even the trees.

At a loss to make sense of it, he finished cleaning up, taking the full garbage bags down to the dumpster.

When he got back upstairs, Laila's door was swinging shut. Mason knocked, his heart hammering as footsteps approached.

The door swung open, revealing a short, bespeckled Asian man. The stranger blinked up at Mason. "Yeah? Can I help you?"

Mason's lips parted. He took a step back. "Is Laila here?"

Confusion wrinkled the man's brow. "Who?"

The fear this was Laila's new live-in boyfriend dissipated. Shoulders slumping in relief, Mason explained. "Laila James. She lives here..."

The man shrugged. "Not anymore, man."

He was about to close the door when Mason forestalled him, gesturing behind him. "Hey, that's my place over there, but I was away for a while. How long have you been living here?"

"More than three months," the man volunteered, sticking out his left hand before retracting it in chagrin.

"Sorry," he said, waving at Mason's brace. "It's, um, nice to meet you."

"Yeah, nice to meet you," Mason said, his mind racing. Laila must have moved out a few weeks after he left. "I guess I have to track her down."

The guy stood there, staring at him. "Okay, then. Bye."

He began to close the door before yanking it back open. "Hey, I do have some mail addressed to the previous tenant. They never came back for it. If you're going to see them, maybe you can pass it on."

"Yes," Mason answered. He had no fucking clue where Laila was, or why she had moved out, but he was going to find her.

His new neighbor disappeared, returning in a minute with a small stack of envelopes, mailers, and magazines. Mason took them all, pressing the bundle against his body to keep from dropping them.

When his takeout finally arrived, he stuck in his fridge. Then he fished out the keys to his Mustang to drive to Gardullo's Gourmet Grocery.

$$\text{\&}$$

Driving one-handed was...challenging. But Mason did it, anyway, struggling a bit to make the sharp turn on Fifth. When he pulled into the grocery's parking lot, he sighed with relief that he hadn't crashed his car.

The cold February wind whipped across his face as he ducked inside the door of the small, privately owned grocery. Laila's bakery counter was empty.

Fuck. Mason hung his head, fighting the urge to kick the wire stand of advertising circulars next to him across the room. A worry that she wasn't here because she had left town twisted his stomach into a knot. He told himself it wasn't likely, but then he hadn't imagined she'd move apartments either.

It's okay, he told himself. Even if Laila was no longer employed here, she had been all through school. Someone would know where she lived now. He would find her.

Mason was about to flag down the store manager to ask him about Laila when suddenly the woman herself appeared from the back of the store.

It was as if the angels in the heavens had decided to take a sideline as lighting directors. A shaft of sun from the front window hit Laila as she walked past the two checkout stands. She wore a sleeveless burnt orange dress that showed off her sleekly muscled arms. Her dark creamy skin looked as if she had a thin sheet of gold pressed over it.

Damn. Laila glowed. Mason put his hand over his heart. He was a little bit afraid it had just exploded.

She ducked behind her counter, bending to fiddle with something before rising, a tray filled with French macarons in her hand.

When she saw him, she stopped short, sending the multicolored pastries flying.

"*Wha—*" she cried out in surprise, snatching up a green-tinted macaron before it flew off the tray. At least half-a-dozen others weren't as fortunate. They hit the floor, scattering all around her in a rainbow of sweet litter.

"Hi," he said slowly.

Laila's gorgeous brown eyes were fixed wide on his face. For a long moment, she simply stared at him. Finally, she blinked, her head jerking back. "H-hi."

"I didn't mean to startle you."

"You didn't," Laila said quickly, then she gave herself a little shake. "Well, you did, but it's okay. I'm just surprised to see you."

Her eyes ran over him, lingering over the sling and arm in the plaster cast as well as the spot high on his cheek that was still shiny after a scab had fallen off.

His face was otherwise unmarked, but given the way Laila gaped at him, Mason half wondered if he'd sprouted horns. *Or she's noticing how much smaller you are.* He was a lot thinner than he'd been, having lost some muscle mass in recovery.

She set the tray on the counter. "What happened to you?" she asked, gesturing to his arm.

"I got hurt. It happened not long after I saw you last," he said. The words felt thick on his tongue. He shut his eyes briefly, torn between turning away because it would be easier to speak and drinking her in.

Hungry for the sight of her, staring won. "I just got back to town."

Laila paled. "Recently?

"Yes. Today, actually."

"You've been gone this whole time?" Laila asked, her voice a touch unsteady.

Mason nodded. "Things went sideways on my last mission. I sort of got blown up."

Her lips parted. "You *what?*" she squeaked.

He managed a weak one-sided smile.

"I'm fine now. Or I will be. But that's why I've been gone so long. I was laid up in a hospital in Mexico City, wearing a cast up to here." Mason gestured to his neck.

Laila appeared horrified. He was almost concerned she was going to faint.

She sucked in an audible breath. "I'm so sorry to hear that. Are—are you in pain?"

"I'm okay."

Her eyes were skeptical.

"Well, I will be fine," he amended.

The light was playing tricks on him. It almost looked like Laila had tears in her eyes, but then she blinked, and the telltale shimmer disappeared.

"I moved out," Laila blurted.

Mason nodded. "I figured that out when I knocked and met our new neighbor—I mean, my new neighbor," he corrected.

There was another long silence.

"Why?" he murmured.

"I...I had to leave," she said, tucking a lock of hair behind her ear. "It was such an expensive place, and my friend Rosamie put our names in the university housing lottery. She got us a room in graduate student housing. It's much cheaper."

"I see." And he did. Between this bakery job and her classes, Mason knew how many hours she worked. Sometimes, it had seemed as if she were dragging herself up the stairs. More than once, Mason had been tempted to pick her up and carry her up himself. *I should have done it.*

A cheaper place would help relieve some of that burden. "How long ago was that?"

His voice was sandpaper rough.

"The week after you left."

He nodded, throat perilously tight. "And your phone? I called you a few times."

More like a few dozen...

"I broke it in the stairwell," she said in consternation. "I have a new one. My old number couldn't be ported to my new carrier."

"Oh." In a way, it was a relief. At least she hadn't blocked him. "I'm glad you're okay, too. I was worried when I saw my plants. I thought something had happened to you."

Laila's brow creased. "What was wrong with your plants?"

He laughed. "They're all dead."

Her hand flew up to her to cover her mouth. "Oh, no! But Mrs. Turnbull was supposed to water them. I showed her what to do step-by-step."

Clearly, Laila had never gotten his note. "I guess she forgot," he said softly.

Laila staggered, leaning on the counter for support. "I can't believe she didn't do it. I even gave her all the money you paid me, too!"

He couldn't help but smile, despite the circumstances. Laila was so adorable in her indignation.

"Is that why you're here? Because of the plants? Are you—" She broke off, swallowing hard. "Are you mad because they're dead?"

"Who's dead, babe?" a man asked at the same time Mason opened his mouth to say no.

"His plants," Laila said as Mason whirled to face the newcomer.

"His *what?*" The guy laughed, causing a few heads to turn. The females in the vicinity paused to admire the younger man.

The brown-haired man was only a few inches shorter than Mason but almost as wide. His chest and arms were muscular, indicating he worked out, although his legs were too lean for real stamina. The guy was strong, but he didn't do manual labor. That much was clear by his preppy clothes and expensive watch.

From his easy and familiar manner—and the '*babe*'—it was obvious he and Laila knew each other.

Mason instantly hated him.

"It's not funny, Joseph," Laila admonished. "Mason had a lot of plants, some very expensive ones, too."

She put her hand to her forehead. "Oh God, the orchids alone were worth hundreds of dollars—maybe more."

There was a slight sway as if she were going to be sick. "Mrs. Turnbull agreed to water them for me. I gave her all the money you'd paid me for the last two times you were out of town. She's a retired teacher—I thought she'd be reliable."

"Babe, calm down. He's not going to sue you over some plants." Joseph smirked, turning to Mason. "You're not, right?"

This time the '*babe*' was reverberating so loud in Mason's mind that he didn't answer right away, making Laila visibly more anxious.

"Of course not," he choked out, forcing a soothing tone. "I was just concerned that something had happened to you. I take it that Mrs. Turnbull is now in possession of my spare key?"

"Yes," Laila said, her eyes going from him to the preppy dude and back again.

The man put his hand out. "Joseph, Joseph Dubey." The way he pronounced his name, stressing the syllables in such an obvious way, raised Mason's hackles.

Even more than his clothes, Dubey's smug confidence screamed *money*. Mason wouldn't have held that against the other man, but there was something off-putting about him. Maybe it was the wafts of privilege. They stank like a fine cologne that made everyone sneeze. It was certainly too much for Mason.

This guy expects everyone to know his name. Mason suppressed a snort. *In his circles, everyone probably does.*

However, Laila was watching him so intently that Mason couldn't be rude. He shook the offered hand with his only available one, letting go as soon as good manners would allow. "Mason Lang."

He refocused on Laila. "I'm sorry you had to move out," he said after a beat.

"You should be." Dubey laughed. "The dorms are tiny. I can't imagine sharing such a small space with another person in the room." Pausing, he gave Laila a meaningful look. "Hopefully, though, she won't have to soon, or at least I hope she won't."

"I'm sorry, I'm not following," Mason said, hoping he was misreading the situation.

"It happens to be our anniversary." Joseph waved Laila forward as if she were supposed to walk through the counter toward him. "I asked Laila to move in with me. And tonight, I'm hoping she'll tell me yes, so we'll really have something to celebrate."

Obeying the causal summons, Laila lifted the flip-up portion of the counter to come around front. A gold locket on a thin chain glinted around her neck. Matching studs adorned her ears.

Laila rarely wore jewelry. But, of course, this was a special occasion. She was dressed up to go out and celebrate her anniversary with this douchebag.

"Congratulations," he said evenly. Inside, his mind was roiling. Had she been seeing this guy before he'd left on his ill-fated mission?

He tried to make his tone casual, but he was only moderately successful. "How long have you been dating?"

"Not long," Dubey answered. There was a tiny smirk as if he knew the answer meant something to Mason.

"It's the three-month anniversary of our first date," Laila clarified, ducking under Dubey's outstretched arm. Her voice was low, almost apologetic, as the man wrapped an arm around her. "Joseph likes to celebrate *every* occasion. He gave me flowers at the one-week mark, and he hasn't stopped since."

The mention of flowers made her face tighten as if she'd just remembered his plants. "Mason, I'm so sorry about what happened."

He waved her apology away. "It's all right. I'm glad you're in one piece. I was...concerned."

Dubey squeezed Laila, pulling her into him a bit tighter. "Babe, we have to get going if we're going to make our reservation in time."

"Oh, yes." Laila winced and bit her lip, hesitating as she reluctantly met Mason's eyes.

"Don't worry about it. They're just plants," he assured her, hating the uncertainty in her expression.

"But—"

"I should get going. Let you get back to your night," he interrupted, discarding his initial plan to linger and grab some groceries. "Congratulations on the anniversary, by the way."

Excusing himself with a murmur, he walked away, heading to his vehicle. It was a good thing it was a sports car.

Mason couldn't get away fast enough.

CHAPTER EIGHTEEN

The next day Laila swore under her breath as a fat stream of water splattered her from the rear awning, sending water trickling down her back.

A sudden storm had rolled in during the early afternoon. She'd hoped it would clear up before she had to empty the bakery's bins, but her shift was almost over, and the weather showed no signs of letting up.

Resigned to getting wet, Laila hauled the full waste bags to the dumpster behind the store, trying not to drag them as she went. The plastic wasn't strong enough to survive the asphalt intact. The last thing she needed was to be forced to pick up the garbage from the ground by hand—again.

She had just heaved the first overfilled bag over the edge of the dumpster when *he* called her name.

Laila spun around. The second bag crashed to the ground, slipping from her nerveless fingers.

Mason stood a few feet away. He must have been waiting for her to come out for some time because he was dripping wet, his golden hair a darker shade of wheat and plastered to his head.

"Hey," he said.

"Hi." Laila blinked, the moisture collecting on her long lashes, making it difficult to see.

There was a long stretch of silence. How was it possible she'd missed him? This impossibly beautiful man had hurt her so much—he shouldn't have the power to affect her. Not anymore.

And yet, it felt like her heart was breaking all over again.

Hungrier than she should have been, Laila drank the sight of him in.

She pointed to his arm. He was still wearing a sling, but the white cast had disappeared. "Can you get that wet?" she asked in a low voice.

He glanced at his sling. "Yes, I had the plaster one removed yesterday. This is just nylon and plastic now—machine washable."

"Oh." Laila picked at the store apron she was wearing. "That's good. It's an improvement," she added lamely.

"Yeah." That was followed by more silence.

"Are you—"

"Why are—"

They both stopped. She smiled apologetically, but she gave up the effort when he took a few steps forward, close enough for her to feel his heat.

"I know I shouldn't be here," he said in a hoarse voice. "You're seeing that guy now, but there is something you need to know."

Laila clutched her apron tighter. "What is it?"

"That night..." Mason broke off, rubbing his face with his good hand. "Actually, the next morning is what I wanted to talk about. What you saw—that girl. Her name is Angie."

Laila flinched. She didn't mean to, but she did. Mason swore under his breath.

"She didn't stay the night with me," he said urgently. "She was there the next morning, but she wasn't invited. Do you understand what I'm telling you?"

Laila suppressed a shiver. She was almost as wet as he was now, but she didn't care. "You...you're saying you didn't sleep with her."

"Yeah," he said gruffly. "I didn't. I wouldn't have. And she wasn't after me for real—she's getting married to Dusty, the man she really wanted, in a couple of weeks. It's not important. My point is that I wouldn't have done that. Not right after you and I... I know that doesn't matter now because you're with someone new, and he seems...great. Fine. But I needed you to know."

"Why are you telling me this?" Was Mason asking for another chance?

He stilled, then rolled his shoulders. "I needed to clear the air. You had to know I have more honor than that."

Her throat was too tight to speak. "I..."

"It's all beside the point. You've moved on," he repeated. "I know it's selfish to come around again after all this time, but I didn't want you to go on with your life thinking badly of me. Because what you think matters to me. It matters a lot."

Pivoting abruptly, he started to leave. He was at the door of his Mustang before she could react.

"Mason!" Laila ran toward him. She stopped short at the edge of the lot. "I—I believe you."

He nodded once. And then he got in his car and drove away.

CHAPTER NINETEEN

Five Months Later

Mason kept his face impassive as Rainer Torsten finished the obstacle course a full fifteen seconds after the rest of the delta team. It was a pretty decent time for a playboy billionaire, but Mason still shot him a warning glance. It wouldn't do to let the other guys think he would accept this kind of performance from them. But for someone as pampered as Torsten, it wasn't half bad, especially in this heat.

He had to hand it to the billionaire—the man had committed to the training. His counterpart, Garret Chapman, had dropped out ages ago.

But Rainer surprised him. He was here every Saturday, rain or shine. Mason didn't take it easy on him either, refusing to tailor the routine to his level or soften it in any way. If Torsten couldn't keep up with the others, then he had no right to be here, even if they spent the six days working here to Rainer's one.

If the rich man's lag widened to thirty seconds, however, Mason might discreetly ask him to tap out. But there was no real reason for it. Torsten had done his best to minimize disruption. He didn't bring his bodyguards to the warehouse and fields where they trained, and he was always on time.

And he was friendly and strangely unobtrusive in a way Chapman, or his bosses, Ian Quinn and Elias Gardner, were not. Though he could never truly stay in the background, Rainer was one of those men who silently observed, never letting on what was going on behind those inscrutable eyes. By reputation, he was a shark in the boardroom, but he was respectful and friendly here.

"Do you have plans for the weekend?" Rainer asked after the recruits had gone off to hit the showers. "I was going to fly down to my place in the Bahamas, and I thought you'd like to come along. "

Mason gave him a sharp look. "You're not coming back next Saturday, are you?"

Rainer appeared caught off guard. Then he shrugged. "No," he said shortly.

He shared a hapless smile that no doubt got him far with the ladies. "Sorry, it's not that I don't appreciate your efforts to train me. It's not even that I'm unwilling to do the work, but I used to travel a lot—business—and coming here every week is starting to get in the way."

That was the reason Chapman had stopped coming. But Mason had always wondered what was keeping Torsten from dropping out. Six months was an eternity for a billionaire in business, wasn't it?

"How did you guess?" Rainer wiped his face with a towel.

Mason shrugged. "You've never asked me or anyone else in the organization to socialize, not even Quinn and Gardner."

"It's not because I didn't want to, but I didn't think mixing with your bosses would be a good look while I was trying to stick to the program. But it's past time I stopped getting in your way. Isn't this team about to roll out soon? Don't you need time to gel as a unit without a fifth wheel that's never going to go out on a mission?"

"Auric has greenlit us," Mason acknowledged. "We're entering the rotation next month—strictly in a support capacity unless we land a softball. But you haven't held the others back at all."

Technically, no job was low risk, but unlike the one where he'd been hurt, some were more...predictable. They were going to start with those. In the short term, his most difficult task as a team leader was going to be making sure the guys stayed icy and on their toes.

"The fact you came on the same day every week made you part of the routine," Mason shared. "But a team doesn't truly gel until they get out in the field. And even though they occasionally give you shit—the guys respect the effort. As do I," he said, putting his right hand out. "If you ever want to drop in when we're in town, feel free."

Rainer shook Mason's hand, obviously realizing it was his right. "How's the arm, by the way?"

"A hundred percent," he said easily.

And it was true. Mason had dived into his rehab routine with a vengeance. He'd checked in with the team's doctor religiously, and he had gone above and beyond the prescribed physical therapy regimens. He'd pushed himself much harder. Mason had been determined to get back to his peak physical condition.

When he wasn't working on himself, he was training the new team. The recruits had been ready and waiting for him when he got back—eight elite men and two women chosen from a small but select pool of applicants. Most were former military like him, but two had come from law enforcement, including a former SWAT sniper.

Mason worked them hard, determined that his team quickly establish itself as one of the elite. But despite being the boss, Mason didn't take it any easier on himself. Once Doc Valentine gave him the all-clear, he ran every mile, did every set of crunches, and every one-armed push-up that his team did.

"Thanks for the effort you put into my training," Rainer continued. "I know I didn't make it easy for you, especially in the beginning."

"You weren't that bad," Mason lied, grinning. The early days of the rich man's training had been...colorful. But his face felt abnormally stretched—a reminder that smiles were rare for him these days.

"You lasted about five months longer than I thought you would," he added a touch more honestly.

Rainer threw his head back and laughed, cementing Mason's good opinion of him. "You never answered my question. How does a weekend in the Bahamas sound?"

"A weekend *where?*" A warm weight crashed into Mason's back as Ransom slung an arm around his shoulders. "Doesn't matter—I'm in."

"Unfortunately, I'm not," Mason said, peeling his friend's arm off. "My buddy is coming to town tonight. Ethan's plane is due within the hour. I have to hit the showers and book it to the airport if I'm going to pick him up on time."

"He's welcome to come along," Rainer offered generously. He ignored Ransom mugging aggressively over the man's shoulder.

"I'm not sure he's in the mood for that," Mason said.

He didn't know the details, but he'd heard Ethan's tone on the phone. They had been friends long enough for him to be able to tell all was not right in Beantown, where Ethan worked as an FBI agent.

"You should go on ahead," Mason said. "And if you feel like company, Ransom mixes a damn fine Old Fashioned. He's also an excellent wingman."

"You're welcome to come along," Rainer said, extending the invitation to Ransom instead. "Although I should warn you, I'm not looking to party this weekend. Just relax, poolside, while admiring the ocean view."

"Sounds great to me," Ransom enthused, nudging the older man with his shoulder. "When do we leave?"

Mason excused himself with a warm goodbye, heading to the showers. The entire way to the airport, he wondered what might be wrong with his oldest friend.

Ethan didn't keep him in suspense long. "She got married," he said grimly as he climbed into Mason's mustang at LAX's curbside pick-up area.

"Who?" Then he remembered. "Oh, that girl—Peyton."

Ethan had mentioned Peyton Carson several times over the years. Not enough to mark an obsession, mind you, but Mason had read between the lines.

"Who did she marry?" he asked, frowning as he pulled into traffic.

"King Asshole himself—and another guy with enough money to buy Heaven itself."

"But not Hell?" The world was full of assholes, but as far as Ethan was concerned, there was only one king—Liam Tyler, his partner Jason's brother-in-law.

"Hell has a cheaper cover charge," the agent said.

"So, who's the other guy?"

"A Nordic billionaire."

Mason chuckled. "Wow."

Ethan slumped in the seat. "I know."

"Two men." Mason shook his head, whistling. "And rich guys at that. At least now you know there wasn't ever a real shot. The girl was obviously after a fat wallet. You're better off."

"Nah," Ethan grumbled. "Peyton's not about the money. She'd be with them without the cash. But you do have a point in a way—I can't be two men."

Mason pulled onto the freeway. "If that's the new standard women are setting these days, we are both shit out of luck."

Ethan snickered. "Do we need to stop at a liquor store? I need a bourbon."

"Don't worry. I've got you covered."

There wasn't much conversation until they pulled up at Mason's new rental.

"When did you move?" Ethan asked, squinting at the suburban split-level.

"When I got back from Mexico."

"I thought you were dead set on staying downtown," Ethan pointed out when Mason gave him the grand tour. "What happened to being able to get sushi takeout at two AM?"

"Got old," Mason said evasively. Ethan didn't need to know that staying downtown for the best take-out didn't seem to matter after Laila had moved out of their building.

"Well, at least it has a yard." Ethan scowled at the bare patch of scorched grass. "I'm surprised you haven't done anything with it."

"I've been busy. Maybe later. For now, the only thing that matters is location. It's midway between Auric's training facility and my physical therapist office."

"Are you still going to that?"

"Not too often. Just the occasional checkup."

He showed Ethan to his room, letting the agent shower while he prepared the grill outside. After steaks and beer, they switched to the promised bourbon, and he showed Ethan the house's chief attraction.

They ducked out of the second-story window on the roof of the garage. The rental was up on a hill, just high enough to get a partial view of the valley below. It was enough. The lights below them stretched out like a blanket of stars.

They took the bottle of bourbon with them.

"How are you actually doing?" Mason asked after Ethan poured himself another, much fuller glass.

"I'm fine—well, I will be fine," he amended after a long pause. The tiniest bit of a slur was creeping into his voice.

"I suppose you think I'm behaving like a jackass—making a fool of myself over a girl I never even went out on a date with." Ethan huffed, rubbing his face. "It's just...did you ever meet someone and see the future? I mean not *the* future, but like a possible future. A really good one."

Yes. Despite the multiple glasses of bourbon, Mason was suddenly sober. "Yes," he repeated aloud, his voice a touch hollow. "I have."

Fortunately, Ethan was too drunk to follow-up. His friend set his drink down before flopping on his back across the warm roof shingles. "I shouldn't have gone to the wedding."

Christ. "You went to the *wedding*?"

Ethan smirked. "I wanted to prove I was okay."

Mason winced. "And were you?"

"I've done undercover work," Ethan reminded him. "Even infiltrated drug cartels. If I didn't have a fantastic poker face, I'd be dead."

"I guess that's best in the long run," Mason conceded. Ethan was tied to Peyton's new husband through his partner. He had to continue mixing with those people. "But it's still a bitch."

Mason couldn't see himself going to Laila's wedding. Not that she'd invite him. Mason had been holding her at arm's length for too long. He'd never given them a chance to become friends like Ethan and Peyton.

"Yeash," Ethan grumbled. "The weddin' was on a private island that groom number two bought."

Fucking A. "Now, that's just obscene."

"They named it after her—Carsonia."

Mason started laughing. Ethan joined him, wiping tears from his eyes.

An image of Mason's version of King Asshole, Laila's new boyfriend, flashed before his eyes. But Dubey was too young for that title. *Prince Douchebag fits better...*

"You know what we need to do? We need to get rich." Mason picked up the bourbon bottle.

His friend thought this was a brilliant idea. "Yes! Let's make some money. Once we're as rich as those guys, we can get any woman we want—quality women." Ethan was definitely slurring now because it sounded more like *'quafily'*.

"What makes a woman a quantified one?" Mason was struggling now as well. *Well, it's a hard word.*

"You know..." Ethan nudged him. "They're nice, and they have...skin."

"They have *skin?*" Mason laughed, leaning over to pinch Ethan's cheek.

"Ease off." Ethan pushed Mason's hand away. "You know what I mean—nice skin. Soft. Healthy. But not spray tan healthy. Skin that, your nose... it shines." Ethan reared up, sliding down the inclined roof about a foot. "But not like greasy shiny."

Lost in a memory, Mason took another swig. "Skin that glows," he said softly.

"*Exactly.*" Ethan waved his hand all over himself. "Glowering shin."

He broke off, burping into his fist. "I thought Auric paid you well. More than an FBI agent makes in any case."

"It does, but there isn't a government pension at the end of this. And I don't want to keep doing merc work for the rest of my life," Mason admitted aloud for the first time. "I want to buy a house, not just rent one—a nice one with a greenhouse. Maybe a pool. And I want the time to be able to enjoy it with someone special. And I don't want them to have to kill themselves working to pay for their share of it."

He didn't blame Laila for choosing Prince Douchebag. Mason had left her to think the worst of him, and he'd been gone for months. To add insult to injury, her guy was obviously loaded and went out of his way to treat her nice.

He gave me flowers on the first-week mark, and he hasn't stopped since.

"I can give her flovers," he muttered.

"So, where do we starve?" Ethan said, his voice abnormally loud. "I mean, start."

"Where did King Asshole and the Nordic billionfare get their mulah?"

"Tyler is in hotels, and I think the Nordician inherited most of his. That and oil deals."

Mason squinted. It was too late to inherit buckets of money. "How about real estate?" he said slowly, taking care to enunciate the words.

"What?" Ethan's eyes were getting distinctly rheumy. Also, the new bourbon bottle was down to its last quarter.

"We should buy and rent houshes and afartments."

"Fart men?" Ethan grimaced. "I don't think anyone will pay for fart men. Unless they have a speshific fetish."

His tongue tangled so much around the last two words that Ethan tripped over himself. From a complete resting position, he managed to flail and slide down the slanted roof. Mason lunged, but he failed to catch him.

Ethan disappeared over the edge. A loud thud followed it.

Swearing incoherently, Mason clambered to the edge. Ethan sprawled on the brown grass in the backyard, just a few inches from the concrete patio.

"You okay?".

"Yeah. Nothing was broken—I think." Ethan said, feeling his legs. "Are you going to go around?"

Swinging his legs over, Mason dropped over the edge, jumping off with the sublime grace of an athlete in his prime.

He landed next to Ethan with almost no sound.

"Or you can do that," his friend deadpanned.

Mason looked down. "You sound more sober."

"Getting there. Falling off a roof helped."

Mason offered his hand. "Let's fix that. I have another bottle of bourbon inside."

CHAPTER TWENTY

Mason knew Ethan thought he was joking about going into real estate, but despite the killer hangover, he remembered their grand plan the next morning. And he still liked it. Ethan was a little more skeptical, but not so much he wouldn't entertain the idea.

Ethan probably thought Mason would forget about it or put it on the back burner as a 'someday' project. But Mason was done with 'someday'. He was determined to make their plan a success *today*, enough so to book a ticket to Boston to scout properties with a real estate agent.

The decision to choose Boston instead of L.A. was a practical one. The L.A. housing market was very cutthroat at the moment. Mason didn't have a nine-to-five job like Ethan. If there were any problems, Ethan wouldn't be able to address them without hopping on a plane.

The gods smiled on their plans. Not two days into their search, they found the perfect six-story building. The real estate agent had written it off as being too rundown, but Mason's extended family did one of two things—they either served in the army or worked in construction. After inspecting it closely, he realized the dilapidation was only surface deep. But despite the relatively low price, it was still too expensive for him and Ethan.

His friend had already gotten a loan to cover his portion. Thanks to his exemplary service record and personal contacts, it was a good one. But Mason didn't want to force Ethan to shoulder more of the responsibility than he had to. So they'd brought in a third investor. Donovan Carter was a friend of Ethan's, and he had more money than he knew what to do with. Donovan agreed to invest on the condition he could have a unit in the building.

This was right when Ian Quinn approached him about continuing as a trainer on a more permanent basis.

"This is going to sound weird," his boss said. "But you being laid-up and taking over training at the facility was a blessing in disguise. We didn't think the recruits would be ready for fieldwork for at least seven or eight months, and you got them ready in less than six."

"Really?" Mason replied skeptically. "I thought that was slow."

"Only because we held you back. Caution is the better part of valor in this line of work. But we got to see you in a different leadership role than we originally intended. And frankly, we can continue to use you."

Quinn leaned in, his hands templed under his chin. "We want to open our first East Coast office in the next few months. We're searching for properties now, something close enough to D.C. to be able to coordinate with our government partners more easily."

"And so we can shop our services more efficiently to them too," Mason said, getting the gist.

"Precisely." Quinn beamed at Mason like a schoolteacher who wanted to slap a sticker on his chest. "Now we've got another two teams to fill, including a smaller six-man unit for specialized ops. We're going to want to have some of our senior personnel at the other office from day one."

Mason frowned. "Are you going to reshuffle the teams?"

"We are," Quinn confirmed. "But only for the people who aren't tied to the area. That means Santos is out. His wife's job isn't mobile. But you, on the other hand…"

"I have no family here," Mason finished.

A flash of dark creamy skin made him drift for a moment. *Stop that.* He hadn't spoken to Laila in months.

"The move will be voluntary. Again—only those who can go will. And, in the meantime, we want you to keep leading your team. However, once we find the right location, things will move very quickly. Given your family background in construction, we'd like you to head this thing up with us. You're going to be our fulcrum—the point on which everything rests. Are you up for it?"

Mason opened his mouth, hesitating long enough to make Quinn raise a brow. "I'm not wrong? You're up for a move, right? Unless there's something I don't know about."

"No," Mason said after a beat. "I have nothing keeping me in L.A."

So that was how Mason started dividing his time between the two coasts. He ended up on another property hunt, helping scout locations for Auric's new base with the same specialized commercial real estate agent.

Isla, the agent, was in her early thirties and single. When his bosses signed on the dotted line, she wanted to celebrate with him...in bed.

"Come on, soldier man," she purred in his ear in the garage of her company's estate office. "I want that cock in my mouth right now."

Her words were like a splash of cold water. There was nothing she could have said to turn him off faster. To add insult to injury, her perfume suddenly made his throat close up.

I must be allergic to it. That was the only possible reason his skin was crawling.

"Maybe next time," he told her, backing away and trying not to look as if he was running to his car. "I just remembered a previous appointment."

He drove away, wondering what the hell was wrong with him. *I'm sweating.* Mason struggled out of his jacket at a red light, throwing it behind him and turning the dial to blast the AC.

It wasn't the first time Mason had turned down an offer he would have normally jumped at. And it wasn't about Laila. She was in the past—he wouldn't think about her anymore other than to wish her well.

He'd accepted a long time ago that she had moved on.

I'm just busy, he told himself. Given his new responsibilities and the way he was jetting back and forth across the country, the length of his dry spell wasn't extraordinary. And it wasn't that he hadn't dated anyone since. There had been a few lackluster dates that hadn't gone anywhere.

I'm just a little pickier these days. Mason was a few years younger than Ethan, but he was old enough to be unsatisfied with a quick lay. That night with Laila had taught him one thing, at least. He was ready for the real thing.

He gripped the steering wheel. That was it then. It was settled—once his life quieted down a bit, he was going to start dating in earnest. But he wouldn't be aiming for casual. Not anymore.

His team had officially disbanded. A few of his people had been reassigned to other teams, but more than half would be coming back to team 2.0, which would be based out near Ashburn, the closest they could get to D.C. without blowing their budget.

Mason was due to move to the East Coast in a few months to oversee the construction of the new Auric base. In the meantime, he had thrown himself into the Boston apartment building renovation, knocking down crumbling plaster in the interior and putting up new drywall. The copper plumbing was sound for the most part as it had been replaced less than a decade ago, but there were few exceptions—shoddy patch jobs done on the cheap in more recent years. The cooling and heating systems were also getting a makeover. Mason wasn't qualified to do that part, but he knew enough to lay the groundwork for the professionals.

During the work, he realized the building still had a tenant—a mother with a baby girl. All the other residents had moved on, but the mom was obviously in a bind, struggling to make ends meet. She was also young, with dark skin and this vulnerability in her eyes that reminded him of she-who-must-not-be-named.

Before Mason knew what was happening, he'd told the tenant she could stay for a few months while she hunted for a new place. He was recalled to L.A. before he could break the news to his oldest friend. Mason resolved to give Ethan a call to confess later—much later.

§&

"I can't believe we're ahead of schedule," Ian Quinn said, slapping Mason on the back on the way out of the conference room.

Mason had spent the last hour updating him and Elias on the progress made on the new headquarters at their downtown office, and it had gone well.

"It helped we're just retrofitting the existing buildings for the most part, not building them from scratch," Mason said.

"Well, I'm still determined to be impressed, so don't burst my bubble," Ian laughed. "And thanks for vetting the construction staff. That was above and beyond."

Mason shrugged in self-deprecation. "I had a head start after doing all that research for the apartment renovation I'm doing with my buddy Ethan. Most companies that do large-scale residential work are experienced with the kind of changes we need at the compound. And scheduling and coordinating the work is secondhand nature by now. The Boston project got me ready."

"I guess we're lucky you decided to go into real estate then." Ian laughed. "Still, it sounds like a good investment. And you're saving us a bundle overseeing the retrofit."

"I'm going to remind you of that come bonus time," Mason said dryly before taking his leave.

Mason was in the mood to celebrate, but it was too early for him to meet up with Ransom or one of the other guys. At loose ends, he drove aimlessly, killing time.

Before he knew it, he was a block away from Gardullo's Grocery.

Fuck. Mason came within a hairsbreadth of doing an illegal U-turn. His instinct was to get the hell away from here, but he changed his mind at the last second.

It wasn't as if he'd never broken this particular rule before. After their last meeting, when Laila had understandably failed to leap into his arms, Mason vowed to stay away.

Now that they didn't live in the same building, it was easy. They didn't travel in the same circles.

But Mason hadn't liked the sight of Dubey. Something about the guy rubbed him the wrong way. So, every couple of months, he would drive to Gardullo's and park in the eye-line of the bakery counter. More often than not, Laila would appear to help a customer or put new baked goods in the display counter.

If he'd wanted to, Mason could have found out where she was living. Working for Auric had taught him a thing or two about researching an op. In their business, they lived and died according to the quality of their intel. Finding her new address would have been a snap.

But he didn't do it. Mason wasn't a stalker. Coming by her work-place wasn't the same—it was a business, open to the public. He was merely concerned about her. Once he was satisfied she was all right, he would leave.

If he happened to miss her and someone else was working the counter, he would duck into the store and buy her pastries from her replacement at the counter. He knew which ones were her specialties. It was like getting a little taste of her, one she never needed to know about.

Mason closed his eyes, ignoring the elephant currently parked on the hood of his car. When he opened them, Laila was leaving the store. Her head was down as she searched for something in her purse.

It was the kind of thing he warned his cousins not to do. Anybody could run up to them while they were distracted. But Laila was just steps away from her store. She was safe enough there, he supposed.

She stood there long enough to push him to act.

Mason opened the car door. This time, he wasn't just going to watch her walk away. He was going to talk to her, find out how she was doing. He would just be catching up with a friend. No harm in that.

Laila had just turned the corner when a low-slung Porsche pulled up right next to her. Dubey stepped out.

He witnessed the second Laila recognized her boyfriend. It wasn't what he was expecting—Laila flinched. Her feet shuffled back as if she were thinking of bolting.

Mason froze, wondering what the hell was going on.

Dubey walked right up to her, putting his hands on her shoulders, his face down close to hers. His back was to him, so Mason couldn't tell what he was saying, but he didn't like the expression on Laila's face.

Her lips moved. Dubey threw up one of his hands, but he kept one on her. Mason could tell he held her tight because when Laila jerked away, her shirt was pulled hard.

Then Dubey did something that had Mason's vision red-tinged with fury.

Dubey pushed Laila. Her head struck the wall behind her hard enough for it to snap forward again. Then the asshole grabbed her by the shoulder and strong-armed her into the car. The Porsche peeled out of the parking lot.

Rigid with rage, Mason clutched the top of his car door. He hadn't moved a muscle during the entire exchange.

Dubey was lucky Mason was at the other end of the parking lot. Otherwise, the abusive fucker would be dead right now.

CHAPTER TWENTY-ONE

Mason pounded on the dormitory door. He gritted his teeth, holding onto his patience with effort as Rosamie took her sweet time opening the door.

"What the fuck, dude?" the tiny Filipina snapped, her big eyes starring daggers at him.

"Where the hell does Joseph Dubey live?" he said, managing not to snarl at her—but only just.

Rosamie crossed her arms and scowled, a mountain of attitude in a pint-sized package. "Who the hell wants to know?"

He clenched his fists. "I'm Mason Lang."

Her brow puckered. "Why do I know that name?"

Mason took a long, rage-calming breath. "I used to live across the hall from Laila, remember?"

The confusion cleared, but her expression turned mulish. "And what do you want, blast from the past?"

"I already said I need to know where the hell Laila is. She lives with Dubey. Or at least that's what her coworkers at the store said. But her last address of record is here with you. She never bothered to change it because they cut her checks right at the store and hand them to her. So, where does that asshole live? His off-campus place—not the frat."

Rosamie narrowed her eyes, impressively standing her ground with her five-feet nothing facing off against his muscled six-foot-three frame. "Yeah, I don't think so, asshat. You had your shot with Laila, and you pissed it away with some wannabe lingerie model."

He raised a finger, pointing it at her face. "That is not what happened, but that doesn't fucking matter—"

"The hell it doesn't," she broke in.

"*Stop.*" It had to be the obvious desperation in his voice that finally made her shut up.

"What I'm trying to tell you is that I just saw that fucker Joseph Dubey slam Laila against a wall before manhandling her into his car." He leaned in close. "So unless you condone that sort of shit, you will tell me where they live—*now.*"

Rosamie drew back, her toasted-almond skin noticeably paling. "That's not true."

Mason threw his hands in the air. "Would I be here if it wasn't?"

She absorbed his words in silence. And then she came to a decision, twisting to grab her purse from a nearby table. "All right, but I'm coming with you."

The drive was twenty minutes with traffic, but each one of those felt like an eternity. Rosamie talked the entire way—alternating between insults to Mason for making the entire story up to threatening bodily harm to Joseph Dubey if he wasn't. She couldn't make up her mind.

But halfway through the drive, she caught his sense of urgency. Her voice took on a strained note. "If he's touched a hair on her head, I'm gonna rip his balls off."

Coming from a woman, those words would have normally made Mason wince in sympathy, but as far as he was concerned, Dubey didn't deserve any. "Not if I get to him first," he growled.

Rosamie gave him directions to a sleek high rise off Pico and Flower. Mason parked the car, snaking a slot across the street when a cab pulled out.

"Joe has a suite on the top floor," Rosamie said as she jaywalked across the street. "His dad pays the rent."

Mason locked the car and ran to overtake her, grabbing her arm and tugging her out of the path of oncoming traffic when it appeared as if she might not clear the distance in time.

Angry horns sounded behind them, but they both ignored them as they rushed inside. It was a high-end building, with the additional security feature of an attendant at the front. The man was supposed to check off and announce visitors. He did a double-take when he saw Mason, but Rosamie waved to the man and he just let them on through.

The suite was on the top floor. Luckily, there wasn't a fingerprint scanner blocking access. Tamping down his anger, Mason decided to let Rosamie take the lead and knock. If Dubey answered the door, Mason might take him down, then and there.

But no one answered.

"Laila, it's me," Rosamie called, pounding this time. "Open the door."

There was a faint scrabbling, and Laila spoke through the wood. "Rosamie? C-can you come back later?"

He could tell from Rosamie's expression that this had never happened before.

"No!" Rosamie tried the doorknob, jiggling it repeatedly. "I'm not leaving."

After an endless beat of silence, the door opened. "I was going to call you actually—it's just that I need to..."

Laila's voice trailed off as she saw Mason hovering behind her friend.

Her eyes were red and puffy, her hair mussed. But the thing that made his vision nearly blackout with rage was her lips. The bottom one was split. The wound was fresh, too, and it was still swelling up.

"It's true," Rosamie spit, blinking fiercely. "He *hit* you."

Laila didn't even look at her friend. Her huge honey-brown eyes welled with tears. "Mason, what are you doing here?"

Before he could answer, Rosamie beat him to it. "He saw you in the parking lot of Gardullo's. He drove me here."

Mason touched Rosamie on the shoulder when she would have continued. Catching his expression, she fell back. He stepped in front of her.

This was the closest he'd gotten to Laila in months. And she was *bleeding*.

"Where is he?" The growl in his voice reverberated in the air, sending out a lethal vibration. It was a voice that promised violence.

Both Laila and Rosamie reacted. The latter shivered.

Mason tried to get himself under control. "It's okay, Laila. It's going to be okay."

She turned away, wiping her eyes, but then wincing as if it hurt.

Mason gritted his teeth, fighting to keep his face impassive.

"He's not here," she whispered, pulling the door open and backing away. They followed her into a spacious penthouse apartment done up in a mishmash of contemporary and sleek minimalist Asian furniture. It wasn't gaudy, but it was definitely trying too hard.

A battered suitcase lay open in the hallway. There were some clothes inside. Something tight uncoiled in Mason's gut. There was no need to convince Laila to leave. She had already decided on her own.

Rosamie was all over Laila, who was fighting not to cry. "Do you want to go to the police?"

Laila thought about it. "I don't know."

"Okay, okay," her friend said, nodding emphatically. "Not a problem. You don't have to decide now. We can talk back at the dorm. Let's just get you packed and out of here."

"She's not going back to your dorm," Mason announced.

Laila's lips parted. He shook his head. "Dubey knows that's the first place you would go. It's wide open—there's no security to speak of. Hell, I just got in there, and no one tried to stop me."

He'd been hopping mad, too. And despite having a murderous glare, the people who passed him on the way to Rosamie's room had just scattered and gotten out of his way.

Mason held out his hand to Laila. "You can stay with me."

She swallowed audibly. "Joe knows we used to be neighbors. I pointed out my old building to him once, so he might know where you live, too."

"If the dorm isn't safe, she can stay with my mom," Rosamie said. "My old bedroom is empty—Mom put her sewing machine in there, but that's better than staying on your couch."

"You'll have your own room," Mason promised. "And he won't find you—I can guarantee that. I moved a few months ago."

He stepped closer to her. "Joseph won't get anywhere near you. I promise."

Laila stared at him with shadowed doe eyes. Then she took his hand. "Thank you."

Rosamie stopped fighting him then. She focused on getting Laila packed up. Even considering how sparse Laila's apartment had been, there wasn't much. It all fit into the suitcase and two garbage bags they grabbed from under the sink.

Mason took a few minutes to go through the apartment, riffling through papers in a vain attempt to find anything incriminating. But there was almost nothing in the desk. Just some utility bills and a few old term papers. There was no second laptop, meaning Dubey had his with him. No gun and no other weapons beyond the high-end kitchen knives.

A man doesn't need a weapon to terrorize a woman, he reminded himself.

Once the ladies were done packing, he shepherded them back to his car, loading Laila's few belongings into the trunk. Fate was on Dubey's side. Mason got Laila and her friend away without the asshole showing his face—or else Mason would have broken every bone in his body.

He decided to drop off Rosamie at her dorm first. Predictably, she put up a fight.

Mason let the small Filipina blister the air before he held up a hand. "I know you think Laila needs you now—and you're right—but you have to think strategically. I don't have a problem with you knowing where I live, but Joseph will come looking for her. He's going to want to know where she is."

"Well, he's not going to find out from me," she protested indignantly.

"Maybe not," he said, glancing at the passenger seat. Laila was quiet, examining her hands. She had that million-yard stare that told him she wasn't even listening. "But let me ask you this—did you ever think Joseph Dubey would hit her?"

His words struck their target. Rosamie bit her lip, guiltily turning away.

"No. I'm the one who pushed her to go out with him," she confessed raggedly. Rosamie reached over from the backseat to put a hand on Laila's shoulders. "I'm so sorry."

"It's not your fault," Laila said softly. "He was supposed to be a catch, remember?"

Mason snorted, but his next words were to Rosamie. They were only a few minutes from the dorm. "Until we get a bead on Dubey and figure out what his reaction to Laila leaving him is, you are not safe either. I'm going to send someone over to your place in case he shows up there."

"Who?" Laila and Rosamie asked at the same time.

Mason pulled up to the dorm. "A friend from work."

CHAPTER TWENTY-TWO

Laila scanned the living room of his rental, clutching one of the garbage bags filled with her belongings to her chest.

"Do you want to take a bath?"

She stared at him as if he were some sort of ghost. "Were you really at Gardullo's today?"

Mason put his hands in his pockets. "I was."

"*Oh*." She sat on the couch—hard—still clutching the bag. When she spoke, her voice was reed thin. "I guess you want to know what happened."

"No."

She jerked, hurt filling her eyes. "Oh."

Mason knelt in front of her. "I just mean I know you want to talk to Rosamie first. I wasn't trying to cut you off from her by bringing you here alone." He reached out to take the garbage bag, then set it aside. "You don't have to tell me anything you don't want to—I learned everything I needed to know about your ex the minute I saw him lay hands on you."

She hesitated, and Mason's gut twisted. "He is your ex now, isn't he?"

"Yes," she gasped. "I'm never going back to him. It's just that I do want to tell you everything, but I don't know where to start."

He reached into her purse, dug around, then handed her the slim smartphone he withdrew. "Start by calling Rosamie. If you don't, she'll be blowing up this phone with calls and texts, which will simply make you more anxious."

He rose, taking her with him. "Let me show you to your room."

Taking her bags and suitcase in one hand, he guided her to the guest room. Fortunately, he'd washed the sheets and made the bed after Ethan's visit. Then Mason left her alone, ducking out to ask Ransom to watch over Rosamie.

Mason added a follow-up text, apologizing in advance for the ass-chewing his friend was about to get from a five-foot-nothing ballbuster.

❦

Ransom swaggered up the girl's dormitory stairs like he owned the place. It was a front, of course. He was hustling, wanting to make sure he got there before little Laila's shithead of an ex-boyfriend showed up looking for her.

There was a significant pause after his knock. Ransom approved. If she were smart, then Laila's friend was eyeballing him through the peephole, making sure it wasn't this Dubey character.

The door swung open to reveal a dusky little pocket Venus. She narrowed her eyes suspiciously, but he could see a glimmer of interest in those dark depths.

"Who the hell are you?" she asked.

Leaning against the doorframe, he crossed his arms. It was a move that made his biceps bulge. Girls loved it.

"I'm Ransom. Mason sent me." He batted his eyelashes. "Hello there, new friend."

The girl's mouth twitched, but then her eyes nearly bugged out of her head. She tried to haul him inside with an ineffectual tug. Ransom helped her along by slipping in the room so she could slam the door shut.

"The manwhore was right! Joseph is here. "

"Manwhore?" Ransom scowled. "Mason isn't a manwhore. It was your girl who left him in the dust when he was laid up in the hospital."

Rosamie put her hands on her hips, glowering right back. "Her phone was toast! She had to switch phone companies, but it was his fault in the first place—"

Their argument was interrupted by a sharp rap at the door.

The little Venus reached for the doorknob. Ransom stopped her with a hand. "Allow me."

Rosamie rolled her eyes, but she backed away with a little game-show-hostess gesture as if presenting the door as a grand prize.

Ransom jerked it open. He looked down his nose at the polo-wearing douchebag on the other side. Except this asshole's clothing was rumpled, a manic light gleaming in his eyes.

"Is this him?" he asked Rosamie.

The douchebag tried to ignore Ransom—a laughable goal. He was over two hundred pounds of whoop-ass.

"Uh, Rose, I need to talk to Laila." Dubey tried to peek around Ransom.

"You aren't getting anywhere near her, *ths asong puki*," the tiny spit-fire hissed in what Ransom guessed was Filipino. "Consider this her break-up message, you *abusive pussy*. And oh, get ready, *asno pagdila kambing*, because I am about to rip your *ass-licking goat* balls off and make them into *Kare-Kare*."

Ransom had to bite his lip to keep from laughing aloud, particularly when she started taking off her earrings in a classic *chingona* girl-fight move.

It was adorable, but also unnecessary. *Ransom to the rescue*. Grabbing the sweaty POS by the shirt, Ransom deadlifted the bastard until they were eye to eye.

"I would listen to the lady," Ransom said in his most reasonable tone. As predicted, Joseph Dubey blanched.

"As of this moment, Laila James is a figment of your imagination,"

Ransom continued. "She's a ghost. If you see her in the street, run the other way. If not, I'll know... and I *won't* be happy."

Unceremoniously, Ransom tossed the guy back into the hall. Unbalanced, Dubey fell on his ass.

"What the hell! Who even are you?" the piece-of-shit abuser sputtered.

"I'm—"

Smiling tauntingly, Rosamie tucked herself under his arm, anger rippling off her in waves. "He's my new boyfriend, so if you know what's good for you, you'll stay far away from me and *miles* away from Laila."

Her attitude was kind of turning Ransom on. He glanced down at his new fake girlfriend.

Not bad, actually.

He was tempted to pat her ass to help sell the lie, but he decided he better keep his hands to himself for now or he might pull a stump back. However, it was very tempting. Rosamie was cute, and she kept it *tight*.

"Very nice," he murmured to no one in particular.

A flash of something crossed Dubey's face. He picked himself up, then indignantly dusted himself off. "Laila and I had a misunderstanding. I admit that the situation got out of hand. I had a bad couple of days is all. This isn't me—I just want to talk to her."

"Not going to happen, asswipe." Rosamie bucked against him as if she were going to go for the douchebag. Ransom hid a grin as he held her back. It took some effort, too. He admired her all the more for it.

Dubey glanced at her, but he wisely kept his gaze on Ransom.

"If I can't talk to Laila, then I can talk to Jasmine? Maybe she will listen and be fair."

"Fair?" Rosamie spat. Her voice rose, her clenched fist rising threateningly. "I'm gonna give you *fair!*"

This time, she did go for the moron. But Ransom had been told to keep Rosamie out of trouble. He just hadn't expected to have to save anyone *from* her.

Ransom plucked the little Venus up, mid-lunge. She blistered the air blue, clawing in Dubey's direction.

The guy gaped at her as if she had sprouted horns. His lips parted as if he meant to say something else.

"Take the hint, motherfucker," Ransom said in warning, letting his voice grow Siberia cold. "Or I'll let her go, and my money is on the lady getting at least one of your testicles before I manage to restrain her."

Dubey closed his eyes, shaking his head. "Tell Laila this is just a bump in the road. I'm going to fix everything."

Wow, this jackass was delusional. That and Ransom had a feeling there was no way Mason would ever let that happen. His best pal wasn't an idiot, and he had a hard-on for little Laila. The fact it hadn't gone away in the time they'd been apart could only mean one thing— it was true love.

"Get the hell out of here," Rosamie spat a final time.

Skin slack and grey, Dubey staggered away. Ransom watched him go with narrowed eyes.

"You can let go now," the spitfire told him, but Ransom wanted the asshole gone before he released her.

Dubey had just disappeared around the corner when Rosamie lifted her arm. Quick as lightning, she grabbed his nipple and pinched hard.

"*Ow.*" Biting his lip to keep from laughing, he set her down, but he quickly sobered.

"Think Laila will file charges?"

Rosamie deflated, losing her steam right before his eyes. "I don't know," she said softly.

"Isn't it better if she reports him?"

"You don't understand." Rosamie sighed. She rubbed her face. "It's complicated."

"I realize she's scared, but if it spares another woman from going through the same thing, isn't it worth it?"

Rosamie's downcast expression didn't change. "Don't you think she knows all this? She's one of the founders of the Night Witches.

Our group is all about protecting other women—but Joseph is a Dubey. As in Lieutenant Governor Dubey. The family is old money. His uncle is a former senator, and Joseph is expected to follow in their political footsteps, too. If Laila makes trouble for him, she could bring the clout of the entire family dynasty down on herself."

Ransom grunted, getting the picture. It was easy for him to poke and prod for justice, but he'd seen the girl. Laila was so delicate looking. Plus, she was shy to boot.

That's probably what makes Mason so crazy. His friend was an alpha guardian. A girl like Laila would flip all of his protective switches into full throttle.

"Mason will make sure nothing happens to her—whether she goes to the cops or not."

Rosamie considered this. "And that's the only reason I let her go with him. I still don't trust him. He might break her heart all over again."

"Mason's gold. You've got nothing to worry about there. Trust me."

She grunted. "We'll see."

Sudden concern tightened the skin around her eyes. "I better call Jasmine to warn her of the incoming asshole—she moved in here after Laila moved out, but she stays with her boyfriend sometimes."

Rosamie stepped to the side and made a quick phone call, but her friend didn't answer. Frowning, she left a detailed message. Then she made another call and then another. By the time she was done, half the women on campus knew that Joseph Dubey was *persona non grata* with the Night Witches as a whole and on Rosamie's shit list in particular.

Ransom made himself comfortable on the small couch crammed between the single beds. When Rosamie glanced up from her calls, she appeared surprised to find him still there.

"Mason's orders were to keep an eye on you," Ransom informed her. "So that means I stay *with* you—at least until we're sure he's not coming back."

"And do you do everything Mason says?" she asked, hands on her hips.

Appreciatively, he allowed his gaze to roam over her curves, lingering in an obvious way on his favorite spots. "Well, some orders are easier to follow than others."

He patted the couch next to him. "Want to watch some Netflix?"

Don't add chill. You want to keep your testicles, he thought, swallowing his chuckle.

Rosamie studied him with narrowed eyes. Then her lip pulled up at the corner. She pivoted on her heel, stomping over to the dorm's mini-fridge. Riffling through it, she pulled out two beers and handed one to him.

"There's not enough room on the couch. You're too big," she said, giving him the same intimate appraisal he'd given her.

Damn, he was really starting to like this girl.

"I guess I'll just have to sit on your lap," she added, cocking her head.

Ransom whistled, fanning himself with one hand.

Yup. He *definitely* liked this girl.

CHAPTER TWENTY-THREE

Laila's eyes flew open. She stared at the unfamiliar ceiling, but she didn't have the confused *where-am-I* feeling. She remembered exactly where she was.

Mason. She was at his new house—with him.

Her brain supplied a mental image of a two-story suburban home. *I can't believe he moved.* Laila had assumed he didn't have the means, but this place was rather large for L.A.

It's bigger than Joseph's penthouse.

Laila's stomach twisted. She didn't want to think about Joe right now—she had brought this on herself. Not the part where he'd hit her, of course. But the fact she'd been there for him to abuse at all.

I should have left months ago. She had wanted to. Laila had known the minute she moved in with Joseph that it was a mistake. But she'd painted herself into a corner through her own sheer stubbornness and stupidity.

Sitting up, she checked the time. Two AM. She was wide awake. *I wonder if Mason has milk.* Having a warm glass before bed was a childhood habit. The effect was almost certainly psychosomatic, but it did the trick more often than not.

Tonight's task was a lot to ask of milk. She doubted it would make a dent, not unless she laced it with a few shots of alcohol. Laila wasn't even sure what would go with milk. Kahlua?

What would Mason do if she woke him up to ask for Kahlua? Shaking her head, she smiled ruefully, knowing he wouldn't have any. Mason probably drank manly booze like bourbon or rye whiskey. Not that she'd dare to wake him to ask for a glass of those either.

As it turned out, she didn't have to. She could hear Mason's low rumble in the distance as she stepped into the hallway. He was in the living room, talking on his cell phone. After she inched around the corner, she froze.

The man wasn't wearing a shirt.

Laila gaped at his perfect torso and the way his chest tapered into those loose flannel pajama pants. He was so sculpted that she was half-surprised he could move. Bodies like his belonged in museums, mixed with the classical Greek statuary. She was glad he hadn't noticed her come into the room. It gave her a moment to wipe her idiotic expression of longing away.

I can't believe I'm feeling this after what happened. Guilt swamped her. The urge to walk over and touch him was so strong, but she didn't have the right. Not to mention the fact that she wanted him at all meant there was something deeply wrong with her. Her only real relationship had ended today in a sudden burst of violence.

Stomach dipping in what signaled the start of a full-fledge emotional tailspin, she started listening to what Mason was saying. It was enough to make her blink and step back, mouth quirking. *Oh, Rosamie.*

"Again, I said for you to *protect* her. I didn't say sleep with her," her knight-in-shining-armor hissed, slashing the air with his hand. There was a pause. He shook his head, closing his eyes briefly.

"Well, don't say I didn't warn you. That one's a hellcat. No—not in a bad way." He broke off. "I don't know, man. For fuck's sake, just be careful. No. I didn't mean that. Of course I know you always use protection. Jeez, man."

He was scrubbing his hands over his face as he turned around.

When he saw her, Mason hesitated before speaking into the phone. "I gotta go. I'd say 'don't do anything I wouldn't do,' but it's too late."

Mason hung up and smiled at her, but it had an edge. "I may have miscalculated when I asked Ransom to keep an eye on Rosamie."

"Ah," Laila said, blushing. She remembered Ransom. A muscled brunet, handsome and flirty. If he was still with Rosamie at this hour...

It's fine, she told herself. Her friend knew a good thing when she saw it... Unlike Laila, Rosamie wouldn't wait too long to make her move. *'Seize life by the balls'* was Rosamie's unspoken motto. Laila wished she were more like her friend. If she had seized Mason earlier, before the redhead and his ill-fated trip...

"Well," Laila said after a moment. "At least we know she's safe. She will be, right?"

"Yeah." Mason nodded. "Although, I should warn you... I'm not sure if Ransom is boyfriend material. You know, if Rosamie cares about that sort of thing."

Laila cocked her head, wondering where Mason was going with this. "Why?"

He shrugged. "Ransom's a bit of a player. Plus, he's a merc."

Like me. He didn't say the words, but she heard them anyway as if he were trying to warn her off. Her heart sank a little. "I see..."

Mason held up his hands. "I didn't mean—"

"I know," she cut him off. Clenching her jaw, she schooled her features—a skill she'd honed over the last few months at those nerve-racking, yet incredibly dull, events Joseph had dragged her to.

Laila had convinced herself that she was over Mason. She believed the lie enough to move in with Joseph, but seeing Mason again in the flesh, being in his house, riddled her determined self-delusion with holes.

But that was hardly her biggest problem. Laila was broke, bruised, and, as of today, homeless.

"Laila, I—"

She put her hands up. "I don't want to talk about us and what almost was," she said honestly. Her brain buzzed, too full to process anything—especially Mason without a shirt. "I have a lot of other things I need to be thinking about. Like where I'm going to go tomorrow. I can't move back in with Rosamie."

Laila had given up her space in the graduate student dormitory to her and Rosamie's mutual friend. She couldn't reclaim it without putting her friend into the position she was in now. And Laila didn't have enough saved for a deposit on a new neighborhood. A room in someone else's place was her only option. Unless one of the Night Witches knew of something, Laila was going to have to spend the next week scouring Craigslist.

I bet these bruises on my face will go over great.

Mason scowled. "You can stay here as long as you need."

Laila hoped it was too dark to see the surge of moisture welling in her eyes. "I don't think that's a good idea."

Mason frowned. "This is the safest place for you."

"And maybe I'll stay for a few days, but it can't be any longer than that."

She glanced up to find him studying her face.

What was his expression conveying—regret?

"Laila, I apologize in advance because this is going to make me sound like an asshole—but I am *not* going to let you leave."

CHAPTER TWENTY-FOUR

Mason suppressed a wince as Laila took a step back. His senses were screaming at him that he'd made a huge mistake.

Look at her face, idiot. She just escaped an abusive ex-boyfriend. Her trust in men had to be in shreds. Acting like a macho gorilla was hardly the way to win her confidence. But he also couldn't stand by and let her walk away. Not again—especially not when she might be in danger.

"I mean, I can't let you go with this situation with your ex unresolved," he said, softening his tone. "I can help."

"I'm not sure anyone can—I don't even know what's going on." She shrugged helplessly, putting her hand on her forehead. "I shouldn't have ever moved in with him."

Mason reached out and touched her, guiding her to the living room sofa. "Because he was abusive?"

"No." Laila put her hands down as she let herself fall back on the couch. She immediately curled up in the opposite corner, hugging a pillow to her chest. "Because he was absent."

"I don't understand."

She was quiet for a minute before asking. "Do you know about him? About his family?"

"He comes from money. His family is politically connected."

"Yeah," she confirmed. "And one of the things they have a tradition of is being part of the Alpha Omega fraternity. Joseph is the president of the local chapter. When he asked me to move in with him, it was with the understanding he would be staying over at the fraternity house on Fridays and Saturdays. He promised he'd be at the apartment with me the rest of the time."

Laila hesitated, but he just waited, schooling his face into impassivity, silently encouraging her to continue.

"I still wasn't going to move in with him. But then he promised me something that convinced me that he was the most genuine and thoughtful person on earth. So I agreed."

"What was it?"

"Doesn't matter." Laila shook her head. "The promise evaporated as soon as I moved in. He got...too busy."

"It wasn't an object—a gift." If it had been a thing he could simply buy, Dubey would have done it.

"No, it was something else," she said. "Something personal."

Laila curled in on herself a little tighter. She didn't want to tell him what it was.

Mason felt a little surge as something clicked into place. *Whatever it is, I'm going to find it, and I'm going to give it to her.*

Laila deserved the world.

"So, he started spending more time at the frat, even during the week when he was supposed to come home to you?"

"Not at first, but soon enough. But he did other things to make it up to me—took me places. Showed me off at his family's functions... political events, fundraisers."

"Showing you off?" he echoed.

"It might have been his way of showing pride in me. He certainly acted like that was it, but I can't help thinking of what Rosamie said about Joe—that he had political aspirations and a woman of color would go over well with his future constituents. It kind of felt like that. Not like he was showing me off as a girlfriend, but like he was...*displaying* me. Does that make sense?" She slumped against the cushions.

Mason couldn't trust himself to sound reasonable, so he just nodded.

"It wasn't just around his family," Laila continued. "He did it at the fraternity, at least in the beginning when he could convince me to go. But I hated the parties, so I told him it was a conflict of interest with the Night Witches and stayed home."

"But even after you stopped going to these frat parties, you still got the sense he was trying to get credit for you?"

She laughed humorlessly. "Yeah. But from who—I don't know. God knows, there are plenty more eligible women, girls with more connections and money. All I've ever done is help found the Night Witches."

"I like your group and what it does," he said. "Good on you."

"Thanks, but it's not like we're big or well-known. But Joe still loved to tell everyone about it—particularly his parents' friends."

Her expression of self-disgust made him want to break things. How dare that white-collar piece of shit make her feel like this.

"Even though I didn't like it, I still went to all the tea and cocktail parties his mother threw...and that's one of the reasons I can't afford an apartment right now."

"How is that?" he asked with a frown. "Was there a cover charge?"

"No," Laila laughed humorlessly.

"Hey, I'm sorry, I didn't mean to tease. Please, tell me."

Laila sank further in the chair. "You're going to think this is stupid, but I needed new clothes."

Mason must have betrayed his surprise, but she waved a languid—or exhausted—hand in front of her face.

"I know how it sounds, but I didn't want to look out of place in front of his rich parents and their friends. I didn't buy much. Rosamie is better with clothes, so I shopped with her, buying some things I could mix and match. I needed to make the most of my money. We went to consignment and second-hand stores, but this is L.A. I think the wardrobe people in this town clean those places out. I spent more than I could afford under normal circumstances but told myself it was okay because I wasn't paying rent anymore."

She shook her head, regret all over her face.

"Laila, honey, that's hardly something to be ashamed of." He reached over to tweak her hand, which gripped the pillow. "Hey, sometimes I have to go to parties to protect a corporate bigwig, some CEOs or a politician. I'm lucky—my company picks up the tab for all my suit rentals. They even pay for the dry cleaning. Suffice to say, I know what it takes to run in those circles, even when you're just visiting."

She gave him a languid smile. "I still feel stupid. My mother always said to keep something tucked away for emergencies. I did try, but I don't think she ever factored in the cost of living in Los Angeles."

"Your stepmom, right? Your birth mother died when you were little."

Laila's thick lashes fluttered. "How did you know that?"

"I listened."

The little line between her brows deepened. "We never talked about her. About them."

Mason hesitated, wondering if he should explain...and eventually said 'fuck it'. He wasn't going to hide how he felt about her. Not anymore.

"I meant I listened when you were on the phone. Sometimes it was in the hall, but, more often, it was in the laundry room. You talked there a lot—I'm assuming it had better reception than your shoebox of a studio."

"You're right," she said slowly. The confusion didn't clear. "But why were you listening?"

Mason took a deep breath. *Stop. You're pushing too hard...* If he wasn't careful, she was going to pack her bags in the morning and decide to crash at Rosamie's. He knew her. She'd sleep on the floor if she had to.

But this was Laila. She deserved the unvarnished truth.

Mason took a deep breath, trying to dance on a fine line. "You think I didn't see you when we lived in the same building. But I did. I saw you. I watched you all the time—I just waited for when you weren't looking."

"Sure you did." Laila wrapped her arms around her knees. It was obvious she didn't believe a word he was saying.

He decided to prove it. "Your mom has memory problems, right?" he supplied, hoping he wasn't making a mistake.

Laila stilled. Wordlessly, she nodded.

"Is she in some kind of home?"

Her mouth dropped open. "Yes. In Chicago...she has early-onset Alzheimer's."

Fuck. He hadn't known the diagnosis was that bad.

Mason inched closer. "That's rough. It must be even worse having to work yourself through school because all your dad's money goes to her care."

Laila gave herself a little shake. "All right, I know I didn't talk about that in the laundry room."

"No, that time you were at work in the break room of Gardullo's," he said. "I used to swing by to check on you after you moved. I thought you weren't there, so I decided to do some actual shopping. Turns out, you were in the break room. I was going to say hi, but I caught you in the middle of a phone call. You were upset, and I didn't want to intrude. I think you were talking to your stepmom's family. Someone was complaining about the amount they had to pay for the care facility because your dad's insurance doesn't pay for the whole thing."

The woman had been talking so loudly he could hear almost everything she had said on her end.

"No, most of it, but not all," Laila replied. "Paula, that's my stepmom's sister, contributes the rest...but at least she does it. I'm grateful for that, even if she does complain about it sometimes, especially when the insurance company payment is late."

"They don't pay it directly?"

"It is supposed to be an electronic transfer every month, but you'd be surprised how often it's late. Paula makes me call them when it is.

She has two kids, and she can't spend hours on the phone haranguing them."

And you're a student working your way through school on your own. But she expects you to do it?

"I miss hearing you sing in the shower," he told her.

There was amusement in her eyes. "I don't sing in the shower."

"You used to," he said quietly. "I think the vent from your bathroom connects up to my bedroom. If I were quiet, I could hear you. I especially liked you doing En Vogue."

Laila's lips twitched, but she caught herself, her hand fluttering up to her mouth. Smiling must hurt.

Mason reached up to touch her chin, just under her split lip. He hated to change the tenor of the conversation, but there were things he needed to know.

"Tell me why this happened."

"I'm not sure." Her hand fell to her side. "I told you Joseph hadn't been around much, but when I tried to call him on it—on him not coming home—he would say he got caught up in frat business. Not always, though. Sometimes, he tried to convince me that he *had* come home. I am a sound sleeper, so he convinced me that I hadn't heard him once or twice.

"Not that it mattered. Things weren't good. I knew I had to leave. I just didn't know how or when to tell him. That and I had final exams and papers due. In the last few weeks, I didn't fight with him about the hours he kept. I tried not to talk to him at all. I just kept my head down and started taking extra shifts at work. I needed to save for a new apartment deposit."

"So conceivably, he could have believed you two were okay?"

"No, he couldn't possibly..." She trailed off, lapsing into silence.

"Why not?" he prompted after a minute.

"Because I wouldn't sleep with him anymore," she said after a long pause.

"*Oh.*" Mason was almost sorry he asked.

"I'm sorry, I shouldn't have mentioned that. Not about se—another guy," she stumbled.

Mason reached out to take her hand. "Laila, he was your boyfriend. You lived with him. Your life went on after our night together. I understand."

Moving on had been a natural step forward for her. He hated her being with another man. He hated the whole situation that led up to it, but he didn't blame her. He wasn't a hypocrite—it could have easily been him. If he hadn't been so busy, he might have started seeing someone else too.

"Anyway," she said. "That's what set him off again."

Mason froze. "Because you wouldn't sleep with him?" he asked in a too-even voice.

"No!" Laila shook her head. "Not that. I meant I tried to call him out on not coming home the night before."

She reached up to rub her temple. "I'm explaining this badly."

"It's okay," he said. "We'll talk until it makes sense."

Laila made a little sound in the back of her throat. "The day before yesterday, I was writing my last term paper. I had finished all my other final exams and lab practicals. This paper is the very last thing I need for my associate degree in respiratory therapy. I stayed up all night finishing it. I was printing it on the office computer when I heard him come in. I didn't want to talk to him, so I went to get ready for work instead of fighting it out then and there."

"But you did later," he guessed.

She nodded. "After I got home from work."

"And?"

Laila put her hands up, her eyes focusing on nothing. "He exploded. I didn't even see the slap coming. And weirdly enough, he seemed almost as shocked as I was."

She raised a hand to her face as if she still couldn't believe Joseph had struck her.

"I fell after he backhanded me," she continued, her fingers tracing her swollen lip. "At first, I thought he was so angry because I said I was leaving."

"But now you don't think that was it?"

"No. Maybe." She shrugged. "But he seemed more upset about the other thing—he kept insisting I was wrong about him not coming home that night. He kept arguing about it. He said I must have fallen asleep because he came home before one AM—that he slipped into the guest room so he wouldn't disturb me and went jogging early that morning. That's why I heard the door when I did. It was him coming back after a run."

"All right," he said slowly. "So, what's he hiding? An affair?"

She shrugged. "That's what I think. After all, he's got a bedroom at the frat. His Alpha Omega brothers would never rat him out to me. Hell, they must get a kick out of it. They claim the Night Witches are 'honored guests,'" she said, raising her hands to make air quotes. "But secretly, they must love it that he hooks up with anyone he wants and gets away with it right under my nose."

"That does make a kind of sense," Mason murmured. But he wasn't completely convinced.

Why would Dubey get violent about this on this occasion if it were something they'd argued about before? Was it because Laila finally said she was leaving? But Dubey had to have seen that coming.

A few minutes later, Laila returned to bed, but Mason stayed up a little longer. Eventually, he crashed, too, deciding there wasn't a great mystery to Joseph Dubey's actions.

Some cowards didn't need an excuse to abuse a woman. Laila trying to walk out on him would have been enough.

The question now was—what was Mason going to do about it?

CHAPTER TWENTY-FIVE

After a nearly sleepless night, Laila woke and pulled jeans and a shirt out of the garbage bags of clothes she'd set on the closet shelves. She found Mason in the kitchen, cooking them a massive breakfast. Her appetite hadn't been particularly good, but he watched her like a hawk, gently bullying her into eating. But she regretted it now. The two waffles she managed to choke down were sitting like bricks in her stomach as she waited for the doctor to finish examining her.

Mason had insisted she see one.

"I know you're still thinking about whether to file a police report, and that's fine," he'd told her that morning. "But we *have* to go see a doctor today. You need X-rays. There might be a hairline fracture under those bruises, or worse."

Laila had hesitated, knowing she'd have to go to campus to use the university's health services. Joseph knew so many people she was worried word would get to him before her visit was over.

If that happened, Mason would wipe the floor with him. Joseph worked out and would likely hold his own against any of his frat brothers. But Mason was a trained soldier—elite and lethal. Joseph didn't stand a chance. She couldn't let it happen. Joe's family had too much money, and far too many lawyers. Mason didn't need that kind of trouble. Not for her sake.

However, her fears proved groundless. Mason didn't take her to her health care provider. He took her to his.

The doctor's office was housed in a small but sleek contemporary building that housed a mishmash of dental and medical offices. When they pulled into the parking lot, Mason told her that the doctor and his nurse, both under contract with his employers, were expecting them.

"These are private physicians," he confided. "Auric is a big chunk of their business, so don't worry. They have everything you could need— even a CT and an MRI scanner. Short of major surgery, they can do everything here."

They shot the X-rays first. Then Laila was led away to an exam room while Mason stayed in the reception area, sitting military straight in one of the padded leather chairs.

He didn't even bother picking up a magazine. Laila could feel his intense gaze on the back of her neck until they disappeared.

The physician, an older man with grey hair, seemed a little taken aback when he saw her, but he conducted a quick but thorough exam with the help of his assistant.

"We don't usually see the men's girlfriends or wives," the PA said as the doctor probed her cheek. "Auric has them on a different insurance plan."

Suppressing a wince, she gave him a tiny shake of her head, trying not to move. "I'm not Mason's girlfriend. We're just neigh—friends."

"So, he didn't do this?" the nosy assistant asked.

Her lips parted. "No. This was someone else. My ex."

The doctor paused, his professionalism unruffled. "We didn't think Mr. Lang was responsible," he said with a pointed glare at the assistant.

"Doesn't hurt to check," the nurse sniffed. "You never know with some of these soldier types."

She turned to Laila. "Are you on any medication?"

"Just…birth control pills." Her voice lost steam toward the end, making it a breathy whisper. The doctor straightened, and the two medical professionals glanced at each other. There was a brief but pointed silence.

"I'm going to check on the X-Rays while Anne takes the rest of your medical history," the doctor said after the two had come to a silent agreement. He excused himself.

As soon as he was gone, the PA asked if she needed a rape kit.

"No," she said, deciding to be honest. "My ex and I haven't shared a bed in several months. I, um, I came to distrust him early on."

She sighed, looking down at her hands. They didn't have a mark on them. When push came to shove, Laila hadn't even tried to defend herself. She'd been too scared, too shocked.

"A cheater, huh?" the nurse said in a knowing tone. The grey-haired woman's abrasiveness might have bothered someone else, but, at this moment, Laila appreciated the no-nonsense attitude.

Too much sympathy would have made her feel even more power-less than she already did.

Laila's shoulders slumped. "I suspect that's the case, but I never got confirmation either way. He always denied it."

"Then, I guess the question I should be asking is if you would like a full STD check?"

"Yes," she said, almost hissing in emphasis. *"Please."*

Laila hadn't been on birth control at the start of their relationship. Joseph had pressured her until she'd agreed to get the pills at the university's health services. But when he'd asked her if it was finally safe to go without other protection, Laila had stalled, using excuse after excuse to put him off.

Her caution and distrust meant the tests were probably unnecessary, but she wanted to be sure.

The nurse gave her a commiserating pat on the shoulder. "I'll put a rush on the results."

"Thank you."

❦

Mason kept hoping Laila would ask him to detour to the police station on the drive home, but she stayed quiet, her eyes locked on the door of the Mustang's glove compartment. She was a million miles away.

He opened his mouth, about to nudge her about going to the cops, when he shut it again.

She agreed to the doctor, and they recorded her injuries.

Laila even told the physicians who had caused them. He knew that because the nurse—Anne—had given him strict instructions not to let the douchebag ex anywhere near her.

In the meantime, they could afford a day or two of indecision. Doc Valentine and his assistant would back up any statement Laila made to the police, even if it took her a few days to work up the courage to contact them.

Be satisfied with her clean bill of health.

The physician had confirmed the injuries were superficial. Dubey hadn't done any permanent damage. That was the priority.

"Are you going to take some time off work?" he asked instead, maneuvering through side streets instead of taking the highway.

Laila jerked, snapping out of her reverie. "I am using some of my vacation days. I texted my boss, although I didn't tell him why. He was a bit surprised. I didn't even take days off for my exams."

She lapsed into silence again. He kept his eyes on the road but kept giving her the side-eye, willing her to speak.

"What you said yesterday," she began. "About watching me. Were you serious?"

He glanced at her, but shifted his eyes to the road. "You know I was."

"Then why?" If he'd been that intent on her, why hadn't he made a move?

A million excuses came to mind, but the one that escaped from his lips was the most honest. "Because I'm a fucking idiot," he admitted with a groan, letting the car coast down the road to his rental.

He was about to pull into the drive when Laila gasped, grabbing his arm. "Mason!"

Mason whipped forward, hitting the brakes when he saw there was another car parked in his space.

The vehicle was a nondescript sedan, but Mason didn't need official markings to know who had come calling. He immediately recognized the bearing and demeanor of the man and woman leaning against the trunk.

"Cops," he said shortly.

Hurt flickered over Laila's face. *"You called them?"* The betrayal in her voice nearly gutted him.

Mason grabbed her hand, squeezing it until she met his eyes. "I did *not.* I would never take that decision away from you. They must be here about something else."

Like quicksilver, her injured expression transformed into fear. "Rosamie!"

Laila shoved open the passenger door, but she got caught in the seatbelt as she scrambled up without undoing it. She fumbled it. Her hands were too shaky to unclip it, so he reached over to do it. Once free, Laila bolted to the waiting detectives.

But it wasn't Rosamie they had come to see her about. It was another friend, one whose name he had heard, but whose face he didn't know.

"Jasmine is missing?" Laila shook her head, bewilderment spreading over her features as the detectives sat across from her at his dining room table.

"When was the last time you saw her?" Detective Silano asked. She was a lean and hard thirty-something with deep grooves bracketing her mouth. Mason bet on those being premature. Behind her, the other detective, introduced only as Boggs, held up the wall.

It took Laila a while to remember the exact day. She had to check her phone's calendar to piece it together, but it soon became apparent they weren't checking because they suspected her and wanted to know her whereabouts at the time of the disappearance.

They were asking because they wanted to know Joseph Dubey's.

The last time Jasmine Elliot was seen was at the Alpha Omega house. She'd been drinking with Dubey and his cousin Bryce Johansen, the vice president of the frat. No one had seen her since.

"Are you sure she isn't at Sam's?" Laila asked, sitting on the edge of her chair. "That's her boyfriend. You should talk to him."

"We spoke to Sam Leeds already," Boggs said, speaking for the first time. "He and his roommate confirmed they hadn't seen Ms. Elliot since Thursday. Mr. Leeds volunteered they'd had a minor disagreement and didn't have plans to see each other. The roommate said they had minor quarrels all the time, but they were good about giving each other space to get over it."

"Then maybe she went to her parents or her sister," Laila said, her tone edgier. "They live in San Diego, and sometimes she just jumps in her car and drives down to see them."

Mason saw the detectives exchange a look, and that was when he knew. He reached out, taking Laila's hand. "You're not trying to trace a missing person, are you?"

The pair across the table exchanged another loaded glance.

"What does that mean?" Laila asked in a thin voice. She watched him with her heart in her eyes.

There was a short silence. "It means they're here because they already found the body," he said gently, squeezing her hand.

It was the only thing that made sense. A college girl missing for a few days would have been taken seriously if the disappearance had been reported, but from what the detectives had said, that hadn't been the case.

And they sure as hell wouldn't have come asking about Joseph Dubey if there hadn't been a body. These were career cops. They wouldn't have poked that hornet's nest unless they had to. But if Laila's friend was dead, then they didn't have a choice.

Laila's breath fractured as she saw the truth written on the detective's faces.

Silano's next words confirmed her worst fears. "Miss Elliot fell off the radar Friday night. Her cell phone was turned off or died around two AM. It was found with her body."

"But you can't find a trace of her, no witnesses who saw her after the frat party," Mason supplied. "Joseph and his cousin were the last people she was seen with alive. Let me guess—the pair are alibiing each other?"

Annoyance flitted across Silano's face. She ignored him, choosing to focus on Laila.

"At this time, neither Joseph Dubey nor his cousin Bryce Johansen are suspects. Both have clean records with several commendations for community service between them. That and several of the Alpha Omega brothers swear they were there all night.
"

Laila's intake of air was sharp. Mason wanted to bang on the table and shout. *Hell, that was it.*

The detective paused, but when Laila stared shell-shocked and unmoving, Silano continued.

"We came to speak to you after interviewing Jasmine Elliot's roommate Rosamie Bautista. Miss Bautista said you might have further information on that."

Swallowing loudly, Laila took a deep breath and nodded. She gestured to her bruised face and told them what had happened to her Saturday morning, and later that night.

"I didn't know why Joe was so insistent that he'd come home that night," she said, looking nauseated. "He was so upset, so angry. It was irrational and out of proportion, or at least I thought so…"

Mason moved his chair until it was flush with hers. He threw an arm around her, pulling her into him. She was cold to the touch under his hands.

"Based on this information, we'll be able to interview Joseph Dubey," Silano said, trying to seem like she hadn't swallowed a lemon.

Mason read between the lines. Dubey had lawyered up with what was doubtless a high-priced attorney. *Hell, he probably has a team.*

"If you wouldn't mind, I'd like to take some pictures of your injuries, to go with your statement." Silano pulled out her cell phone.

Jaw firming despite the lost expression, Laila nodded, murmuring her assent.

"I took her to my doctor this morning," Mason told the detective.

"He took X-Rays as well as pictures. I can have them sent them to you."

"Do that," the officer said, her tone a touch more gracious than before. "But we still need our own."

With that, she stood and ushered Laila to push her chair away from the table. Silano walked around her, taking pictures from several angles. They left a few minutes later.

Laila's drawn face worried him. So was her continued silence. He pulled her into the living room, throwing a blanket over her. She let him fuss over her, but she didn't react until he tried to press a hot chamomile tea into her hands.

"No, thank you," she said, still unfailingly polite despite her obvious heartbreak. She pushed the mug away, piercing his soul with her big brown eyes.

"Mason…will you hold me?"

"You never have to ask." But Mason didn't hug her. That wasn't enough to soothe the yawing ache inside him. He sat next to her, pulling her bodily into his lap.

Laila was startled, but it only took her a minute to relax, melting into his arms as if she'd always been there.

"I'm sorry about your friend," he whispered into her hair.

"So am I," she said, shuddering despite the tight hold of his embrace. "Because it's all my fault."

CHAPTER TWENTY-SIX

Laila knew what Mason was going to say before it was out of his mouth. She could tell by the way his body stiffened, growing still underneath her.

"No, it's *not*. If your ex is involved—and we don't know that for sure—it has nothing to do with you."

Laila tried to climb off his lap, but Mason wasn't having any of that. Collapsing against him, she shuddered, trying to absorb his warmth. When she found her voice, it sounded as if she'd gargled with rocks.

"They wouldn't even *know* each other if it weren't for me. The only time the other Night Witches set foot inside Alpha Omega house was to help another girl get back to her dorm room. They would never have stayed to drink or party there, not until I started dating Joe."

Mason's hand fisted in her hair before he gentled his hold, cupping the back of her neck possessively. With light pressure, he tilted her head back.

"That is not on you. You didn't do anything wrong. Any time a woman walks into a room with a man, she is at risk, whether she knows it or not. A place full of men will never be safe—definitely not a frat. Hell, I've been to college. Even a sorority isn't a safe space. Nothing you did or didn't do would have changed that."

Except the Night Witches *did* know that. Or at least they used to. As much as she wanted to deny it, she had been responsible for that line blurring.

"If I had told Jasmine about the problems I was having with Joe beforehand, she might not have gone there that night." Laila swallowed, wondering how the hell her throat had become this raw.

"I didn't even tell Rosamie. I was worried she'd blame herself because she encouraged me to go out with him. And because I didn't tell her, I didn't tell anyone. Which was stupid—if I had just been a little more open with my friends, then Jasmine might still be alive."

"We don't even know what happened that night. Not for sure. It's possible she went somewhere else after the frat."

"You don't believe that, and neither do I. Not after the way the cops acted," she said. "They seem fairly sure Alpha Omega is where she was last seen. And with the way Joe behaved…"

Laila pressed her cheek against his T-shirt, trying desperately to shut off her brain. The material was impossibly soft, considering how new it appeared. The only way her cotton clothing became this smooth was after a thousand washes later, usually when it was just about to fall apart.

Mason's hand cupped the back of her head. "We're going to figure this out."

It was the '*we*' that penetrated the cocoon of regret and self-recrimination.

"No, Mason. I can't drag you into this mess. You letting me stay here is enough."

It was more than enough, in fact, possibly too much. Mason was a good man, strong and capable. He had the training to protect himself and her. The urge to lay her problems at his feet was so tempting, but the sheer strength of her desire meant it was wrong.

She'd gotten herself into this mess.

She'd have to be the one to get herself out.

♨

Mason didn't want to let Laila go, but the doorbell rang, so he allowed her to push away. She sat on the farthest edge of the couch. Resisting the urge to reach out and touch her again—his perpetual struggle—he walked away with a low 'excuse me' to answer the door.

Rosamie blew in like a hurricane with Ransom close on her heels. The minute she and Laila saw each other, they burst into tears. They fell into each other's arms, proceeding to have a conversation conducted in subvocal whispers.

Wary and gun-shy in the face of feminine tears, he and Ransom backed away by silent mutual agreement.

Moving to the kitchen, Ransom started ransacking Mason's fridge. He handed him a beer before cocking his head at the women on the couch, visible through the passthrough window. "What the hell language is that?"

Mason shrugged. "It's English with a heavy girl accent."

Opening the beer, he clocked the mark on Ransom's neck. "Thanks for keeping an eye on Rosamie. Although judging from the hickey on your neck, it's not that much of a hardship for you."

Flushing, Ransom touched his neck—in the wrong spot. "This was before she found out about her friend. Since the police came, she's been alternating between making calls and crying, but that's understandable given that they were roommates. It's pretty messed up. So is your girl's face." Ransom leaned on the counter, raising a brow. "Are we gonna hunt down the bastard who did that to her, or what?"

"Don't tempt me," Mason growled, tightly clenching the neck of his beer. A small but ominous crack forced him to relax his hold.

"I was planning on it," he admitted after a moment. "But I don't want to muddy the waters. If the police are looking at Dubey as a person of interest in this death, then kicking the living shit out of him will just complicate this clusterfuck."

Ransom sniffed, then took a swig of his beer. "Do you think they're going to be able to pin anything on that asswipe? Rosamie says he has more money than God."

"The money is a problem. But no one is untouchable." Mason's eye gravitated back to Laila the way it always did. She was nodding at something Rosamie was saying.

He took another sip of his beer. "Patience is a virtue."

Mason gave the girls the better part of an hour together. He hoped it would give them time to get the sharpest part of their grief up and out of their system before deciding that was wishful thinking.

That was going to take time, lots of it. Mason's thoughts were on grief and how everyone experienced it in different ways, but that still didn't prepare him for the sight that greeted him when he walked back into the living room

"We have to make some plans..." His voice trailed off as Laila twisted to face him. Her adorable little mug was twisted, her fingers pulling down her lower eyelids. But that wasn't half as bad as Rosamie.

The small Filipina was pushing up her nose with one finger. She'd somehow managed to flip both her upper eyelids inside out.

"Woah." Ransom skidded to a stop next to Mason. Then he burst out laughing. "I never met a girl who could do that, too." He then flipped his own eyelids up, making a snorting sound echoed by the diminutive Filipina.

Suppressing a shudder, Mason pointed to Laila. "You, still adorable. These other two knuckleheads, however, are *grotesque.*"

"Sorry," Laila said, rubbing the tear tracks off her cheeks with the heels of her hands. "It's just something stupid we do to make ourselves feel better."

He put a hand up. "You do whatever you have to do."

Ransom held out two beers to the ladies.

Fishing a tissue out of her purse, Rosamie wiped her face in straightforward, no-nonsense swipes. "Got anything stronger, playboy?"

Mason turned, fishing bottles of port and whiskey from the chest that served as his liquor cabinet. Laila took the port. Rosamie, predictably, the whiskey.

He took a seat on the other couch, outlining his concerns. "Rosamie, it may not be the best idea for you to stay in the dorm alone. Is there someplace you could go?"

Rosamie frowned. "I'm not going to let that asshole chase me off campus."

Laila took a sip of the port, coughing. "Are you sure you want to stay in that room without Jas? You have to move out next week, regardless."

"What?" Ransom perked up.

"It's the end of the quarter," Laila explained. "The summer session starts in two weeks. We have to be cleared out of the graduate dorm a week before so they can clean before the incoming students. Our dorm will be filled with high school students doing special programs for college credit."

"I thought you were done with classes."

"I am, but Rosamie is not," Laila said.

"I move back in with my family in summer," Rosamie said in a flat voice that spoke to her enthusiasm level. "To save money."

"I was going to stay on with Joe this summer while I searched for jobs in my field," Laila said, her eyes dropping to her hands. "But before that plan, Rose and I were going to try and sublet a place together. Maybe we should try again."

"*No,*" both he and Ransom said it at the same time.

Ransom tsked. "It's not a good idea, doll face," he said, sitting on the couch's arm next to the Filipina. "If some shit went down, then you two living alone is a security risk. I mean, look at you. I know you can throw a punch, but you're kind of a shrimp."

Scowling, Rosamie flipped him off.

"You can stay here with Laila if you want," Mason offered.

Please say no. Please say no.

"Maybe during the day and shit, when we are both training," Ransom said. "But Rosamie is going to crash at my place. Aren't you, darling?"

Rosamie smirked. "The hell you say."

"What?" Ransom lifted his arms, throwing out his most charming grin.

Mason almost smiled before he remembered the circumstance, but when he checked Laila, he let the gesture bleed onto his face. There was definite amusement in her eyes, but it was muted.

"You don't want to bring trouble home," she told her friend softly.

Rosamie gripped her hand. "This is *not* your fault. And I'd like to see that piece of shit get through my mom. She'll tear Joe a new one in like four different places."

Ransom laughed, but Laila nodded. "Yeah, that sounds about right," she murmured.

"You're just trying to scare me," Ransom sniffed. "She's going to love me."

"Who said you were meeting my momma?" Rosamie asked, her head drawing back.

The two got lost in their banter, which was equal parts sniping and flirtation.

Laila quietly slipped away from them, refilling her glass of port. She let him usher her into the kitchen, where she leaned back against the counter. "Thank you for inviting her to stay, too. I know she's not your favorite person."

"Why do you say that?"

"Um." A tiny crease appeared between her eyes. "Well, granted, I haven't seen you interact all that much, and the first time was under tense circumstances…but you kind of stiffened up just now when you saw her."

Not to mention the fact Rosamie admitted pushing Laila to go out with Dubey. *She was probably very vocally anti-Mason too.* However, given how things had looked from her perspective, he really couldn't blame the woman.

Plus, he and the shitkicker did have one thing in common. *We both love Laila.*

Well, there was maybe more than one thing.

"I do like her," he said, straightening in realization. "Because

Rosamie is your Ransom—and believe me, having a Ransom at your back is always a good idea."

Her nose wrinkled and she huffed lightly, almost laughing. "So, the stiffening is involuntary?"

His eyes widened. "Oh no, it's intentional. For the record—I always brace myself when Ransom comes around. You should, too."

❦

A few days later, Laila waited until Mason left for his training session before going into his bedroom to curl up on his bed.

She knew she shouldn't. He'd made it before he left. There was no way she'd be able to get those military-precision corners right.

Or I could ask him if I can sleep here. She knew he would let her. He wanted her.

Laila didn't understand it, but she could tell. There was a heat in his eyes when he looked at her, but only when he thought she wasn't watching. If she took him at his word, he'd always worn that look, even back in their old building.

Except Mason would never ask her to share his bed again. He would never take advantage of the situation or her vulnerability.

Laila buried her face in the bedding. *So stop being vulnerable. And stop being a creepy stalker by smelling Mason's pillows.*

Forcing herself to stand, she smoothed the sheets. Good to his toes. That was Mason. *Damn.* Was it wrong to wish he were just a little bit bad?

No sooner had she thought it that she was swamped with guilt, one that backed up and ran over itself.

I am not Joseph's girlfriend anymore, she told herself sternly. Their relationship had been over the second he struck her.

But she hadn't told him so to his face...

Laila knew she didn't owe him that. She didn't owe him anything. Nevertheless, she felt as if she had missed something—the opportunity for a clean break.

I should have ended things weeks ago. Hell, she should have never moved in with him in the first place. Part of her had known that. If she'd listened to that instinct, maybe Jasmine would be alive.

That thought was another gut-punch, but Laila deserved it.

Nevertheless, she physically pressed her hands to her stomach, breathing in slowly until the band of compression went away. Mason was right. She couldn't keep doing this to herself.

Laila made her way to the kitchen, intending on preparing a small breakfast. She found her phone on Mason's charging base on the passthrough counter. He must have put it there for her.

The passthrough was her favorite feature of the house. She liked being able to see the living room from the kitchen and vice versa. Her least favorite was the shelves in the closet. Improbably wide and too high for her, Laila had a difficult time organizing her clothes without bunching everything in the front. But it was a small inconvenience. She was just glad to be here with Mason.

Wondering if it was worth rearranging her clothing again, she picked up her phone and started when she saw the number of messages received.

Only the two newest were from Rosalie. One was a short and sweet text from Mason telling her he'd prepared pancake mix, and he'd left it waiting for her in the fridge. There was also a voicemail from Detective Silano, telling her they hadn't been able to get Joseph to make a statement. His lawyers were stonewalling.

The rest of the messages were from Joseph.

She sat on the floor where she stood, scrolling through the texts. Most were pleas to meet. None mentioned Jasmine or a visit from the police. Shaking her head, she racked her brain. Laila had to do something—*anything*.

Then she frowned, considering the phone in her hand.

When Ransom dropped off Rosamie, she had a plan.

CHAPTER TWENTY-SEVEN

Rosamie grabbed her arm, gripping it tight before relaxing and letting it go with a loud whoosh.

"Sorry," her friend apologized when she saw she'd left nail marks on Laila's forearm. "I thought I saw him."

"Yes, me too. But it was only someone who kind of looks like Joseph," Laila assured her.

They were across the street from her ex's building, watching the lobby from the busy window seat of a taco shop. The man who'd just rounded the corner and passed them had been close in height with similar coloring, but his features had been far sharper. Nevertheless, the resemblance had been close enough to nearly give her a heart attack.

"Have there been any sightings of him on campus?" she asked, willing her racing heart to slow. She spoke without turning, her eye on the distant figure of the security guard in the lobby of Joe's building.

Rosamie hunched over her phone.

"Not today, but according to my spies, he was at the frat all last night. He's been there every night this week, sending the pledges on stupid missions and partying like nothing is wrong."

She wrinkled her cute snub nose. "In fact, according to Juan, he's been drinking a lot more than usual at those things."

"Yes, you mentioned that." It was part of the reason Laila had decided to break into Joseph's apartment.

It's not breaking and entering if you have the key, she reminded herself.

"I can't believe you want to do this," Rosamie said after a pause. "I'm the one who comes up with the crazy plans—not you."

"It's not *that* crazy," Laila whispered, checking over her shoulder furtively. It was irrational, but she kept expecting Mason to appear over her shoulder, his handsome face glowering in disapproval.

Oh, you know it would be much worse than that. Mason would be furious if he found out she was putting herself at risk this way. It both warmed and terrified her.

"We have to do this," she said aloud. "I think we are the only ones who can."

"*How?*" Rosamie asked. "We're not exactly crack detectives. As far as I can tell, your plan begins and ends with getting in and out of Joseph's apartment without being seen. Are you seriously expecting to find some evidence lying around? It's not like the party was here—it was at Alpha Omega."

"I'm aware of that. And I don't expect Joseph to have left anything that could incriminate him on purpose, but you said so yourself—he's partying a lot at the moment. I may not know him as well as I thought I did, but I know enough. Joe's drinking and rallying the frat brothers around himself in a desperate effort to pretend everything is all right. When the alcohol clears, he's going to come to his senses, then we'll lose our opportunity."

"To do what again? I'm still lost."

Laila took out her cell, then showed Rosamie the picture.

Rosamie's mouth flattened. "Why are you showing me a poorly drawn cartoon penis?"

"Do you not see the map?" Laila gestured to the picture again.

Rosamie squinted at the screen. "Oh, yeah. It's the campus, right?"

"Yes. It's one of those GPS-generated images." Laila set down her phone. "He sent me this a few weeks ago. It was a frat stunt. They all ran around campus, trying to make obscene pictures. But he didn't know how to turn on the GPS tracking so it generated an image like this, so I did it for him."

It was one of the last civil interactions they'd had.

"I'm hoping he left it on," she said, aware her hopes were pinned on a very flimsy premise.

"What if he has his phone at the frat?"

Laila shrugged. "If he does, then I'm going to steal his laptop. He has it set to backup over the air to it daily."

Rosamie nodded, understanding lighting her eyes. "And I'm guessing you know that because you set that up for him too."

"He is something of a Luddite."

Joseph had always had people to do the little things for him growing up. Now he either simply paid them or relied on his charisma and connections. People tripped over themselves to help him. It had made her a little uncomfortable when they were together. Now she downright hated the way the world worked.

Like you were any better than his groupies. But at least her efforts to be a good girlfriend served a purpose now. If they could provide her with a clue, she might find a way forward out of the twisted mess.

"What will Mr. Muscles say when he finds out what you did?"

"You mean what *we* are doing," Laila reminded Rosamie pointedly. "And I'm hoping we find something concrete so he can say *congratulations.*"

Her friend raised a skeptical brow. "Like that will ever happen. I think it far more likely he's going to spank you—*hard.*"

Rosamie's very pointy elbow poked Laila in the ribs. "Try not to enjoy it too much."

Laila huffed. "And I think *you* are projecting. Also, now I know entirely too much about your new relationship."

Rosamie snorted. "Somehow, I don't think either Ransom or Mason are going to pat us on the head. But at least you aren't trying to do this alone." She tugged on her purse strap. "It's also a good idea we're packing."

They didn't have guns. Though Rosamie had gone to the shooting range once or twice with her old boyfriend, Laila didn't know how to use one. Instead, she had Rosamie's stun gun. It was the handheld kind that had to be had pushed against your assailant, so she'd asked Rose to 'borrow' something that didn't require getting up close and personal from Ransom's collection.

Unlike Mason, who didn't appear to keep any weapons in his house, Ransom was something of an aficionado. He'd shown off his firearms to Rosamie. Although he kept them locked up, there were some he didn't secure—like the projectile stun gun that could be shot from a distance.

Laila nudged Rosamie, urging her to her feet. The security guard was on the move, about to take his lunch break. "Remember, if Joseph is there, don't let him see the stun gun. We're only there to pick up my forgotten textbooks."

The ones she had already sold back to the campus bookstore. But she didn't think Joseph knew that. It wouldn't occur to him to sell any of his books back at the end of the quarter.

With affected casualness, they crossed the street, entering the lobby. Laila paused at the mailbox, tempted to check for her mail as she put on her winter gloves to avoid leaving fingerprints.

"No," Rosamie reminded. "If we do find his phone or computer, he will eventually miss them. And you don't want to let on that we were ever here."

"Good point," Laila muttered, eyeing the camera at the entrance of the hall that led to the elevators.

"This camera and the ones in the elevators are the only ones here, but it doesn't cover where we're standing."

"So, what do we do?"

Laila pressed a finger to her lips. On silent feet, she edged along the wall, making sure to stay out of the camera's range.

There was a small, upholstered bench a few feet from the corner.

Dragging it without looking as if she were dragging it, she let go of it just underneath the camera.

"Keep an eye out," she said, taking the opaque silicone caps out of her bag. She'd grabbed them from Mason's kitchen. They were meant to close up bottles of varying sizes, but she hoped one would fit the camera like a lens cap.

"Is anyone watching?"

Rosamie hurried to the door. "Nope, go ahead. But *hurry*."

Fumbling a little, Laila stretched the cap over the lens...and it popped right off.

"Are you sure there is no sound?" Rosamie stage whispered.

"No, they are pretty old closed-circuit," she said as she struggled with the next largest cap—this one was far too big. *C'mon.* They couldn't afford to be caught on camera.

Besides the single man posted in the lobby, the rest of the building's security features were minimal and mostly just a showy deterrent. It hadn't bothered Laila much when she was living here, because something was better than the nothing she'd had before.

"What if we just push them up high and crawl underneath, you know, heist-style?" Rosamie suggested.

It was a good idea, but when Laila tried, neither the camera nor the arm it was perched on moved. "They must screw these things into position. I think we need a screwdriver."

Frustrated, Laila tugged at the single exposed cable. She sighed with relief when the tiny green LED flickered and died. "Or we can just unplug it."

"Okay, get down from there before someone sees you."

Positioning the cable so that it barely made contact, she scrambled down. With luck, the guard would just believe that the cable slipped out on its own. "This way," she said, ushering Rosamie past the elevator to the stairs.

They made it to the top floor without further incident, although they were both out of breath by the time they got there. Pausing in front of Joseph's door, Laila pulled the smaller stunning device out her bag, slipping it into her more accessible front pocket. Giving her a sharp nod, Rosamie pulled out the larger one, posing with it like Charlie's shortest Angel.

Laila grinned, but it was shaky. Sucking in a deep breath, she reached for her key. But she didn't need it.

The door was unlocked. Holding her breath, she pushed it open.

❦

"Are we too late?" Rosamie's eyes widened on the disarray that used to be Joseph's pristine apartment. "Did the police already raid the place?"

"Um..." Laila closed the door behind them. She bent to pick up an empty bottle of vodka. "Something tells me that's not it."

The place looked worse than the frat on a Sunday morning. There were empty bottles and dirty glasses and dishes scattered on almost every surface. The round table near the entrance was on its side, dirt from the potted plant that normally stood in the middle of it spilled on the glossy marble floor. The plant itself had been kicked into the living room, a trail of black soil flecked with white marking its path.

"Joseph must have moved the party here at some point."

"Do you think he's still here?" Rosamie grimaced. "Or anyone else?"

Laila shrugged helplessly. There was no one in sight. "Let's just hurry."

They began to go room to room, searching under and between couch cushions for the phone. Laila had to pick her way through the detritus, thinking Joe must have had a big party, but the more she went over the mess, the less convinced of that she became.

For one, the discarded pizza boxes and half-full food containers were all from different places. There was no evidence of a single bulk order, the kind shared among party guests. The only thing that could have conceivably been shared by multiple people was alcohol. The sheer number of bottles was enough for three or four people. To think Joseph may have drunk all this on his own in just a few days—big chunks of which had to have been spent at Alpha Omega.

Her stomach twisting, she caught Rosamie's eye. Laila waved at the empty bottles. "I think he's trying to drink himself to death."

Rosamie's dark eyes flashed. "Because he feels guilty—now we know for sure he's involved. Otherwise, he wouldn't be acting like this."

Laila wanted to protest. A tiny voice in her head still wanted to defend Joseph, but she didn't. She couldn't. Rosamie was voicing the same thoughts she was having.

"Let's check the bedroom," she suggested.

With a terse nod, Rosamie took out the stunner. She held it up like a cop about to go into a raid.

The siren's sounded the second she made the comparison. Jerking her head around, she rushed to the window.

"Oh-my-God." Rosamie was right behind her. But her friend's shoes were far more slippery. They lost traction on the slick marble floor, sending Rosamie crashing into her. Gritting her teeth, Laila checked Rose's forward progress before she banged into the window.

"Thanks," Rosamie murmured. "Are they getting closer?"

Laila craned her neck, but she couldn't see any cruisers. "I don't think so. They must have been on the other block."

She turned around too fast, inadvertently striking a beer bottle she hadn't seen with her foot. Horrified, she watched it fly across the floor.

Squealing in dismay, Rosamie grabbed her. They held each other's hands, both cringing as the bottle hit the couch and rebounded with a clatter, setting it spinning in a circle.

Laila didn't know her heart had stopped until the bottle slowed to a stop, and no one ran out to confront them.

"I guess he really isn't here," Rosamie said, risking raising her voice a fraction. "Although I'm surprised he hasn't had the maid stop by."

"Yeah," Laila agreed. Joseph employed a cleaning service. A rotating team of five no-nonsense Hispanic women came every Sunday. Judging from the mess, they had skipped this week. "He must have canceled them."

"*Uh-huh.*" The attitude-laden acknowledgment told Laila exactly what Rosamie thought of that.

It wasn't real evidence, nothing they could take to the police, but both knew this kind of behavior was out of character for her normally carefree and privileged ex.

A few more minutes of searching yielded nothing. Eventually, there was only one more place to check.

Laila jerked her head in the direction of the bedroom, her hands damp under her gloves. By silent mutual accord, she and Rosamie tiptoed to the bedroom door. Turning the handle, she pushed it open and peeked inside.

The hairs on the back of her neck stood on end, and she fought the urge to turn tail and run.

They had been wrong. Joseph *was* home.

Freezing, Laila threw out an arm, checking Rosamie's progress once more.

Joseph's six-foot frame was splayed over the bed. He was lying face-down, shirtless, wearing only a pair of cargo shorts with his bare feet hanging over the edge. An empty beer bottle sat a few inches away from his hand. A few more were scattered on the floor, but thanks to the plush white carpeting surrounding the bed, they hadn't broken. However, judging from the smell in the room, it appeared as if they'd still been partially filled when he dropped them.

Rosamie's nails dug into her arm. *Let's go,* she mouthed, her eyes nearly bugging out of her head.

That was Laila's impulse, too, but they were already here. And Joseph wasn't moving. His breathing hadn't changed at all since she'd opened the door.

Whether his recent behavior had something to do with Jasmine's death, Joseph was making himself vulnerable now. And there was no way to know how long that would last.

"*If he's here, so is the phone,*" she mouthed, shaking off Rosamie's restraining hand. Her friend made the tiniest of squeaks in protest, but Laila shushed her with an admonishing finger.

Slipping out of her shoes, she proceeded in her socks. Rounding the bed, she checked the nightstand, hoping Joe's phone would be charging inside the drawer through the cables built into the high-tech design.

It wasn't.

Grimacing, she stepped closer to the bed to check to see if it were in his pockets. But they appeared flat to her eyes. Unless it was underneath him, then it wasn't in the bedroom either. Crouching, she brought her eyes level to the bed, trying to see if she could see it poking out underneath him.

Joseph groaned, turning his head in her direction. Laila froze. If he woke up right now, they would be eye to eye.

Rosamie waved wildly from the doorway. Holding her breath, Laila backed away, acknowledging the fact she'd probably pushed her luck to the limit. And then her eye fell on the open bathroom door.

The cell phone was lying on the bathmat next to the toilet as if it had fallen out the last time Joseph used the facilities.

Moving like molasses, Laila shifted, inching along until she was inside the bathroom, bending to get the phone. Grabbing the device, she nearly died when it slipped out of her slippery gloves. She caught it just in time, trapping it against her thigh before it hit the floor.

Why didn't I spring for the leather instead of the cheap cotton?

Getting ahead of herself, she began the seemingly endless journey back to where Rosamie waited. Her friend wasn't making a sound, but Laila could see the flare of her nostrils as if she were breathing fast. The stun gun was out and pointed at Joe's prone form. Edging around Rosamie, Laila closed the door of the bedroom, sparing a moment to thank whoever had oiled the hinges.

"C'mon," she whispered, toeing her shoes back on. Though she half-expected it, Joseph did not wake to chase them down. After cracking the door a sliver to make sure the hallway was empty, they slipped out, closing it carefully. Then they ran down the hall as if the hounds of hell were after them.

Rosamie waited until they were at the stair entrance to speak. "Girl, you are insane! I can't believe you did that."

Clutching the phone, Laila started to reply, but her words turned into a strangled scream when muscled arms plucked her friend out of the air, a large hand covering Rosamie's mouth.

CHAPTER TWENTY-EIGHT

Mason reached out to grab Laila before she tumbled down the stairs in shock.

Guilt flared like fireworks in her caramel-colored eyes. Her head shot up to Ransom, who had snatched up Rosamie mid-step, wisely covering her mouth so she wouldn't make a ruckus.

"I am going to spank you *so* hard," Ransom growled in Rosamie's ear.

"See, I told you," Laila hiss-whispered before she caught his eye. Abashed, she looked down at her feet.

Jaw tight, Mason's words came out in a growl. *"Not here."*

Pointing down the stairs, he marched their motley crew down to the ground level. But instead of heading to the front doors, they moved down the hall to the emergency exit. With a sharp nod at Ransom, he signaled his wingman.

With a grunt that had nothing to do with how heavy she was, Ransom put Rosamie down, whipping out a small leather folio holding his specialized tools. In less than a minute, his partner had disabled the alarm on the door.

They were outside in the alley in the next minute, but he didn't let

Laila or Rosamie explain until they were blocks away in the parking lot where he'd parked his car.

"Now that we're clear, would either of you like to explain what in the living hell you were doing in Joseph Dubey's apartment?" He looked them up and down, noting the gloves and caps covering their long hair. "Dressed for a heist no less? You are aware that breaking and entering is against the law, right?"

His voice was a cold whip, a tone reserved for men in his unit who disobeyed orders.

Laila flinched, but he didn't soften. He was too angry.

How could she have come here? They didn't know if Dubey was involved in her friend's death, but knowing she had willingly gone to his apartment had sent Mason over the edge.

What was worse—there had been no warning, no build-up. It was like getting hit by a truck and being sent over a cliff he hadn't realized was there. Laila could wreck him without even trying.

For a man known for his control and calm under fire, it was an unsettling realization.

"It's not breaking and entering if you still have a key," Rosamie pointed out in a small voice when Laila continued to stare at the ground.

Mason ignored Rosamie. "*Laila.* What the hell were you trying to accomplish?"

She took a deep breath, lifting her chin to meet his glare. Her expression was steady. "Detective Silano called. The investigation is dead in the water because they can't even question Joe. His family's lawyers are stonewalling."

Ransom grunted, pulling Rosamie's back against his front. "I'm sorry, babe. I'm sorry for you both."

Mason shot him a glare. "Somehow, I doubt Detective Silano encouraged them to investigate for her."

His voice was still sharp enough to make Laila swallow nervously. "We have a very small window before Joseph either asks for his apartment key back or has the locks changed."

"And just what did you think you were going to find? A signed confession?" The edge in Mason's voice could have performed surgery. He didn't like the way Laila cringed away from him, but his blood pumped hot. All he could picture was Joseph's big hands wrapped around her slender neck.

"No… I was after this." She flicked him a glance under her lashes before pulling out a sleek cell phone. It wasn't hers.

He groaned aloud. "So, we can add theft to the list of charges?"

"I'm with Mason on this one," Ransom said, making a sour face. "The fact that you two got in and out without being seen—"

"Which we don't know for sure they did," Mason interrupted, instinctively moving to block Laila from sight as a pedestrian passed them on the sidewalk.

Pausing, Ransom held up a finger. "Which we don't know you did," he acknowledged. "But getting the phone is pointless cause these things can't be unlocked without a thumbprint or the PIN. Unless you also severed Dubey's thumb in there as well, we're SOL because those things aren't as easy to hack as on TV."

"That won't be necessary," Laila said, her shoulders straightening. "I know the passcode."

Mason raised a brow, and she reddened. "I thought he might be cheating. I decided I couldn't move out without proof, so I paid attention long enough to memorize it. But I never worked up the courage to actually look."

Rosamie threw her arm around Laila, surreptitiously checking her watch. "We're going to return it after we check it."

Mason scowled. "You are *not* going back."

"But we have to," Laila protested. "Before he wakes up…"

Mason closed his eyes as a wash of red swamped his vision. There was a long beat of silence. When he spoke, his voice was dangerously low. "Are you telling me that Joseph is home right now?"

Laila bit her lip, but both women stayed resolutely silent.

Ransom cleared his throat to break the tension. "All right, what's done is done—let's make the most of it."

He plucked the phone out of Laila's hand. "As for this, having the code is good. What would be better would be to clone everything on it. And we happen to know someone who can do that."

Mason frowned. "Who?"

Ransom smirked. "You know who I mean—you vetted all the recruits."

Realization dawned, but his expression didn't lighten. "We hardly know Toya."

The woman in question, Toya Almari, had a strong background in intelligence in addition to being an experienced special-ops agent. Ian and Elias had considered it a coup when they'd convinced her to sign on with Auric. Mason had trained her along with the other newbies, but their relationship was distant. He wasn't her boss since she was destined for another team.

They definitely weren't on friendly enough terms for Mason to ask her to break the law.

"How do we know she would be willing?" he asked, acknowledging the woman had the requisite skills.

Ransom, however, was certain that she would help. "I've talked to her. Trust me. She'll do it."

And to Mason's surprise, she did. What shouldn't have surprised him was Laila and Rosamie's fascination with the former special-ops agent.

It took less than a half an hour for Toya to come down and meet them, a black bag full of gear at her side.

When Ransom tried to explain why they needed the phone's information, she'd held up a hand. "This one said a girl died and this phone might shed light. That's all I need to know."

"We also have to return the phone. The owner is passed out at the moment, but that might not last long," Laila said before Rosamie began to pepper Toya with questions on what she was doing.

Toya patiently answered most. She copied the phone's data to her computer and held on to it, promising to send it a report of any relevant information after she had decrypted and cleaned it up, separating user data from the phone's operating system. "Don't worry about putting the phone back. I'll do that."

Mason frowned. "Copying it is more than enough. You should let me return it."

"No, *I* should," Laila said. "It'll be simple with the key. I can just toss it back on the couch or inside the door."

"*No.*" Both Mason and Ransom said it at the same time.

"Which is why I will do it," Toya said, suppressing a laugh as she held up the phone. "No offense, but you two are way too conspicuous. And you ladies are familiar faces as well from what I've gathered. But I have some experience in this sort of thing."

"But—"

"Trust me," she said, putting a hand on Laila's arm. "I know how to blend."

Mason put out his hand. "I owe you one."

"I know," Toya said, the corners of her lip lifting. "And I will collect," she added, shaking on it.

Laila threw her arms around Toya. "Thank you."

"You're welcome, darlin'," Toya said, patting her back and squeezing her. "I hope it helps."

CHAPTER TWENTY-NINE

"Do you think Toya would come drinking with us?" Rosamie poked her head between the seats. Mason gripped the steering wheel of the Mustang, the cords in his neck standing out in stark relief.

Laila bit her lip, willing her best friend to shut her mouth.

"Isn't it a little soon for you to be planning a girl's night out?" Ransom observed from the backseat. "You know...under the circumstances."

"Jasmine's boyfriend has planned a pub crawl for her memorial— all her favorite places." Rosamie shrugged, trying to make herself smaller as Mason twisted to frown at her. "You never met her, or you'd realize how much she would have liked that."

Mason grunted noncommittally. His hands were still tight on the wheel, but at least it no longer appeared as if tendons in his neck were going to burst.

Rosamie was about to say something else, but Laila twisted and shook her head in warning.

She said nothing as he drove them all to Ransom's place, promising to let them know the minute Toya sent them the report in a halfway civil tone. She thought it promising, considering how angry he was, but once they had dropped off the others, he continued to drive in stony silence.

It stretched and stretched, making her skin feel tight.

"How did you figure out what we were up to?" she asked, desperate to break the tension stifling the air.

"Ransom called me because one of his tasers was missing," he said, jaw tight. "No one but Rosamie has been in his place. When you didn't pick up your cell, we put two and two together. I canceled today's practice session, then drove like a bat out of hell to get here. Ransom met me out front. No one was at the desk, so we just went in—past a disabled security camera."

"You noticed that, huh?"

His lips pursed. "I'm not about to compliment you for taking precautions when what you did was flat-out insane. What would have happened if Joseph woke up? He might still realize you were the one who came by and swiped the phone. You could be arrested."

"With the hangover he's sure to have, he'll think he lost it himself. Plus, I took back up," she protested weakly. "Also, I did have the key."

That and the person who had given her that key had still been texting her as of yesterday, begging to see her.

"Then you should have given it to *me*."

"You going in would have ended much worse, and you know it," she argued. "If you'd seen Joseph in the flesh, you would have dragged him out of bed and beat the crap out of him," she said, finally snapping. "Go on and tell me I'm wrong."

Mason's mouth firmed, his profile tightening until it was almost ascetic in its severity. But he didn't argue with her, not until several miles had passed.

When he turned to her, his light blue eyes were luminous, as if lit from a fire within. "If you ever put yourself at risk like that again, I will put you over my knee."

Laila scrunched down into the seat. "Now, you're stealing Ransom's lines."

Mason exhaled very loudly and deliberately. "Laila, don't test me."

Deciding silence was the better part of valor, Laila stopped trying to defend herself. Mason was too worked up. That and it was hard to truly argue with him—not because she was afraid of upsetting him, but because part of her still couldn't believe she'd done what she had.

Laila wasn't stupid. She was aware she had taken a big risk. But she also knew she had the best chance of finding out whether Joseph had anything to do with Jasmine's death. She was the only one with access.

The rest of the drive passed in silence. Laila alternated between telling herself she did the right thing and panicking the police were going to be waiting at Mason's with handcuffs.

His phone buzzed. He picked it up, keeping one hand on the steering wheel. After glancing at it, he handed it to her. There was a text from an unknown number.

Item copied and returned.
    Instructions to download the file to follow.
    This message will self-destruct.
    JK. Delete this if you know what's good for you.

Sighing with relief, Laila hugged the phone to her, deleting the message as instructed. A few minutes later, Mason pulled into his driveway.

Laila hurried inside, intent on getting to her room before he could start another argument. She made it to the bedroom door when Mason grabbed her and spun her around. His arms wrapped around her, his mouth covering hers before she could think.

It had taken one touch for his anger at Laila to transform into desire. All he'd meant to do was stop her from running and hiding in her room, but the second his hand touched the bare skin on her arm, he clutched her to his chest and kissed her—hard.

Too hard.

He broke the kiss, pulling his head back. "Your lip—"

"Is fine," Laila said, reaching up to pull his head back down. Her mouth covered his, her small tongue breaching the seam of his lips.

Her taste, both exotic and sweetly familiar, filled his mouth, making his pulse pound and igniting a sharp hunger for more.

Something that felt like relief swept over him. Laila was here, and she was warm and willing in his arms. Mason could indulge as much as he wanted.

A little whimper escaped Laila. He stopped, inhaling deeply because it wasn't a protest. It was a sound that spoke of a need almost as strong as his own.

Overcome, he started to strip her. His hands were rough, but she didn't object. Laila was too busy trying to tug off his shirt. Helping her, he yanked it up, tossing it away before stopping to pull down her black jeans. They landed next to his shirt.

She was down to her bra and panties when his patience ended. He gathered her up. Laila instinctively wrapped her legs around his waist. A few steps forward let him pin her against the wall, his mouth devouring hers.

Laila was so petite it was easy to lift her high, her lace-clad breasts level with his mouth. He tasted her through the cups, wetting the material with his tongue and tugging with his teeth until her nipple was poking stiffly through it. Shuddering in response, Laila's nails raked his back, digging in with just the right amount of pressure.

He used his teeth to pull the bra cup down, his mouth settling on the exposed caramel skin before taking the chocolate tip into his mouth. Laving it with his tongue, he shifted to support her with one hand, so the other was free to stroke. He ran his palm up and down her thigh before shifting her panties aside, working his fingers between them to touch her heated folds.

"Mason," she gasped, her hands scrabbling down to try to reach his zipper.

"Wait." If she did what he thought she was going to do, this would be over too fast. He'd been waiting too long.

Setting her down, he pressed her shoulders against the wall before bending. Hooking his fingers into the waistband of her panties, he pushed, following them down. Kneeling in front of her, he nudged her legs apart, wasting no time. His mouth settled on her heat, licking and closing his lips over her clit.

Laila jerked, crying out. She might have fallen if the wall wasn't supporting most of her weight. Pinning her legs open with the bulk of his body, he held her straining and shivering body while his mouth worked, tongue and lips and teeth moving obsessively...gluttonously.

Salt and sugar in one.

The months of abstinence came rushing back. He broke, giving in to the need. Mason had gone without because only this woman would do. Then Laila was crying his name, urging him up. Tearing at his jeans, he pulled out his already-throbbing erection.

"Please."

Laila didn't have to ask twice. Picking her up again, he urged her legs back around his waist as he thrust home.

Tight velvet wrapped around his cock, an agony so sharp and sweet a cry escaped him, too.

Mason flexed, withdrawing and pushing back in with a groan, repeating the sweet torture until he'd set a steady and demanding rhythm. Pulse pounding in time with his thrusts, he let instinct take over, letting loose the reins of his hunger the way he'd only ever been able to with her.

Laila urged him on with whispers and hushed moans that seemed to directly tap into that primitive part of his brain, the one that wanted to consume and possess every inch of her.

So that was what he did. That painful period of want and loss was over. His sweet sugar was here, melting all around him. He was taking her back, making her his, with each hard thrust.

Mason wanted to last, but each deep, penetrating stroke brought him closer to the edge. He fought to hold on a little longer, but pleasure this intense wasn't meant to last—his heart might give out. Then Laila shuddered, her entire body clamping down on his shaft with a keening wail she couldn't stifle.

His rhythm stuttered and broke. Losing control, he pistoned in and out, grinding against Laila as his cock throbbed, pulsing. Hot seed jetted as his orgasm tore through him. Pinned to the wall, Laila took all of him, her arms pulling him in tight.

Enervated, Mason leaned forward, pressing his forehead against the wall above Laila's silky shoulder. Suddenly, it didn't matter how much he worked out or how fit he was. He was buried in Laila, and he couldn't catch his breath.

She still panted too, little shivers coursing through her body. Her channel pulsed around him. Although he was spent, he could already feel his hunger stirring again. With Laila, it was never too far.

Peeling them off the wall, he lifted Laila, working her up and down on his cock, which was already hardening in her warmth.

Gasping, Laila twisted to look at him. *"Again?"*

"Again," he told her before lowering his mouth for another soul-devouring kiss.

They had a lot of time to make up for.

CHAPTER THIRTY

It took three more lovemaking sessions to blunt the edge of his hunger long enough for him to let go of Laila. Arms shaking slightly in the aftermath of his last explosive climax, he collapsed next to her on his bed, having carried her in there somewhere between rounds three and four.

Round two had been on the floor just in front of his bedroom door. That was after walking through the ground floor of the house, lifting Laila up and down on his shaft so they could leave their mark on every room. She was so much smaller than him, so it was an easy task at first—up until he'd burned through all his strength and stamina in the most pleasurable way possible.

Still short-winded, he pulled an equally spent Laila across the mattress into his arms, spooning her until her breathing slowed.

He kissed the back of her neck. "I missed you."

Laila twisted around to face him. "I missed you, too."

Pressing his lips to her forehead, he lapsed into silence, letting his fingers trail over the soft skin of her back, enjoying the feel of her hands touching him. Lazily content, he smiled when she pressed her lips to his chest.

"I like that you're so big," she said between kisses. "You make me feel small."

"You are small." He laughed, but it faded fast.

Noting the change in his expression, Laila frowned. "Did you hear your phone? Is it the file?'

"Um, no, it's not that." He'd left the phone with his pants. They were somewhere on the floor of the living room, or was it the hall?

Mason reached out to cup her cheek. "I just realized we—I— didn't use anything. I'm so sorry, Laila. You know I'll always protect you. I got carried away."

She reached out to rest a hand over his heart. "Don't be sorry. If I get pregnant, we'll get married. Once we have one baby, we should start on two and three. I want at least three kids."

"Okay, great," Mason put an arm behind his head with exaggerated casualness.

Laila burst out laughing. "*Okay?* Just okay? I was *kidding.*"

"I know you were, but I like the sound of three babies with you. I was thinking more along the lines of two, but we could just as easily have four."

"Hey, I said *three.*"

Grinning, he shook his head. "Even numbers are better. That way, we can avoid middle child syndrome."

Laila bit her lip, shaking her head. "It's not going to be an issue—at least not just yet. I'm on the pill. I, uh, started a few months ago."

"*Oh.*" She took the pills for Dubey.

She winced, hesitating.

He touched her arm. "It's okay. Tell me."

"Well, um, Joe wanted me to start. He wouldn't let up until I made an appointment to get some with University Health Services." Laila's lips pulled down. " But you should know that even though I caved and started taking the pills, I never trusted him enough to rely on them. I always made sure he used other protection."

She broke off and pulled a pillow over her head, so her next words were muffled. "God, I hate this. I never wanted to bring him up again. Not here—not in this context."

Mason pulled the pillow off. "It's normal to discuss sexual history. In case you were wondering, mine is all clear."

"Well, your doctor said I have a clean bill of health. They ran tests when you took me to see them, and they sent me the results already."

He pulled her back to him until she was pressed flush to his chest. "Then we have nothing to worry about, right? Well, except for agreeing on the number of kids we'll eventually have."

Laila took a long look at him, then she reached out and pinched him.

"Ow," he said, laughing. "What was that for?"

"You can't be real. Mason, you are too good to be true."

Warmed heart and soul, Mason pressed another kiss to her forehead and decided to keep going down the line of her neck. "I hope you still feel that way after we've been married a few decades," he said between long sipping kisses.

Cuddling close to rest her head on his chest, she murmured, "I don't think that's going to be a problem."

§❧

Mason picked up the phone without checking the caller ID. "Yeah?" he asked, stirring his sauce so it wouldn't stick.

Determined to cook for Laila for a change and equally determined to impress her, Mason pulled out the big guns. He was making his grandmother's sausage ragù sauce, the one whose ingredients were a closely guarded family secret. It was the only recipe in his repertoire that took hours, plural. If he didn't eat take out, Mason's meals were simple things that took less than a half an hour to prepare.

However, the ragù was worth every minute, or so he kept telling Laila whenever she asked. Giving her some garlic bread to tide her over, he juggled the phone when Ransom practically yelled in his ear. "Did you check the file Toya sent?"

"No, I'm cooking," he replied, checking over his shoulder, but Laila wasn't in the kitchen. Figuring she had gone to set the table, he lowered his voice. "What about the file?

"What are you cooking?" As usual, Ransom had been distracted by the mention of food.

"My grandma's ragù and linguine."

Ransom whistled. "Now I know you're in love."

Mason didn't deny it. What was the point? "What was it about the file?"

"I'll tell you when we get there."

He scowled. "You're coming over?"

"We are now. We'll be there in twenty."

Hanging up with a shake of his head, he called to Laila, warning her to set two extra place settings.

The sauce was finally ready by the time their self-invited guests arrived.

"The file was mostly gibberish," Rosamie said, passing the salad to Laila. "I guess it's the code for the OS, but I only took a quick look. Toya knew we were in a hurry, so she just did a data dump. We will have to scour it ourselves."

"I think I can speed up the search. I took enough coding classes before switching to respiratory therapy to tease out what's part of the operating system from the call logs. What I don't know is how the GPS data will be formatted. I'm going to have to do some research," Laila said, putting her hand over her wineglass before Mason had a chance to serve her. "So, it might be a long night for me. I think I should skip the wine."

Rosamie nudged her hand off before she reached for the other bottle he'd put out—the Chardonnay. "A search like this needs wine. Lots of it. Don't worry. I won't let you go to sleep."

The Filipina flicked her lashes at him. "Red wine makes her sleepy. White makes her wired."

Mason mock saluted. "Then, I'll go get the corkscrew."

It took most of the bottle of wine for Laila to work through the data. The girls settled on the couch in the living room while he and Ransom crowded on the armrests behind them.

"The only person he called that entire day was his father," she muttered at some point.

"No incriminating calls?" Rosamie asked, her shoulders drooping.

"Except one of the calls happened at one forty-nine in the morning."

There was a beat of silence as the foursome absorbed that. "It makes sense," Mason said. "Who does a spoiled man-child go to when he gets in over his head?"

"I'm not sure I agree with the man-child part, but there were definite signs of being spoiled and going to his dad for advice whenever there was a challenge on the horizon," she said.

"I guess killing someone would qualify," Rosamie said darkly.

Laila grimaced. Mason could tell she wasn't convinced he'd done it, but this circumstantial evidence pointed in that direction.

"It's not enough for a jury," he said. "The fact he called his father at that hour doesn't prove anything. It could easily be dismissed as a drunk dial."

"A drunk dial that lasted eleven minutes?" Rosamie peered closer at his computer screen.

"That does seem a bit long for a drunk dial," Ransom observed. "But it might just be long enough for daddy dearest to call someone on another line and put a plan in place."

"That might be true, but it seems odd that it would be the last call. If they were getting rid of Jasmine's body, wouldn't there be more calls to coordinate?" Rosamie asked. "For something like this, I'd imagine Joseph would have the phone glued to his ear so that he could get step-by-step instructions."

"Maybe he did," Laila pointed out. "They might have wised up and switched to one of those apps that delete your messages. Which I should have thought of before..."

Mason rubbed her back. "It could be something else. Didn't you say Joseph has a cousin at the fraternity?"

"Yes," Laila said, straightening. "Bryce. I kind of forgot about him."

"We should all be that lucky. Bryce is the worst." Rosamie's mouth tightened. "But if you asked me if he could be involved with something like murder, I would have said no. He's a butthead, but harmless.

Do you think it could be some other Alpha Omega, and they're covering for them?"

"I'm not sure they'd get their hands dirty for anyone but each other," Laila observed thoughtfully.

"It does sound as if they'd be each other's go-to man for help, considering the blood tie. No matter how tight they are with their frat brothers, I doubt they'd go to such lengths for anyone else—not for something like this. Is that your impression, too?" Mason asked Laila.

She appeared to think it over. "Yes. Unless they are old friends with someone else there, someone who is a part of their parents' inner circle, too, but I can't remember anyone special. I don't think any of those friendships at the frat are that deep."

"Maybe not, but do you think the opposite is true? Would a frat member cover for them?"

"That's far more likely," Laila said. "Given the family's money and political connections, I can see one of their many hangers-on covering for one or both in the hopes of collecting a big favor someday."

"Or an outright bribe," Rosamie groused. "Any luck with the GPS data?"

Laila groaned. "I can't make heads or tails of it."

"Then don't waste more time on it," Ransom said. "I'm sure Toya could tear it apart and inside out a lot faster. Since you mentioned it when you met her, she's probably been working on it and is waiting for us to ask for it."

"Why wouldn't she just send it along?"

"So she can collect another favor for the cleaned-up data," Mason said with a sudden grin. "The woman is an operator."

Mason and Ransom's guess proved true. Toya had been waiting for their call. She also collected another marker.

"Is it terrible I like her even more for that?" Laila asked Rosamie.

"No. Toya is a badass who knows her worth," her friend said, holding up her glass as if toasting the absent woman. "If anything, it's deepened my girl-crush."

Laila pored over the data again. Unlike the jumble of code she'd been trying to decipher, the date had been meticulously organized into a spreadsheet with date and timestamps.

"He did leave the frat," Laila said, comparing two clusters of data. "And it's not on campus, more like ten miles away. I can tell by comparing it to all that cartoon penis data."

She pointed to a cluster of GPS data points that were generated last month.

Rosamie wrinkled her nose. "Does it really form a penis?"

"A curved one, but yeah."

Rosamie threw her head back, laughing, and tapped Ransom with the back of her arm. "Like yours!"

"Hey…" Ransom leaned way over, grabbing her chin to bite her on the nose. "You like that."

Mason covered his ears. "La, la, la," he began to sing. "We don't need to know this."

Laila laughed, but abruptly stopped, appearing surprised to find amusement under the circumstances. But she shook off the melancholy to give him a small smile.

❧

Mason—the only one who didn't have a second glass of wine—drove them all out to the GPS coordinates.

"It's a bar," Laila exclaimed with a scowl.

"And not a nice one at that," Mason added. *The Stag and Stars* had the name of a classic English pub, but it more closely resembled a run-down dry cleaner than anything else. "I don't see this as a place Dubey, or his cousin, would frequent."

Joseph and his cousin looked more like a sports bar patrons—high-end ones, with the occasional rooftop bar to impress the ladies.

Rosamie's face was dark. "Why would they come here at two-thirty in the morning? Especially when they would have to get behind the wheel to get here."

"Not drinking. The last call at this dive is at two AM. " Ransom squinted at the sign in the window. "Are we sure this is where they came? It's nowhere near where Jasmine's body was found."

Laila pointed to the map they'd printed out. "They came to this parking lot, at least. It's roughly where the coordinates dead end before they head back to campus again, and none of these other places seem more likely."

She had circled this as the area Dubey's phone had pinged. The radius covered the surrounding blocks. They'd already driven up and down the neighboring streets. The region was a jumble of apartment buildings and small shops that wouldn't have been open at that hour.

Laila had figured out the range after calculating probabilities that left a wide margin of error, but the bar's parking lot was dead center. "We should drive around and document the entire area, just in case we missed some glaring detail," she said, taking out her phone to snap some pics of the bar. "Maybe we'll see something that makes the trip out here make sense."

Mason circled the bar parking lot so Laila could take pictures of all sides, then they backtracked their earlier route, taking snapshots of all the possible destinations. None appeared more likely than the bar.

"Ransom and I will come back here tonight around closing time," Mason promised Laila. "We'll double-check with the bartender that the posted closing time is the real one."

"Thank you," she said, but she couldn't feign much enthusiasm—not that Mason blamed her. They had driven here in high hope of finding a smoking gun...and they hadn't found one.

CHAPTER THIRTY-ONE

Mason watched Laila from the passthrough. He was making dinner again, and she was going over something on her computer, occasionally running her teeth over her fully healed lower lip in a way that made him want to go over there and do it for her. But he didn't want to disrupt her focus.

A little over a week had passed since their excursion to the *Stag and Stars*. They'd contacted Detective Silano to 'suggest' they look at traffic cameras in the general vicinity of the bar on the night in question.

After acting on the tip, the good detective called them back. "How the hell did you know Joseph Dubey's vehicle was in that neighborhood?" she asked point-blank in a conference call with him and Laila.

Laila had tried to hedge, but Mason decided that, in this case, the truth would not serve justice. He'd told the detective the girls had heard the rumor from a fellow student who'd heard it from a friend of a friend. "I wouldn't be surprised if that original 'friend' were in the frat. I hear the rats are leaving that particular sinking ship."

Despite being officially into the summer session, Alpha Omega was quietly put on probation until the case on Jasmine Elliot's death was closed. Despite there being no legal charges in the works, a cloud of suspicion hung over the fraternity, one that wouldn't be cleared until the exact timeline was nailed down. However, Laila was cynical that anything would come of it.

"I bet they won't even lose their charter. The Dubeys aren't the only wealthy patrons. There is a whole slew of elite and upper-class families on their alumni rolls," Laila shared in a depressed tone, curling into his arms after the call with the detective. "Unless Joe or Bryce suddenly break down and confess, I predict the school will hush everything up again in the fall. Jasmine's death will be nothing but a cautionary tale or reduced to a mere rumor."

Mason hated to agree with her, but he'd been around the monied class long enough to learn how the world worked. He didn't offer platitudes. Instead, he offered her the only thing he could—himself.

Whenever he wasn't at work, he was with Laila, spoiling her whenever he could. He cooked their every meal, bought her treats, and generally made sure she didn't have to lift a finger. He didn't even let her load the dishwasher. Her sweet bewilderment at being taken care of only made him love her more.

"You know you shouldn't be getting me so many little presents," Laila told him laughingly as he forced more gourmet chocolate on her as they sat together on the couch. "It never pays to set the bar so high so early in a relationship, at least that's what my stepmother used to say—usually when my father forgot to bring her flowers on their anniversary. But at least he never forgot her birthday," she added with a grin.

"Well, I'm very good with dates thanks to Google calendar," he said, putting an arm around her.

"Are you seriously never going to let me back in the kitchen?" she asked, gesturing to the coffee table, which held the remnants of their steak dinner.

"Well, if you feel like baking again, I'm not going to stop you. Especially if you feel a yen to make those rocky road brownies or lemon squares," he said with a winsome grin. "Or the bread pudding, you know the one with the chocolate mixed in? And—"

Laila put her arms around him, interrupting his growing list. "How about I bake all of it, every recipe I know?"

Mason grinned at her. "Only if you feel like it…"

Laughing at how transparent he was, Laila cuddled close. Savoring the closeness, he held her quietly.

"I have to go to work next week."

Startled, Mason glanced down at her. "What? Why?"

She shrugged. "I've used all my vacation days."

"But—"

Laila put her fingers on his lips. "Mason, it's wonderful you're letting me stay here rent-free, but I have to make money. I have a cell phone bill and a stepmother to help support. I don't contribute much there, but what I do makes a difference. My boss has given me all the leeway he can."

"Then quit. I make enough money for us both. It's too dangerous for you to go into Gardullo's. Dubey or any of his cronies can come and harass you whenever they want. Does your manager understand that he might have to get between you and someone who wants to harm you?"

Laila was dismayed. "Do you really think that would happen?"

"It's a possibility we have to consider." Mason rubbed the back of her neck. "Besides, didn't you just graduate? You could give notice at Gardullo's and focus on finding a job in your field…on the East Coast."

"The East Coast?" she echoed.

Mason rolled his shoulders. "I should have brought this up sooner, but I've been asked to relocate for work. The company I work for is opening a second office there. I also have that apartment renovation project there—although that's covered for now."

"Covered how?" Her face was the picture of consternation.

Mason grimaced lightly. "Um, well, I was supposed to be there helping, but I called my buddy, Ethan, and told him I couldn't go. I need to be here now. But it's okay. It turns out our third investor, Donovan, has some relevant experience, so I called him in. He said he was way overdue for some time off and was happy to go."

That last may have been an exaggeration, but Donovan was a good guy. He didn't argue when Mason explained the circumstances.

Laila frowned. He'd told her about his project with Ethan and Donovan before, but he hadn't gone into that much detail. "I thought you said he was a doctor."

"He is, one who has built clinics in Africa." He held up his hands. "It's perfect, really."

"And the East Coast move?"

"It comes with the promotion I got earlier this year, but if you don't want to move over there with me, I can speak to my bosses. They've heard some of the details through the grapevine and offered me paid time off, but if you're not willing to leave L.A., I would rather turn it down. Because I don't want to move without you."

Laila was quiet for a moment. Each second felt like an eternity, but she took his fingers, lifting them to press a kiss to the back of his hand.

"I want to be wherever you are. Being on the East Coast would put me closer to my stepmother, but I'm afraid of leaving Rosamie. If we move with this unresolved, she might become a target by default because she's the only one here."

Mason had thought about that. "I'm not sure that's true. You're the only one who can directly refute Joseph's statements about where he was that night. Rosamie's knowledge is all second hand. You are the one who would have to testify he hurt you to force you to establish an alibi. That puts the target on your back, not Rosamie. Besides, from what I've gathered, Ransom is all over bodyguard duty. I never thought I'd see him give up his player ways, but this is Rosamie we're talking about. She doesn't take his shit. I think he needs someone like that."

Laila was thoughtful. "Do you think so? Or are they being forced together by the circumstances—mutual danger fostering a false closeness? Wasn't that the plot of *Speed*?"

He chuckled, bending to press a hot kiss to her lush mouth. "Even if that were the case, it sounds as if Ransom's thinking of going the distance this time. He hasn't had a long-term relationship in a while, but even if this thing with Rosamie blows up, he'll still keep an eye on her. It may be one of the more surprising things about him—not one of his exes has ever had a bad thing to say about him."

"Really?" Laila wasn't skeptical, just a little surprised.

Mason used his free hand to stroke her cheek. "I don't know how he does it. They never get mad at him. Maybe it's because he's too much of a goofball. Most of the women he dates aren't looking for anything long term. That and he's the type of guy who will help you move. Although, all you need to do is buy him a six-pack—no need to date him."

Laila smiled. "Something tells me that he won't help us pack up this place if we move all the way to Boston."

Something tightly coiled deep in his gut unfurled. Mason pressed his forehead to Laila's. "Does that mean you're coming with me?"

"I—yes. Yes, I will."

When Mason abruptly let go, she almost fell flat on her face against the couch cushion. Baffled, she watched him run out of the room.

"I'll be right back," he called. He'd returned before she had a chance to get upset. And when he kneeled in front of her holding a small black box, she lost her ability to breathe.

Mason held it up. "I've been holding on to this for a while. I wrote to my cousin to ask for it when I was in the hospital."

He opened the box to reveal a beautiful art deco ring with a sparkling oval diamond in the center. Laila gasped aloud, reaching out to stroke the delicate leaf-and-vine design of the silver band.

"This was my grandmother's. It went to my cousin Nate since he was the first to marry, but his wife is a jewelry designer who opted to wear a piece she made instead. Nate has a band that matches her ring. But I always liked this one. It's what I picture my wife wearing."

Tears glinted in Laila's eyes. The awe on her face was more than he'd hoped for. "It's absolutely perfect."

Mason's answering smile was blindingly beautiful. "Laila, will you marry me?"

She threw her arms around him. "I thought you had already asked by giving this to me."

He squeezed her tight. "Some words need to be said aloud."

Pressing kisses all over his face and neck, she hugged him back with all her strength. "Then yes, yes, and *yes*."

Mason grinned. "You know, there's another context where I'm fond of hearing those words..."

He lifted her hand, pressing a kiss against her palm just above the stone. "I want to see you in this and nothing but this," he said before stripping her bare.

Soon, she wore the ring and nothing else.

After tugging down his pants, Mason pulled her onto his lap. Laila's slick folds slid over his stiffening length, the silky wet heat burning him up.

He slid into her tightness with a groan. His hands moved over as he murmured endearments, urging her until she was riding him fast and hard.

Pulling her into him, he tongued her breasts as her vicelike grip nearly sent him over the edge, but he was missing that tell-tale flutter.

Reversing their positions, Mason came down over her, taking Laila to the floor.

"This is what you really want, isn't it, sugar?" he whispered, pinning her arms on either side of her head. "You like being covered by me, taking me deep and hard. It's what that tight little pussy needs to get off."

"Yes, I do," she admitted raggedly, clutching at him with sweaty hands. "I love it."

Whimpering, Laila clamped her legs around his back as he ground against her, giving her the blunt and straightforward domination she seemed to need. "Please, never stop."

Goddamn, she was perfect. Mason wanted to throw his head back and shout it to the skies. Instead, he crushed her to the carpet, riding her with open possessiveness.

Throbbing now, he drank in her cries, reveling in the feel of her naked sheath gripping and spasming around him.

"Mason, *now, now.*" She came with a broken shout, her entire body shaking and trembling underneath him.

"That's it, sugar, milk me dry," he ordered as he finally let go, pumping everything he had into her greedy, pulsing core. The shudders racked him, the pleasure so intense it was almost painful. It was as if he'd come with his entire body, his bones and muscles dissolving and then being reknit—this time with Laila's DNA weaved into them.

It was a damn good thing she'd just agreed to become his wife, because he could never let her go now.

The realization was stunning and fucking scary at the same time... But he could deal because he wasn't in this alone.

Collapsing to the side to avoid crushing her, he fought to catch his breath, one hand splayed over Laila covetously.

Mason didn't move for a long time. Then he gathered his fiancé's lax and sated body in his arms and carried her into the bedroom.

CHAPTER THIRTY-TWO

Laila was still floating on a cloud the day after Mason's proposal, especially after the hardest part had been weathered.

"I can't believe you're leaving me!" Rosamie had wailed when she heard the news.

"We will visit a lot, I promise."

"Not enough," her friend pouted, squeezing her tight until Ransom convinced her to let go with a hit-and-run kiss that had Rosamie clutching the air after him.

The still-together couple had come over in the evening for dinner. Ransom being Ransom, he'd passed the invitation to all their current and former Auric teammates, and, suddenly, it was a party. Laila didn't recognize any of the faces, but that didn't stop them from embracing her as if they'd known her for years.

"Everyone is so friendly," she commented to Julio, who Mason had introduced as his friend Klein's boyfriend.

"That's because we feel like we know you already," the friendly Hispanic man said enthusiastically, lifting his refilled champagne glass to clink against hers. By that point, she and Mason had been toasted so much she felt as if her blood was half champagne. Laila felt light, almost fizzy with joy.

"Mason has been pretty tight-lipped about his love life. The first time we heard he had one at all was when he started asking for you at the hospital," he said, leaning in conspiratorially. "It was the great mystery of the year—*who is Laila?* We were all dying to know. But when Mason was lucid again, he clammed up. Luckily, Ransom has no such restraint. We've been rooting for this."

He put his hand on her shoulder. "You know we were all very worried when he was hurt earlier in the year. Even though he's been promoted out, he's one of the team's rocks, part of the foundation Auric is built on."

Taking advantage of the group's preoccupation with their drinks, Laila drew Julio aside to a quiet corner.

"You have a very deep loyalty to them all, don't you?"

"They deserve it," he told her.

"Do you ever worry about the danger of the job?"

"I do," he admitted. "Mason getting hurt shook me up. He's so solid. You just can't imagine he'd ever be vulnerable. My partner Louis and I talked a lot about safety around that time, and my fears for him and our family. Auric trains its people well, and they don't take any chances. Louis insists he's safer now than when he was in the army or would be as a cop."

"Was he also a police officer?"

"No, but Santos was for a while after the army."

"I hadn't realized that." Mason had proudly introduced her to his former team leader, who'd brought his wife to the celebration.

"What about the other thing? About Auric?" she asked in a quieter voice. Her eyes flicked to the crowd of big, boisterous men and their partners. "I trust Mason enough to know he'd never work for bad people, but do you ever have any misgivings about the company? You hear things about some private security firms being bad actors."

Louis's chest puffed out, but he didn't seem offended. It almost appeared as if he approved of the question. "Auric isn't like that. Not with Elias Gardner and Ian Quinn at the helm. Louis has told me how they turn down sketchy jobs that seem legit on the surface. They've gotten rather good at sniffing out shitty people. Even once they expand, they're going to stay small enough to keep an eye on things. And if they don't, every man has an out clause. It's in their contract."

Laila's brow furrowed. "What kind of out clause?"

"It's kind of like an old-fashioned morality clause they make actors sign. But in their case, the men have to agree never to do anything that goes against the founding principles laid out in the Auric charter. The novel part is that it goes both ways. If the company ever takes a job that makes the men cross that line, the men, too, get to walk away without having to worry about finishing out the rest of their contract."

Her lips parted. "That's amazing...and comforting."

Julio nodded. "You'll see when you meet them. Elias Gardner and Ian Quinn both served. They understand the concerns that a man might have when going into this line of work. I've heard Ian say more than once they wouldn't want to hire anyone who didn't worry about their employer crossing the line."

Feeling a whole lot better, Laila was far more enthusiastic about meeting the Auric founders. Both made an appearance midway through the festivities, congratulating her and Mason with genuine warmth.

Ian Quinn hugged her. "Welcome to the family," he said before wishing them well and saying goodbye so he and Elias could attend a previous engagement.

The party didn't wind down until after midnight when Mason kicked everyone out so they could begin their 'private celebration'. He even used those words, much to her blushing embarrassment.

"It was the only way to clear the room," he swore afterward, running his finger up and down her hot cheek.

The single touch was enough to send electricity across her face. It traveled down her body. Laila put her arms around Mason. "Well, I would hate to make you a liar..."

Her hands slipped under his shirt. Beaming, Mason whipped it off, tossing it on the floor.

Laila burst out laughing. "How are you real?" She stroked the expanse of golden muscles on his chest. Maybe someday she would grow jaded, living with such beauty on a day-to-day basis, but she didn't think so—not when his insides matched his outsides.

She never got an answer. Mason's mouth was busy. It moved up and down over her neck, sending waves of enervating pleasure down her body. Her legs gave out after a minute, but it didn't matter because she was being carried out of the kitchen.

"We're going to have sex in the bedroom?" she asked when Mason dropped her on their bed. Her man was usually too impatient to make it all the way to the bedroom. Mason usually just pinned her up against the nearest wall, but something could definitely be said for the bed...

Mason flipped her over, his big hands stroking her skin as he pulled off her pants and panties in one go. Her bra and shirt were next, but Mason thought better of discarding the shirt. It ended up tied around her wrists.

Laila squealed when he tickled her backside, but it turned into a shudder when he ran his roughly callused palms over the tender skin.

"*Mason.*"

"Yes, sugar?" His hands were moving between her legs, teasing and probing while his mouth pressed hot kisses across her cheeks.

"I can't," she panted. "Too ticklish there."

"I think you can, sugar," he replied, the caramel drawl nearly doing her in. Holding her still for his mouth, he licked her up and down, pulling her backside up to his lips, his arms wrapped around hers to hold her down.

Her breath hot against her knees, Laila moaned. Then he clamped his hands on her thighs, working her back and forth on his tongue.

Laila tried to crawl away—it was too intense. But Mason wasn't about to let her go. Instead, he moved over her, covering her body with his as he guided his thick length into her body.

Face pressed to the mattress, Laila cried out. She was warm and wet, more than ready thanks to his mouth, but the feel of him was too good.

"That's what you really want, isn't it, sugar?"

"*Yes.*" Laila tried to push back against him, but Mason wasn't about to relinquish control. He kept her still, penetrating her with slow and steady strokes. Torn between heaven and hell, she squirmed and panted, flexing her muscles to hold him inside her as long as possible.

"Do you need more, sugar?" Mason's voice sounded amused.

"Are you going to make me beg?"

Mason curled over her, his body curved around her to maximize skin-to-skin contact. "No," he said, his deep voice making her nerves buzz. "My job is to give you what you need...exactly how you need it."

Pulling her onto her knees, she braced herself as Mason pulled out and thrust back in, repeating the motion until he was fucking her fast and hard, his thighs slapping against hers.

Her first orgasm hit her fast, crashing over her and sending her screaming into the mattress with bone-rattling shudders.

"That's one, sugar," Mason said, rearranging her lax limb so she sprawled on her back, legs spread. His mouth covered her breast, teeth grazing her nipples in turn.

"But I'm not through with you yet. I'm going to need a few more of those orgasms before I'm done—the ones where you scream my name." Tasting the soft skin under her breast, Mason murmured. "That sound good to you, sugar?"

Still too weak to move, Laila laughed. "I don't know if I can survive another one of those."

"Don't worry, sugar." Mason pressed a hot kiss to her stomach. "I'm going to help you."

Her future husband was true to his word. He did help...three more times.

❧

Laila called her manager at Gardullo's to explain she wasn't coming back. "I feel terrible leaving without being able to work out a two-week notice," she told him.

"It's sooner than we planned, but I understand. Plus, it's not like I didn't know this was coming. Once you got a job at a hospital or clinic, we were going to lose you anyway," he told her, having already been resigned to that fact. "And as long as you left your recipes, Shirley is happy to take over, but there were a few she hasn't gotten right yet. I hate to ask, but I don't suppose you can make a few batches of your specialties, can you? Your regulars have been asking for them."

So that was how Laila started baking in Mason's kitchen. His oven was large, considering it was for domestic use, but the size didn't compare to Gardullo's commercial ovens. It required her starting early in the day so she could make many small batches of her specialties.

"Wherever we live after this, whether it's that apartment in Boston I told you about or somewhere else, I'm going to make sure you have the biggest and best oven money can buy," Mason promised after watching her set up tray after tray of cookie sheets in preparation for today's orders.

"A regular one will be fine—you have no idea how much a high-end oven can cost," she admonished, quoting a figure that made him do a double-take.

"Well... maybe we'll keep an eye out for a refurbished oven," he said with a wrinkled nose before kissing her goodbye and leaving for the Auric facility to teach a marksmanship class.

After he left, Laila mixed her killer oatmeal chocolate chip and pecan cookie dough, putting the lot in the fridge to stiffen the dough while she made her *petit four* batter. Hours later, she took a break for lunch, vowing she could compromise on the brand of her oven, but she couldn't live without a well-ventilated kitchen.

Unfortunately for her, the kitchen windows of the rental faced west with an unrestricted view of the valley, so it received a full blast of afternoon sunlight at this time of the year.

Sweating profusely, Laila fanned herself with a junk mail flyer. She had already pulled the gauzy white curtains closed on the windows, but it hadn't helped as they were mostly decorative.

Laila could hardly blame Mason for not noticing how poorly situated the kitchen was for baking. She doubted the owners had used it much at all except at breakfast and dinnertime when the light wasn't so harsh.

Wiping her damp brow, Laila put the last loaded cookie sheet in the oven, lowering the temperature to give herself a good twenty minutes before she had to pull them out. That was more than enough time to shower. Laila wanted to be fresh and clean when Mason got home.

Although why I bother, I'll never know, she thought with a grin. He was just going to get her all hot and sweaty again.

Laila had just pulled out her short bathrobe when she heard glass breaking. Frowning because the sound was too loud to be at the neighbors, she hurried to the living room. Nothing there was disturbed, but she caught movement out of the corner of her eye.

Someone was behind the curtain of the kitchen door window. She could see a man-shaped shadow. Frozen, Laila watched as a large, hairy hand reached through the window, groping for the doorknob. The sound she heard must have been one of the small glass panes set in the door being broken.

Laila ran forward, her split-second reaction to go for one of the kitchen knives. She pictured herself stabbing at the hand while screaming her head off to alert the neighbors, but then the door began to swing open.

Aware it was too late, she spun to run out the front door, but someone was there, too, jiggling the doorknob.

Oh my God, it's a hit squad!

Laila ran to grab her phone in Mason's bedroom, snatching her purse at the same time. Thrusting her hand inside, she clutched the sleek little stun gun she'd borrowed from Rosamie.

It won't do much good against two men, her brain managed to supply above an increasing buzz that sounded remarkably like static.

A crash followed heavy footsteps. They were getting closer.

Acting on pure instinct, her panic-ravaged brain didn't even think. She bolted to the closet, flying up those high and wide closet shelves she hated. Laila squeezed into the corner of the highest shelf, the one where Mason kept blankets and his spare duffle bag. Praying she was completely concealed, she pulled the blanket and duffle over herself.

She couldn't even close the closet door from here, but as long as she wasn't visible, maybe they would pass her by, guessing she had somehow slipped past them to escape outside.

Too scared to move, she kept her phone pressed to her thigh with one hand, her purse clutched in the other.

I have to get the stun gun out. If she were discovered, they would drag her out of the closet. She had to have her only weapon out and ready to use.

It's not the only one. Wrenching her eyeballs to see her phone's screen without moving her head, she texted Mason, *911.* Then she turned the phone to silent before dropping it next to her so she could use the hand to feel around the bag's interior for the stun gun.

Her hand closed around the weapon's base at the same moment the door swung open. The sound of it banging against the wall made her blood freeze. Laila desperately clenched her muscles, suddenly worried she would pee herself and the smell would give her away.

Holding her breath, she waited as they searched the room. From the bangs and grunts, it almost sounded as if they had flipped the bed, tossing it to the side to make sure she wasn't hiding underneath.

Blood rushed through her head. It was so loud she was deafened by it.

Calm down. It would help if you calmed down.

Focusing on her breath, she worked to keep from gulping the air. The slightest noise could mean her death.

Then she heard the wail from the kitchen. The fire alarm had started, but she'd been so freaked out she was only noticing now. Her cookies were burning—she'd been hiding for longer than she realized.

"Laila!"

Startled, she jerked. That was Mason. Fingers moving like molasses, Laila edged away from the duffel bag so she could peek beyond it.

Laila almost cried out. One of the intruders stood just below her. Nerves screaming, her heart almost stopped when she saw him raise his gun, his legs bending to crouch behind the door.

Mason wouldn't see him there. Seeing the nightmare in her mind, Laila quietly lifted the duffle and blanket, their combined weight making her muscles shake as she set them away from her, attempting to untangle her legs so she could climb down the shelves.

Praying the man wouldn't hear the creak of the wood over the blaring fire alarm, Laila swung her leg over the edge. A trickle of wetness ran down her thigh, but Laila didn't stop climbing until her feet were back on the floor.

There was no way he wasn't going to see her, but Laila forced herself to walk, stun gun out as if she were a priest holding a cross to ward off evil. She was almost directly behind the intruder when Mason appeared at the threshold.

Out of time, Laila lunched forward, pressing the button of the stunner to activate its potent voltage.

Finally hearing her, the man spun, meeting her halfway. His move closed the distance, so the stunner pressed right into his neck.

"*Laila.*" Mason's hand closed over the stunner as the man jerked, his bulk and the door trapping him so he couldn't fall to move out of range.

Despite Mason's superior strength, Laila didn't let him pull the stunner away until the gunman had collapsed, slumping against the corner.

Hands ran over her face. Mason touched her everywhere as if to convince himself that she didn't have any bullet holes.

Then he turned and took care of the intruder, searching his bag of gear for some kind of restraints.

"Don't worry. The other one is already down."

Trembling from head to toe, she watched in a daze as he grabbed the duffle from the top shelf. He pulled out long plastic zips, using them to hogtie the bad guy while keeping up a steady stream of conversation.

She didn't hear any of it. Not until the sirens sounded in the distance.

Then she burst into tears. "Mason, I was so scared I peed a little," she gasped as he clutched her to him.

He laughed with tears in his eyes—he was so relieved she was speaking again. "It's okay, baby. You have time to change before the cops get in here."

§.

A freshly showered Laila sat in the circle of Mason's arms as a veritable swarm of police officers milled around them. Her haziness was finally clearing up now that she'd finally stopped trembling.

"It's shock, baby. It's normal," Mason had explained when she'd started shaking after the fact. He'd refused to let go of her, holding her close the entire time he'd been explaining to the cops—even when the cops had tried to separate them to get their statements independently.

The responding officer hadn't liked that very much, but Mason had stood firm until Detective Silano arrived, taking over the questioning.

"I have a good feeling about this," she said after electronically fingerprinting the man Laila had tased. But the detective didn't elaborate, and Mason was too focused on getting them both out of there to argue much.

They ended up spending the night at Elias Gardner's spacious Carbon Mesa house.

"This is a real honest-to-God mansion," she told Mason excitedly after they had been shown to a sumptuous guest room that rivaled any five-star hotel room Mason had ever seen.

"Ian and Elias are cousins, but they grew up in different worlds. I've always thought that it was to Elias' credit that he followed in Ian's footsteps instead of his father's."

She was about to ask Mason what the Gardner family business was when she caught sight of his face.

"*Hey,*" she said, walking into his arms. "I'm okay. I wasn't hurt today."

Mason swore under his breath, but he wasn't angry. His blue eyes were soft but intense as if there were lit from a fire within. "That's because you're incredibly smart and so fucking brave. You thought strategically. You knew you couldn't outfight them, so you hid, but you managed to keep the high ground."

He pressed her closer, his hands working under the T-shirt she was wearing to settle warm and heavy against the bare skin of her back.

"But," he sighed, "you should never have been in danger in the first place. I would never have left you if I thought they would be able to find you. I'm only glad I didn't stop at the main office as I'd planned."

Laila tugged his head down, pressing a brief but hard kiss to his lips. "You can't watch me every minute of the day. The important thing is I'm okay." She hung off his neck, letting him bear her weight until his strong arms picked her up, cradling her to him. "Not to mention the vast majority of the time, *you* are going to be the one in danger. And I won't be there to save you then. We're both going to have to learn to deal with it."

Mason cocked his head at her. "*Hey*. You did save me." He sounded stunned.

"You don't have to sound so surprised," she chided, but then laughed when he growled and tossed her on the bed.

The mattress was so thick she barely felt the impact. Laila tugged at Mason's shirt as he crawled over her.

"Wait," he said as she kissed the delicious line of his strong jaw. "We still don't know how they found you."

"That's tomorrow's mystery," she said, finally succeeded getting his shirt off. "Right now, I need you to touch me."

Mason kissed her, but his demeanor didn't lighten. "Laila, baby, you are my life," he told her. "I know there are no guarantees in life, but I'm going to spend the rest of my days taking care of you. If anything ever happened to you—"

Laila silenced him with a kiss. Mason's protective instincts were too deeply engrained. She was never going to convince him that she was all right using words. She was going to have to show him.

So that was what she did…again and again.

CHAPTER THIRTY-THREE

"It took a few hours, but he cracked," Detective Silano told them.

Mason had brought Laila to the police station, agreeing to come only after the detective had assured them her assailant had been transferred to central booking.

They sat in the detective's crowded office, their two chairs crammed against the wall catty-corner to the desk instead of across—or else the door wouldn't have been able to close.

They soon learned why she wanted privacy.

"Who is he?" Laila frowned at the mug shot of a sallow-faced dirty-blond man in his late fifties.

"Elmer Lugge. Elmer and his cousin own the Stag and Stars."

"So this is connected to the bar," Mason grunted, putting his arm around Laila.

Detective Silano nodded, pushing another paper toward them. This one was a picture printed out on plain printer paper, but it was wrinkled. The detective had slipped it into an evidence bag. "He was arrested with this on him."

Laila looked down at the picture, then gasped. Mason picked it up. It was blown up and grainy, but it was a clear picture of Laila in the passenger seat of his car. Her phone was in her hand. It was right after she'd taken a picture of the front of the bar.

"How the hell did they get this? There were no cameras outside that dive."

Silano picked up the bag with the printouts. "Once we saw this and worked out the angles, we found the camera. A grate concealed it. It feeds into a ramshackle system, but we studied the entire video. There are cameras trained on the front and rear entrance. They pick up most of the parking lot. Your Mustang passed close enough for them to get your license plate. We found your plate number scribbled on a post-it in the office trash can."

"This pit has an office?"

"It's an ancient metal desk in the storage room with a lot of crap piled on top of it."

"I see." Mason scowled at the mugshot. "So, what is this asshole saying?" he asked before noticing the expression on Laila's face.

"What's wrong?"

"You already changed your address with the DMV?" There was a tinge of disbelief in her tone.

Mason rolled his shoulders, discomfited. "Babe, you do that when you move—within ten days is the rule. I moved *months* ago."

"But no one does that on time." She still appeared inexplicably bewildered.

"Laila, baby, it's the rules," he said before taking her hand in his.

"Right." Now, Laila seemed amused. She turned to the detective. "Can I ask—the last time you moved, how long did it take you to update your address?"

The detective smiled. "Coincidentally, I did it last month."

"And when did you move?"

"Two years ago."

The ladies exchanged a private smile.

Mason's lips compressed. "Well, now I'm sorry for being so diligent if that's how they found us."

He twisted to face Silano again. "Although... I'm a little surprised the proprietors of the Stag and Stars to have the connections to run a license plate."

Detective Silano's dour face broke into a grin. "And that's how we knew they had connections, starting with the Stag. Elmer and his brother don't own the bar. The real owner is hidden by a few clever layers of paperwork—shell companies."

Laila frowned. "So, who owns it?"

Silano held up a finger, checking the papers on her desk. Mason knew all this was for show. She was enjoying herself too much. "It's why it took a few days for us to call you in. We had to double and triple check this because the name is Oscar Johansen."

"*Wait.*" Laila sat up straighter. "That's Bryce's father, isn't it?"

Detective Silano nodded in confirmation. "Yeah, do you know him?"

Laila glanced at him before looking back at the detective. "He was at all the Dubey functions. He was kind of rude, though—always on the phone in the background. More than once, he would catch Franklin's eye and draw him aside for these little conferences. I was introduced to him at least three times before he bothered to learn my name."

"Well, that tracks with what we know of him," the detective said. "Oscar isn't Franklin's brother. He went to college with him, then married Franklin's younger sister. He's got a law degree he doesn't use except to bludgeon people with it. He negotiates contracts for Franklin and manages the people around him. Closest we can tell is he's sort of permanent family fixer. And he's a distant cousin to Elmer Lugge."

"*Ah.*" Mason exhaled sharply.

"Yeah." The detective picked up a file. "Elmer and his cousin—who is not related to Oscar, by the way, both have rap sheets, mostly small-time stuff. But they cleaned up their act over five years ago when they took over the bar from the previous owner. Rumor has it the bar was payment for some work they'd done for someone important. They've bragged more than once that they have friends in high places."

"So that's their connection to Joseph," Laila said. "We knew that whenever the boys got in trouble, they would call one of their dads."

Mason silently agreed. But how quickly they got help *didn't*, not really. They were able to get rid of Jasmine's body too fast. But if Oscar had a pair of criminals indebted to him—a built-in clean-up crew—then that rapid timeline made sense.

A pained expression crossed Silano's face. "There is something you should know. According to Elmer, Joseph Dubey and Bryce Johansen wanted Jasmine Elliot out of the Alpha Omega fraternity when they couldn't rouse her because she'd had too much to drink. Elmer was supposed to take her inside the back way of the Stag and Stars so people would see her."

Silano broke off to rub her head as if she were getting a headache. "We know now there was more in her system than just alcohol, but the ME's results aren't clear on how that contributed to her death."

Laila nodded, her expression sickened.

"But after the case of alcohol poisoning last year, Joseph and the others couldn't afford to call an ambulance. Alpha Omega had almost lost its charter back then. Another case of alcohol poisoning, involving a woman this time, would have freaked them out. They wanted to dump her in a bar to make it look as if she'd gone there afterward and kept on drinking, effectively passing off the responsibility onto someone else—on Jasmine herself."

Mason stood, tugging Laila out of her chair. Bewildered, she resisted until he bodily picked her up, sitting back down with her wrapped tightly in his arms.

"*Oh.* Thanks."

He passed a hand over her hair, but his words were for the detective. "I take it something went wrong with Oscar's master plan."

"You could say that." Silano leaned back in her chair, letting out a disgusted sigh. "The frat cousins dropped the girl off, doing a quick handoff in the back parking lot. Joseph told them to call an ambulance, then they were gone. But Elmer said he touched the girl, and she was already cold. He figured the girl had been dead when they called, but the two frat brats, as he called them, didn't want to cop to it. Since he had a record, he decided following the plan wasn't in his best interest—not if the girl was already dead."

"So he dumped her in the park," Mason finished.

Silano rose. She came around her desk to lean against the front. "I don't know what would have happened if Elmer had stuck to the plan —if medical intervention would have worked."

Mason's stomach sank. He knew what was coming.

Laila tensed in his arms. "What are you saying?"

"There was dirt in Jasmine Elliot's lungs. It matches the soil in the park she was found in."

Laila's sob was ragged. She understood, had instantly grasped the meaning. "Because she was still alive."

"Yes." Sighing, Detective Silano closed her eyes briefly. It was a tired sound. "Elmer was wrong about her being dead before the hand-off. I didn't want you to hear the details at the trial, but thanks to you, there *will* be a trial."

"We hope," Laila muttered, despondent. "But even if we get that far, they won't go down for murder. You might get Oscar for conspiracy, but Franklin? I don't even know what you would charge Joseph and Bryce with."

"Involuntary manslaughter. That's something that will follow them for the rest of their lives."

"Maybe…if you can get a conviction." Laila leaned into him.

"We're negotiating to bring in Joseph Dubey and Bryce Johansen. I don't think these boys have the fortitude to stand up to an interrogation."

Mason held Laila close. "Assuming their lawyers let them speak at all."

Silano put her hands up. "I'm not going to lie. Even with Elmer's testimony, it's going to be an uphill battle. But I'm going to take whatever victories I can get because, in this job, there aren't that many."

With that bitter truth, Silano excused herself after getting called to the bullpen by a uniformed officer.

"It doesn't feel like enough, does it?" Laila's shoulders slumped. "And what's worse, there will be people who blame Jasmine for going to the party in the first place, or because she was drinking to begin with."

"Anybody says it's her fault, we'll sic Rosamie on them."

That won him the tiniest of smiles.

"Let's get out of here," Laila said, rising to her feet.

Following her, Mason threw an arm around her shoulders. "Silano is right—we focus on the battles we can win. The fact this happened at Alpha Omega *after* they had a case of alcohol poisoning means it should be shut down. Permanently. And the people who tried to hide it deserve everything that's coming to them. Even if Joseph and Bryce don't get jail time, well, Jasmine's family has a hell of a civil case. I don't know what their situation is—"

Mason was going to elaborate on what the Elliots could do with a cash award when someone cried out, "*Laila!*"

Reacting instantly, Mason pushed Laila behind him, putting a hand out when someone charged toward them. And then she clutched his arm. "It's Joseph," she said in his ear.

Rearing back, Mason grabbed the guy by the neck, slamming Dubey against the wall.

"Don't even think about touching her," Mason hissed at the familiar stranger as cops swarmed around them.

Joseph Dubey didn't look like the smug golden boy Mason remembered. Though his clothes were clean, he was disheveled, his face red and puffy.

"Mason, let go of him." Laila shook his arm, sounding distinctly nervous as a crowd of officers pressed in.

"This asshole's family sent someone to kill you—" he snarled, aware of an annoying buzzing in the background. It sounded like a subspecies of irate lawyer, ranting at the edge of the crowd.

"I did not do that!" Despite being held by the neck, Joseph was nowhere near breathless. *Which just means you should squeeze harder.*

Detective Silano chose that moment to wade through the crowd. "Mr. Dubey has consented to come in and give a statement," she said, mugging at him furiously before pitching her voice low to growl, "*Get your girl out of here.*"

Mason chanced a glance at Laila. She wasn't even looking at him. Her gaze was fixed on Joseph, her face nearly bloodless.

Shoving her ex away like the piece of trash he was, Mason roughly let him go, transferring his now-gentled hold to Laila. Not wanting her to spend another second in her abuser's presence, he began to usher her out.

"Wait, *his* girl?" Joseph stared at Laila with lost puppy-dog eyes. It made Mason want to kick him.

But Laila twisted in his arms. "Joseph, tell them the truth about Jasmine. Tell them how she *really* died. She deserves that."

Her voice shook, but her conviction—the sheer emotion—cut through the air like a knife. Even the lawyer shut up.

Mason had her out the door before anyone could reply.

CHAPTER THIRTY-FOUR

Mason's face was grim as they exited via the police station's main entrance.

"I didn't interrupt a necessary confrontation, did I? You're not going to be talking to a therapist someday about how I ruined your one chance at closure?"

"I'll let you know when I calm down," Laila said, reaching out to brace herself on his arm.

Her pulse pounded, and her legs were so weak she was having trouble standing. Breathing hard, she bent, instinct making her put her head between her knees.

Swearing, Mason picked her up, ushering her to a bench just to the left of the doors.

His arms went around her as she fought to regain her composure. Laila squeezed his biceps, her head pressed to his chest. But despite his attempts at comfort, she was still trembling.

"I'm sorry," she said after a few minutes. "I had no idea I was going to fall apart like this. Even though I had no plans to see him, I thought I was prepared. I was just fooling myself."

Laila had pictured herself confronting Joseph a million times. In her imagination, she had been brave and aggressive, getting in his face and slapping the shit out of him. The reality had been so different. Just the sight of him had knocked the breath from her lungs. She had felt small and violated all over again.

The fact she'd found her voice and gotten any words out was a victory, she told herself. But her reaction now that he was out of sight —the way she was clinging to Mason—made her feel weak and pathetic.

Mason disagreed. "Do you know what I saw? I saw a strong, brilliant, and beautiful woman confront her abuser. And you made the most of it—telling him to do the right thing for Jasmine when you could have focused on what he did to you. I wouldn't have blamed you. Had it been me, I wouldn't have had the wherewithal or selflessness to say anything like you just did. I would have just started swearing and not stopped."

Her lips quirked in a wan smile. "Had you been in my shoes, you would have defended yourself when he tried to hurt you—and you would have wiped the floor with him...although, honestly, I'm having a lot of trouble seeing you two as a couple. You're not really each other's type."

Snorting softly, Mason pressed a kiss to her forehead. "Why don't we get the hell out of here so you can have a bubble bath and I can beat the hell out of the punching bag I have in the garage?"

"That sounds like a good plan, but I have a better one."

Closing her eyes, Laila leaned against his chest. She shut out the police station, letting the sun and the warmth of Mason's embrace warm her chilled bones. With a voice that grew in strength and firmness, she detailed a scheme that involved candles and her decadent hot fudge sauce, followed by even hotter sex in the shower.

Mason's hand gripped the back of Laila's neck reflexively. It took him a minute to find his tongue. "You are the most amazing fucking woman in the world. You know that, right?"

Laila's chin jutted out. "Because I want to lick chocolate off your naked body? Mason, honey, there isn't a woman alive who wouldn't want to do that."

"She's right about that!"

Mason jerked. A middle-aged woman in a meter maid uniform at the edge of the parking lot grinned at him and gave Laila a thumbs-up before getting into her little cart and driving away.

Laila giggled.

He cleared his throat, his cheeks flaming. "What I meant to say is that I know it can't have been easy, trusting a man again after what happened with that asshole," he said, jerking his thumb behind him to indicate the station and its current occupant.

Silano better not let that worm wriggle off the hook.

"You make it easy," Laila said, those golden-brown eyes seeing right through him to capture his soul. "I trust you with my life."

"Good, because I want all of it—the next eighty years at least."

Her brow puckered. "So we are planning on living past the century mark? Together?"

"Damn straight we are." He laughed until Laila smiled. "And you know what?"

"What?" Laila asked, her heart in her eyes.

"It won't be long enough—I'm going to love you for the rest of our lives and into the whatever comes after."

Despite the emotional rollercoaster of their day, Mason felt like he was on top of the world. The scene in the police station had gotten ugly at the end, but it was *over*. Plus, Laila had handled seeing her ex with grace and strength. They still had some legal hurdles to overcome, but whatever happened, they would face them together.

Laila's fingers twined in his filled him with a sense of rightness. It wrapped around him like a second skin. Forget the high after a successful op—all he needed to feel fucking invincible was to hold his girl's hand.

Smugly self-satisfied and nearly bursting with pride in the woman at his side, he escorted her across the street. Since the lot around the station was reserved for squad cars and parking enforcement vehicles, Mason had parked the Mustang on a side street in a metered slot a few blocks down. They took their time, both aware on some level that this was it—they were about to start their life together.

When they passed a shop window full of women's designer clothes, he tugged Laila closer to it, pointing to a red number that was both elegant and sexy. She laughed when he told her it would be perfect on her. She tugged him away after catching sight of the price tag hanging from the sleeve, but Mason made a mental note. He had to take Laila shopping and out to dinner...do normal couple things their history and circumstances had kept them from doing. They were overdue for some fun.

It took them nearly twenty minutes to make it down two blocks. The car was across the street. He led Laila into the street when the light changed, and that was when he heard it—an engine accelerating instead of slowing down.

The black SUV had tinted windows, and it had been specially modified. Mason recognized it as a high-end model favored by drug lords and politicians across the country.

He processed that in the split second he had to react.

Mason shouted a warning to Laila, pivoting and throwing himself at her, wrenching back toward the curb they had just stepped off. There was the impact of his much larger body against her small one, and then they were flying.

Instinctively rolling, he managed to twist in midair, so they crashed down with him on the bottom. The impact knocked the wind out of him twice, once when he hit the ground and again a second or two later when Laila landed flat against his chest. But his shoulders felt the difference—this wasn't the blacktop of the road, he had made it to the sidewalk. Gasping in pain and relief, he rolled and rolled until they hit something—the wall of the building on the corner.

"Are you okay?" he asked Laila, his voice half an octave higher than normal.

Dazed, she shook her head. "What happened?"

He started to pull them up, rearing back to shake off the hand of a bystander. Belatedly realizing the man was just trying to help, he apologized, but he pulled Laila behind him anyway. Scanning for additional threats, he did a rapid assessment.

"Get inside there. Call Silano!" He pointed at the door a few feet away—a chain drugstore.

"I'll be right back," he yelled, running in the direction the SUV had taken. It was almost four in the afternoon. There was too much traffic for the driver to have made a quick getaway.

And it hadn't. *I can fucking hear it.*

Legs pumping, Mason sprinted across the street, barreling down the block full tilt. The SUV turned at the corner, and Mason leaped over a chain that separated a parking lot from the sidewalk. Weaving through the cars, he kept running, determined to cut through it.

At the corner, he ran around a dumpster, crashing into a trash can. He fell into the sidewalk, scraping the skin of his palms, but he didn't stop to think. Mason acted.

Training kicking in, he rolled to his feet, grabbing the trash can lid as he went.

The SUV plowed through the intersection, blasting through a red light. It was getting too big a lead.

An image of Laila's face flashed through his head as he threw the lid, spinning it like an Olympian discus thrower. He hadn't consciously aimed through the window, but it sailed through anyway.

Mason didn't know if it hit the driver or merely blocked his view, but the result was the same. The SUV veered sharply to the right—sending it straight into the heavy metal base of a streetlamp.

The sound of crumpled steel and breaking glass rent the air. The SUV's horn blared. Inside, he could see someone flailing behind the bright white of the deployed airbag.

He also caught a glimpse of something else his training had taught him to search for—the cold glint of a gun. The driver held it as he tried to get out from behind the partially deflated airbag.

Fuck. Mason had to disarm the assailant before the man could get out of the car. The surrounding office buildings were emptying, and the sidewalks were filling up with office workers and lookie-loos coming to check out the accident.

Too much collateral damage.

He tensed, preparing to launch himself into the vehicle, when a small hand grabbed his arm.

"Here!" He spun on his heel to see Laila holding something out to him.

"*Laila.*" The one word held everything—equal parts fear for her mixed with his love and intense frustration she hadn't listened to him. How *dare* she put herself in danger?

Turning back to the SUV, he threw open the door, grabbing the gunman's arm and bringing his own down on it with enough force to break a bone.

The dark-haired assailant screamed as Mason hauled him out into the ground with a shout. "Laila, get back!"

"Oh my God, it's Oscar."

"What?"

"Oscar Johansen—he's Bryce's dad."

Of course. The fixer.

"Get Silano," he gritted out as he kneeled on Oscar's lower back, holding him down without crushing his lungs, aware that, despite his anger, he needed the fucker to talk.

Laila held up her phone, an active call displayed on the screen. "Don't worry. She's on her way."

CHAPTER THIRTY-FIVE

Laila was as mad at Mason as he appeared to be with her. How could he think she was going to just hide in a damn drugstore while he ran after the bad guy, *unarmed?*

Okay, so he hadn't needed her stun gun. She'd never seen anyone do a karate chop in real life, and it had been impressive as hell. Laila had heard Oscar's bone snap, and though the sound made her wince in retrospect, she barely registered it at the time. The scream that had followed had caught and kept all of her attention.

That Mason had executed the move in the tight confines of the SUV, generating enough force to break a bone, had amazed the EMTs and the cops who came with Silano to make the arrest.

Laila paused, remembering her gleeful grin as the detective caught sight of Oscar Johansen laid out on the floor with his hands cuffed behind his back like a gift Mason was presenting to her.

"Christmas came early," she declared, repeatedly slapping Mason on the back.

The detective had wanted to hug him, Laila knew, but the woman had restrained herself.

Can't say I blame her, Laila thought, peeking at Mason from the corner of her eye. He was digging under a cabinet, his sculpted derriere within touching distance. But Laila kept her hands at her sides, mostly because he was mumbling about needing to check her out.

He rose a minute later with a canvas first-aid kit in his hand.

"Come over here," he said gruffly.

Laila crossed her arms. "No."

Mason stepped back, eyes flaring. "You could have cuts and bruises. I need to check you out."

Standing as straight as she could, Laila held out her hand. "Only if I check you out first," she said, gesturing for the kit.

Mason scowled at her. "What?"

She pointed at his scraped hands. "You're hurt worse than me."

"Laila—" he began.

She held up a hand. "I won't let you until I see your hands."

Growling something under his breath, he handed the kit over. "I will comply," he said primly. "But after this, I expect *full* cooperation."

"We have a deal," she said with an equally formal inclination of her head, gesturing for him to take a seat on the couch.

Once he was seated, she opened the bag, setting the disinfectant, antibiotic ointment, and bandages on the coffee table. Being extra gentle, she cleaned his scrapes, blowing on the disinfectant she applied. When she looked up, his eyes were fixed on her face, his expression warm now.

The muscles in her neck relaxed, making her realize just how much tension she had been carrying since their almost-silent car ride home. *I won't be tense next time,* she vowed.

There would be other occasions when she and Mason argued, even fought. She never had to be afraid of him when he was angry. Her brain had known that before, but her body needed a little more convincing. That would come with time, and they were going to have lots of it. Nobody—not Joseph or Franklin or fucking Oscar Johansen —was going to take it away from her—from them.

"I just flashed forward to our future, seeing you kissing our kid's booboos and making them better."

The soft words clashed with her militant mindset, making her crumble into a mushy pile of goo.

"I will always try to protect you," he swore as she wrapped a white bandage around his hands, just enough to cover the scrapes while leaving him with full mobility. He ended up looking like a boxer getting ready for a bout.

"I know that," she said, pressing a kiss to his wrist. "But you need to get used to me protecting you, too."

"If you promise me the next time won't involve you running out in the open when there is a gunman around, then yes," he said, the words clipped despite his obvious effort to let go of his anger.

Pretending she hadn't caught his tone, she stood. "I trust you have no other injuries I need to examine?" she asked in her most professional how-may-I-serve-you voice, the one she saved for Gardullo's high-end customers.

The corner of his mouth quirked, his annoyance fading. He knew she was teasing him. "No."

"Good."

Laila pulled her shirt over her head.

Mason's head jerked back, his eyes fastened on her breasts, which were lovingly cupped in the dusty-rose lace bra she'd found on sale.

When she undid the fastening of her jeans, shimmying out to reveal the matching pink panties, Mason's lips parted, his hands reaching out reflexively to claw the air as if he couldn't help himself.

Laila stepped into his outstretched hands. "You needed to take a good look," she said, pitching her voice low.

"*Holy hell.*" His voice was all gruff and gravel. It sent a frisson of anticipation across her skin, making private places tingle.

Shedding her bra with more haste than grace, she took his hands, putting them on the sides of her breasts. She shivered as he cupped her, the bandages abrading her nipples.

Putting her hands over his, she slid them down her waist to the elastic of her panties. Guiding him, she used his hands to push them down. Stepping out of the lace, Laila moved to straddle Mason, but he held her up. "*Wait.*"

He stood and yanked at his clothing, setting what had to be a world record for stripping. Naked, he crashed back on the couch, pulling her on top of him with hot, hungry hands.

Laila closed her eyes, her head falling back to expose the vulnerable line of her neck. Mason's mouth flamed up and down the tender skin, liquifying her bones.

Mason's hands closed on either side of her face. His head drew back to stare into her eyes. "No matter how much of you I get, I always want more."

His breath fanned over her face, the bite of peppermint and the cedar of the soap he used like a drug to her senses.

Her mouth took his, slanting over his lips, drinking him deeply. Pushing away, she moved down his chest, kissing and licking her way down his body.

She pushed his thighs apart, making room for herself before grasping his cock in her hands. His intake of breath was sharp. Mason's entire body jerked under her firm grasp.

"You're so thick," she said, pressing a kiss to the side of his rigid organ. "I sometimes wonder how we fit so well, but we do."

Another kiss, this one open-mouthed. A hiss escaped Mason's lips.

"I never thought I would enjoy this," she said, letting the flat of her tongue stroke his length. "But with you, I want it. I want to consume you, take you inside me every way I possibly can."

Mason's hands buried in her hair as she sucked the tip into her mouth. She kept him there, moving her tongue around the sensitive rim of the flared head. And then he was moving. His arousal popped out of her mouth, and she was flying through the air. Mason caught her against his body. Her back hit the couch cushion. He covered her —his hair-roughened skin stroking her flushed and damp silkiness.

"I need you," he breathed in her ear, his voice edgy and sharp with hunger. His hands pulled her legs apart, widening them for an invasion she welcomed with every fiber of her being.

But when his shaft touched her damp warmth, he was gentle and sure, always careful not to hurt her. Her body opened, defying the laws of biology and physics as she stretched to accept him, her hands digging into his back.

Pulsing around him in welcome, she thrust against him, working herself against his thickness, making Mason swear. The veins in his arms and neck bulged as she undulated like a wave, rising and falling to meet him as he stood still with effort, her rock in the ocean.

The friction building, her every nerve ending firing, she rose one final time, using her hands to press him close so she could grind against him.

"Sugar—I can't wait. *I can't.*" Inside her, Mason swelled. He shuddered, his rigid control breaking. He thrust inside her hard and fast until her sheath pulsed around him, making her cry out, her vision fragmenting as her orgasm splintered her like breaking glass.

Mason hauled in a shaky breath and grunted, his thighs slapping against her as he finally let go, coming with a burst that flooded her with heat. Fucking her through his climax, Mason finally collapsed on top of her, his breath harsh as his shaft pulsed twice more before finally coming to rest.

It took him a minute, but, eventually, he shifted, lifting her limp body so she rested on top of him. And he managed to do it without breaking their connection. He was still inside her, soft now, but that was good. She never wanted to let him go.

"I think I'm an addict," he murmured, his finger tracing the skin of her hips, trailing over the taut globes of her ass.

Laila hummed. "As long I am your drug of choice, I have no problem with that."

He laughed, his fingers tightening on her curves. A little squeak escaped her before she could stop herself.

Frowning, Mason rose, his finger tracing over a tender spot. "You *are* bruised."

Laila twisted her neck, but only Linda Blair had a chance of seeing that part of themselves.

"My rear has plenty of padding. It will be fine."

Mason's hand stroked over her other cheek. A sudden grin brightened his face. He was almost too handsome to look at—blinding like the sun. "Let me kiss it and make it better."

Laila giggled, bending her legs to cross them at the ankles behind her. "Maybe if you let me kiss yours, too—and don't tell me you don't have any. You took most of the impact."

"I have no idea if I'm bruised."

Scoffing, she whipped her head back and forth. "No way. I love you, but I don't believe what Ransom and your teammates say about you—you're not superhuman."

Mason's hand cupped her cheek. He leaned forward to press a long, soft kiss to her lips before drawing back so he could speak.

"Trust me, sugar, I'm feeling no pain."

"Because of my wonderful analgesic effect?" she teased, tapping her toes together.

"No. Because you just told me that you loved me for the first time."

Laila cocked her head at him. Was it really the first time? How could that be right? She'd lived and breathed with the emotion from the moment she'd laid eyes on him.

"But you knew that already," she said, no longer needing to protect the truth. "You've always known. I've always loved you—since the day we met."

A suspicious glint in his eye, Mason pressed a much harder, much deeper kiss to her lips. "It seems I needed to hear it out loud."

EPILOGUE

Rosamie banged the picnic blanket for emphasis. "And then the lawyer tried to trip *me* up, to try to discredit Laila before she even took the stand."

Her friend's loud and indignant voice almost shook the leaves on the tree next to them.

They sat in the shade, protected from the sun's bright rays. Below them, the green hill was starting to brown in the summer heat, but the deer that inhabited the Forest Lawn cemetery were still out in force, grazing on the other side of the narrow lane.

Earlier, a hearse had passed, leading a caravan of mourners to a plot to the east.

"Jasmine's parents chose a beautiful spot," Laila observed.

"*Laila,* don't talk about her as if she isn't here," Rosamie chided, patting the plaque with Jasmine's name on it in silent apology.

"You're right. I apologize, Jasmine," Laila said, patting Rosamie's hand as well in commiseration. "Go on with the story."

"All right then," Rosamie said, resuming her tale. "And then the smarmy-ass lawyer tried to get sneaky with me, implying all sorts of shit. I told the fucker where to go and came this close to getting slapped with a contempt of court, but the judge settled with just giving me a warning because of the circumstances. But the real kicker came when the asshat finally called Laila to the stand."

Rosamie's eyes closed, reliving the moment. "I don't know how the hell it happened—the gods must have been smiling on us—but every single one of Auric's security teams was stateside that day. But I didn't realize that until Laila walked into the courtroom, and they all stood. It was like they were coming to attention. They all moved at the same time, completely in sync. I got chills. Literal chills. Ransom was there, too, in his suit looking so fucking hot I just—"

"Rosamie, *focus.*"

"Yeah, sorry," her friend said, apologizing to Jasmine's plaque. "Back to the courtroom. Again, all those warriors stood, showing Laila their support. It was so fucking breathtaking and damn *in-ti-mi-da-ting*," she said, drawing out every syllable.

Laila nudged her. "You forgot to tell Jasmine how Frederick Dubey tried to hire them."

"Oh, yes!" Rosamie gesticulated, slapping her forehead. "The fucker did! Joseph's dad tried to hire Auric on some bullshit protection detail. It was a thinly disguised bribe—as if the Dubeys were hoping Auric would somehow turn on Mason and Laila. But Ian Quinn told Dubey where to stick it."

"He did," Laila confirmed, wiping a smudge on the plaque with a napkin.

"And so did Elias Gardner, which seemed to shock the hell out of Franklin because their fathers were like part of the same lacrosse team in college or some stupid fuckery like that—as if that's supposed to make them the same. Elias was a Navy seal. Franklin is a *politician*," Rosamie finished with a delicate shudder.

Laila smiled, deciding not to remind Rosamie how she'd pushed Laila to become a future politician's wife.

But a career in Congress was no longer in Joseph's future. Not after the way he had broken down on the stand. In a halting voice Rosamie swore was an act, Joseph repeated what Elmer had told

Detective Silano—Oscar was the one who had come up with the plan to hand Jasmine off to the Lugge cousins.

From across the courtroom, Joseph had pleaded with Laila to understand that Jasmine was meant to get medical attention all along. Then he had started crying, tearfully confessing he still loved her.

Mason hadn't like that at all. Neither had Laila, but she'd expressed only pity, taking Mason's hand when he placed a territorial arm around her shoulders.

"The judge gave Elmer and Oscar the max, but Joseph and Bryce probably won't serve their full terms," Rosamie finished sadly. "And Franklin didn't even get charged."

"On the bright side, he's going to have a hell of a time getting reelected," Laila said, hugging Rosamie to her side.

"True," her friend admitted. "He's too tight with Oscar for people to believe he didn't know anything."

"Yes. The press is tearing him apart."

"Well, it was stupid of him not to resign after the shit hit the fan," Rosamie sniffed.

They sat there a while longer, telling Jasmine all about Rosamie and Ransom's hair-raising island vacation and Laila's New Orleans wedding.

Rosamie threw herself on the ground. "Oh God, the food. I still dream about those crayfish."

"The best part was the honeymoon."

Rosamie smacked her. "Don't rub it in. Ransom's mission is taking forever and a half. I am *frustrated*."

"Actually, I meant the return leg from Europe where we had a two-day layover in Chicago, and Mason took me to see my mom."

"What?" Rosamie sat up. "I didn't know he did that."

"It was a complete surprise," Laila said, growing tearful all over again. "Mason blindfolded me at the airport, then we took a rental car. I thought he was taking me into the city, but when he whipped the blindfold off, we were at my stepmom's care home."

"Aw," Rosamie said. "I can't believe he did that. Were you hinting at a trip there?"

"No. I hadn't mentioned it at all," Laila said, recalling the emotional scene.

Laila had thrown her arms around Mason's neck, tears streaking down her cheeks. She'd never told him that Joseph had dangled the possibility of visiting her mother to get her to move in with him.

He promised to take her, might have even been sincere at the time, but he'd put the trip off twice, not realizing he was shredding her heart each time. After that, she'd stopped reminding him of his promise.

Laila had never mentioned visiting her stepmother to Mason. But, somehow, he had known without having to be asked. He was good at that—knowing what she needed before she acknowledged it aloud. Sometimes before she realized the need herself.

The sun had begun its descent when the friends finally headed out to where Rosamie had parked Ransom's car. Rosamie rested her head on Laila's shoulder as they walked. "When does your flight leave?"

"Day after tomorrow." Laila and Mason were living in a small house near Auric's second training base. She had even met his oldest friend Ethan and the man's gorgeous new wife. The couple lived in the apartment building Mason had invested in. After she saw how it had been refurbished, she desperately wanted to live there as well, but it was too far from the Auric base to be practical. For now, they were renting it out, putting the money away. Laila told Mason the cash was for their next European vacation. He would reply that it was for the deluxe oven he wanted to buy her.

"You'll meet us for dinner at the hotel, right?" Laila nudged Rosamie as they climbed into the vehicle.

"As if I would ever turn down dinner at the Caislean. I hear their chef made a deal with the devil—his scallop risotto is that good."

And the meal was divine. They ate and drank, Mason's elite VIP card getting them special treatment from the staff.

Effervescent from the fine wine and company, she walked unsteadily in her heels toward the elevator that would take them to their room after saying goodbye to her best friend in the world.

"We'll see her again soon," Mason promised. "You know you can always join me when I come to L.A. for a training mission."

"I can do that now, but I'll be too busy with work soon." It had taken her a little while, but Laila had landed a job in a children's clinic that suited her, helping patients and running diagnostic tests on kids and babies, which was a bonus she hadn't expected.

The job allowed her plenty of time to pursue her passions—spending time with her gorgeous, virile husband and baking. Though she had always enjoyed it, she found new pleasure baking for her expanded circle of loved ones.

That included all the Auric people now. Rosamie hadn't been the only one who got chills the day of the trial. She'd almost cried when she saw them all—each merc telling her through their bearing that they would stand between her and any danger.

Even Toya had been there, sleekly dangerous in an all-black tailored suit. She'd slipped a note in her hand as Laila walked up the aisle. It said, *Kick their asses.*

Laila could have gotten through that terrible ordeal of the trial on her own. She knew that. But having Mason and the Auric people there had bolstered and strengthened her in ways she could never have foreseen.

She'd eaten the high-priced attorney defending Oscar for lunch.

And Laila hadn't stopped or slowed down since. Neither had Mason.

These days, none of the Auric people left on a mission without one of her signature treats tucked into their gear bags. She even shipped them to the L.A. training facility by overnight delivery. Ian Quinn was happy to foot the bill ever since he discovered a weakness for her lemon-and-poppy seed cookies.

"You're not worried I'm going to make your personnel fat and slow?" she'd teased when he'd told her that he'd cover the costs.

"That's what we have your husband for—Mason knows how to whip them into shape," Ian had said with an easy smile.

Finally alone with the man in question, Laila slowly stripped him of the tie he'd worn to the hotel's Michelin-starred restaurant.

Humming a nonsensical tune, she pushed Mason down on the edge of the bed. "The first time I stayed here, when you brought me, I lay down on a bed just like this and pretended you were with me."

Light sparked in his eyes. His big hands moved up her back, undoing the zipper of her dress. "How did you pretend?"

Shimmying out of the silky gown, she kicked it aside before taking his hand and moving it down the length of her body. She made him cup her breast, the fingers under hers trailing fire down her body to her satin-covered mound. "It went something like this," she whispered.

The rest of their clothes melted away as she joined him on the bed, glorying in his touch, the feel of his skin, and the warmth of his hard body over hers.

Long minutes of intense pleasure melded into one another. She took Mason inside her, again and again, each time refusing to let go until he'd broken, splintering in her arms the way she always did in his.

After her fourth orgasm, Mason collapsed next to her on the bed, a sated golden god. Laila curled against him. Her hands stroked his chest, her legs rubbing against his.

"I still kick myself for not coming to you that time I brought you here," he confessed. "I wanted to. But I told myself I was protecting you by leaving you alone. I was so concerned with saving you from the dangers of my job that I left you exposed to the dangers of the world. I was a fool."

She grinned at the ceiling, her body still coming down from the blistering heights he took her to. "We've been married for over eight months. I can't believe you're still beating yourself up about those early days. And don't get me wrong—I love that you protect me. But I can take care of myself, too."

"I know that. My wife is the ballsiest, most bad-ass baker in the world." Mason rolled on top of her, caging her with his arms. "But I will regret every day that I knew you and didn't do this," he said, lowering his head for the deepest and most possessive kiss of her life.

The caress reverberated through her, sinking into her very skin, transmitting his love and need more effectively than words.

Laila wrapped her arms around his neck, pressing her forehead against his. "Then it's a good thing we'll never have to be apart again. We have the rest of our lives to make up for any lost time."

His grin took her breath away. "Damn straight we do, sugar."

THE END

The Mercenary Next Door is the second installment of a spin-off series. If you want more romance read the award-winning Singular Obsession books!

Or get the next installment of Rogues and Rescuers on sale now!

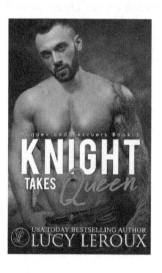

Not all queens want a knight to rescue them...

To the outside world, Caroline Wentworth is the new cold and cutthroat CEO of the struggling Wentworth Hotel chain. Always dutiful, Caroline lived by her father's constraints, squeezing into the suffocating mold of the perfect southern socialite. Since his death, she runs the show and makes the hard calls he refused to face, earning her the title of 'Ice Queen' from her employees.

FBI Agent Isaac Rivera is used to assertive people, but he's met his match with Caroline. Convincing this driven and overworked woman that she's in danger is his hardest mission yet. Just when he thinks he has her where he wants her, Caroline blindsides him again with her determined independence. Refusing to back down, Caroline has a hotel to save, and can't possibly get sidetracked by an irresistible FBI agent. With danger looming and his heart burning, can this Knight thaw the fiery Ice Queen?

ABOUT THE AUTHOR

Lucy Leroux is another name for USA Today Bestselling Author L.B. Gilbert.

Seven years ago Lucy moved to France for a one-year research contract. Six months later she was living with a handsome Frenchman and is now married with an adorable half-french toddler. Her family lives in California.

When her last contract ended Lucy turned to writing. Frustrated by the lack of quality romance erotica she created her own.

Lucy loves all genres of romance and intends to write as many of them as possible. To date she has published award-winning paranormal, urban fantasy, and gothic regency novels. Additionally, she writes a bestselling contemporary series. The 'Singular Obsession' books are a combination of steamy romance and suspense that feature intertwining characters in their own stand-alone stories. Follow her on twitter or facebook, or check out her website for more news!

www.authorlucyleroux.com

amazon.com/author/lucyleroux
facebook.com/lucythenovelist
twitter.com/lucythenovelist
instagram.com/lucythenovelist
bookbub.com/authors/lucy-leroux

Made in the USA
Middletown, DE
03 March 2024

50744226R00146